D0945746

The Wanderer

Other books by Knut Hamsun published
in Condor Books

PAN, *translated by James W. McFarlane*

VICTORIA, *translated by Oliver Stallybrass*

MYSTERIES, *translated by Gerry Bothmer*

Knut Hamsun

The Wanderer

Under the Autumn Star
&
On Muted Strings

Translated by Oliver and Gunnvor Stallybrass

A CONDOR BOOK
SOUVENIR PRESS (Educational & Academic) LTD

English translation Copyright © 1975 by Farrar, Straus & Giroux, Inc.

First published in the U.S.A. by
Farrar, Straus & Giroux

First British Edition published 1975 by
Souvenir Press (Educational & Academic) Ltd,
43 Great Russell Street, London WC1B 3PA
Reissued 1992

All Rights Reserved
No part of this publication may be reproduced,
stored in a retrieval system, or transmitted,
in any form or by any means, electronic,
mechanical, photocopying, recording or otherwise,
without the prior permission of the Copyright owner

ISBN 0 285 64787 3

Printed in Great Britain by
The Guernsey Press Co. Ltd, Guernsey, Channel Islands.

Contents

Under the Autumn Star

I

*Y*esterday the sea was as smooth as a mirror; it is smooth as a mirror today. The island is having an Indian summer. Such a mild, warm Indian summer! Yet there is no sun.

It is years since I knew such peace, perhaps twenty or thirty years; or perhaps it was in a previous life. Whenever it was, I must surely have tasted before now this peace that I feel as I walk around in ecstasies, humming to myself, caring for every stone and every straw, and sensing that they care for me once more. We are friends.

As I follow the overgrown path through the forest, my heart trembles with an unearthly joy. I remember a spot on the eastern shore of the Caspian where I once stood. The place resembled this one, and then as now the sea was calm and torpid and iron-gray. I walked through the forest, I was moved to tears of rapture, I kept saying, Dear God, to be here again!

As if I had been there before.

But if so I must have gone there, once upon a time, from another age and another land, where the forest and the paths were the same. Perhaps I was a forest flower, perhaps I was a beetle and made my home in an acacia tree.

And now I have come to this place. Perhaps I was a bird and flew these enormous distances. Or a seed in some fruit sent by a Persian trader.

There now: I am clear of the city, with its noise and bustle and newspapers and people; I have fled all that, because the summons came once more from the rural solitude that is native to me. "You'll see, it will all turn out well," I say to myself, and am filled with hope. Ah, but I have fled like this before, and returned again to the city. And fled again.

But this time I am firmly set on finding peace at all costs. For the moment I am lodging here in a cottage, with old Gunhild as my landlady.

The mountain ashes scattered among the conifers have started to shed their berries—heavy clusters of ripe coral-colored berries that fall to the ground with a thud. They harvest themselves and reseed themselves, they squander each year their incredible superabundance; on one single tree I count more than three hundred clusters. And here and there among the hills stand stubborn flowers that refuse to die, although in truth their time is up.

But then old Gunhild's time is up; and does she die? She behaves for all the world as if death was no concern of hers. When the fishermen are messing about on the beach, tarring their traps or painting their boats, old Gunhild goes up to them with lackluster eyes and the shrewdest of business minds.

"How much is mackerel today?" she asks.

"Same as yesterday."

"Then you can keep your mackerel."

And Gunhild makes for home.

But the fishermen know full well that Gunhild is not one to play-act at going: she has been known to walk all the way up to her cottage without one backward glance. And so "Hi there!" they call after her: let's make it seven mackerels to the half dozen today, for an old customer, that is.

And Gunhild buys her fish . . .

Hanging on the lines to dry are red skirts and blue shirts and underclothes of immense thickness; all spun or woven on the island by such old women as are still alive. But hanging out to dry, also, are those delicate sleeveless slips whose wearers are so apt to turn blue with cold, and those mauve woolen vests which resemble twine when stretched. Where do these monstrosities come from? From the city, of course, bought there by daughters in service, by the young girls of today. With careful, infrequent washing they will last for exactly a month. And their owners find themselves deliciously naked as the holes begin to spread.

But there is none of that nonsense about old Gunhild's shoes. At suitable intervals she takes them to a fisherman of similar age and outlook, and has the uppers and soles permeated with a powerful concoction of grease against which water stands no chance. I have seen that stuff being boiled up on the beach: it is made of tallow, tar, and resin.

Yesterday, as I strolled along the beach looking at driftwood and shells and stones, I came upon a fragment of plate glass. How it came there is a mystery to me; to look at it is like looking at an illusion or a lie. It is hard to imagine a fisherman rowing it there, leaving it there, and going away again! I left it where it lay, thick and plain and commonplace—from the window of a streetcar perhaps. Time was when glass was rare, and bottle-green—God bless the olden days when anything was rare!

And now smoke is rising from the fishermen's huts on the southern tip of the island. It is evening; gruel is being prepared. And when they have eaten their supper, decent folk go straight to bed, in order to be up again at dawn. Only the young and foolish continue to slouch around from cottage to cottage, dragging out the time, heedless of their own best interests.

II

A man landed here this morning; he has come to paint the house. But old Gunhild, who is very old indeed, and crippled with arthritis, gets him to start by chopping a few days' supply of wood for the stove. I myself have offered, time and again, to chop that wood; but she thinks my clothes are too good and has steadfastly refused to give me the ax.

The imported painter is a stocky little man with red hair and no beard; I watch him cautiously from a window, to see how he goes about his work. When I see that he is talking to himself, I steal out of the house and listen. If a blow goes astray, he contains himself and says nothing—unless he grazes his knuckles, in which case his irritation vents itself and he says, "Damn! Damnation!"—then looks quickly around and starts humming, to camouflage what he has said.

Why, I know that painter! Only he's no bloody painter—it's Grindhusen, one of my mates from the road-building days at Skreia.

I go up to him, make myself known, chat with him.

It is many, many years since we built roads together, Grindhusen and I: a pair of callow youths who danced along the roads in the sorriest shoes and ate such food as we could scrape up money for. But whenever we had some money to spare, we would throw an all-night Saturday dance in honor of the girls, with our mates as hangers-on, and the woman of the house growing rich on the coffee she sold us. Then we would work with a will for another week, impatient for Saturday to come around again. As for Grindhusen, he was after the girls like a red-haired wolf.

Does he remember the old days at Skreia?

He looks at me, sizing me up, reticent; it takes me a little time getting him to share my memories.

Well, yes, he remembers Skreia.

"And do you remember Anders the File, and Corkscrew? And Petra?"

"Which do you mean?"

"Petra. Wasn't she your sweetheart?"

"Well, yes, I remember her. In fact, I ended up getting hitched to her."

Grindhusen starts chopping again.

"You got hitched to her?"

"Well, yes. That's the way it was. But what was I going to say—ah yes: looks like you've become a big shot, eh?"

"Why do you say that? These clothes? Don't you have a best suit?"

"How much did you pay for that lot?"

"I don't remember, but not a great deal—I couldn't tell you exactly."

Grindhusen looks at me in amazement and bursts out laughing.

"Don't you remember what you pay for your clothes?" Then he turns serious, shakes his head, and says, "No, I suppose you don't. That's how it is when you're well off."

Old Gunhild comes out of the cottage, sees us passing the time of day by the chopping block, and tells Grindhusen to start on the painting.

"So you've turned painter now," I say.

Grindhusen doesn't answer, and I realize that I oughtn't to have said that in front of a third person.

III

For a couple of hours he daubs and smears, and soon the cottage's northern wall, facing the sea, is a gleaming new red.

During the midday break I go out to Grindhusen with a shot of brandy; we lie on the ground, talking and smoking.

"Painter? I'm not *exactly* a painter," he says. "But when someone asks me if I can paint the wall of a house, I figure I can manage that. And if someone asks me if I can do this, that, or the other, I reckon I can manage that too. Hey, that's a mighty fine brandy you've got."

His wife and two children were living six or seven miles away; every Saturday he went home to them. There were also two grown-up daughters, one married; and Grindhusen was already a grandfather. When he had given Gunhild's cottage its two coats of paint, he was to go to the parsonage and dig a well; in the country there was always something that needed doing. And when winter set in and the earth froze solid, he either went logging in the forest or took things easy for a while, until some job or other appeared from nowhere. His family was not too large nowadays, and something would turn up tomorrow as surely as it had today.

"Now if only I had the chance, I'd buy myself some stonemason's tools," says Grindhusen.

"Are you a stonemason too?"

"I'm not *exactly* a stonemason. But when the well's been dug it will have to be lined, that's obvious . . ."

I wander about the island as usual, thinking of this and that. Peace, peace, a heavenly peace speaks to me in muted tones from every tree in the forest. Why, there are hardly any songbirds left, although a number of crows wheel noiselessly from perch to perch. And the rowanberry clusters fall with a thud and bury themselves in the moss.

Maybe Grindhusen is right: maybe it's a universal truth that something will turn up tomorrow as surely as it has today. It's two weeks now since I saw a newspaper, and I'm still alive and well, and making great strides toward inner peace: singing, flexing my muscles, standing bareheaded as I gaze at the stars in the evening sky.

For the last eighteen years I have sat in cafés and complained to the waiter if a fork was not quite clean. Here in Gunhild's cottage I complain about no forks! Did you see Grindhusen, I say to myself: how in lighting his pipe he held the match till the very end and never burned his leathery fingers? I notice, too, that when a fly crawls over his hand he simply lets it crawl; perhaps he never even feels it. That's how a man should be where flies are concerned.

That evening Grindhusen takes the boat and rows away. I roam the beach, singing a snatch or two, throwing stones far out over the sea, hauling driftwood ashore. The stars are out, the moon is up. An hour or two later Grindhusen returns, with a good set of stonemason's tools in the boat. Those are stolen goods, all right, I think to myself. We each shoulder a load and hide the tools in the forest.

By now it is night, and we go our separate ways.

The next afternoon sees the painting of the house completed; but to make up the day Grindhusen agrees to chop firewood until six o'clock. I take Gunhild's boat and go out fishing, in order not to be around when he leaves. I catch no fish; I keep shivering and looking at my watch. Surely he must have gone by now, I say to myself; and around seven o'clock I row home again. Grindhusen has reached the mainland and shouts good-bye to me from there.

A ray of warmth pierces me through and through; it is like a summons from my youth, from Skreia, from a generation back.

I row over to him and say, "Can you dig that well on your own?"

"No, I'll need someone to help me."

"Take me!" I exclaim. "Wait here, I'm just going back to settle up."

I am halfway across before Grindhusen calls out, "No—I need to hurry—night's coming on. Besides, you're not serious, are you?"

"Give me five or ten minutes. I'll be right back."

And Grindhusen sits down on the beach: he remembers that I have some mighty fine brandy in my hip flask.

IV

It was a Saturday when we came to the parsonage. Grindhusen had finally, and with many misgivings, taken me on as his assistant. I had bought provisions and working clothes, and stood now at the appointed place, clad in a smock and top boots. I was free and unknown; I soon learned to walk with long, slow steps, and as far as my face and hands were concerned, I already had a proletarian look. We were to live at the parsonage and cook for ourselves in the washhouse.

And so we started to dig.

I did my full share, and Grindhusen had no complaints. "You'll make a real good worker yet," he said.

After a while the priest came out to us, and we raised our caps and bowed. He was a mild, elderly man with a deliberate manner of speech; the wrinkles that fanned out from his eyes were like the remnants of a thousand good-natured smiles. He was sorry to bother us, but his poultry were a perfect nuisance, straying into the garden year after year; perhaps we could come and do something about the garden wall first, or rather one particular section of it?

Grindhusen answered, Why, of course, that could certainly be fixed.

So we went and sorted out the tumbledown wall, and while we were busy with this, a young lady came out and watched us for a while. We raised our caps again, and I thought how lovely she was. Then a teenage boy came out to have a look, and plied us with questions. I guessed they were brother and sister. The work went on apace, while the youngsters stood and watched.

Then it was evening. Grindhusen went off home, while I stayed behind, spending the night in the hayloft.

The next day was Sunday. I didn't dare put on my town clothes for fear they should look too smart on the likes of me; but I gave yesterday's outfit a good going over. I spent the mild Sunday morning strolling about the parsonage grounds; I chatted with the farmhands, and joined them in chaffing two of the maids. When the bell began ringing for church, I sent to ask if I could borrow a hymnal, and the priest's son brought me one. From the tallest of the farmhands I borrowed a jacket; it was on the small side, but by taking off my smock and vest, I made it into a passable fit. And so I went to church.

The inner peace that I had been building up during my stay on the island proved quite inadequate as yet: as the organ tones swelled out, I found myself wrenched from my context and ready to burst into sobs. "Shut your trap!" I told myself—"it's only nerves." I had chosen an isolated seat, and I hid my emotion as best I could. I was glad when the service was over.

After dining off the meat that I had cooked for myself, I was invited into the kitchen for a cup of coffee. As I was sitting there, in came the young lady from yesterday. I stood up, bowed, and received a gracious nod in return. How charming she was, with her youth and her dainty hands! When I got up to go, I forgot myself and said, "Thank you so much for your kindness, most gracious lady!"

She looked at me in astonishment, wrinkling her brows and slowly turning crimson. Then she turned and flounced out of the kitchen. She was very young.

Now I'd really messed it up!

Sick at heart, I crawled up into the woods to hide. Impertinent fool that I was, not to have held my tongue! Abysmal old windbag that I was!

The parsonage buildings lay on a little slope, topped by a wooded plateau, with here and there a clearing. It struck me that this plateau was the proper place to dig the well, with a pipe leading down to the buildings. I made an estimate of the height and felt confident that the fall was sufficient. On the way home I paced out the distance, and made it about two hundred and fifty feet.

But what business of mine was the well? Let us not be caught off guard like that again: turning genteel, blurting out affronts, acting above our station.

V

On Monday morning Grindhusen returned and we started to dig. Out came the old priest again: would we mind putting up a post for him on the road up to the church? He needed this post—there used to be one there, till it blew down—needed it for nailing up notices and announcements.

We put up a new post, taking pains to see that it stood as straight as a sentry; then we crowned it with a hood of zinc.

While I was busy on this hood, I got Grindhusen to suggest that the post should be painted red—he still had some red paint left over from Gunhild's cottage. The priest, on the other hand, wanted the post white, and Grindhusen echoed him obsequiously; so I pointed out that white notices would show up better against a red background. Whereupon the myriad wrinkles around the priest's eyes melted into a smile, and he said, "Yes, you're absolutely right."

That smile and those few words of assent were all I needed to make me proud and happy in my inmost being.

The young lady came up and addressed a few words to Grindhusen; she even joked with him, asking him who this red cardinal was that he was installing up here. To me she said nothing, nor did she look my way when I raised my cap.

Dinner was a sore trial. Not that the food was poor; but the way Grindhusen ate his soup, and the glistening pork fat around his mouth, filled me with disgust.

What will he be like eating porridge? I reflected hysterically.

When Grindhusen stretched himself out on the bench for an after-dinner nap, still in the same greasy condition, I let him have it and shouted, "For goodness' sake, wipe your mouth, man!"

He looked at me, then wiped his mouth with his hand.

"Mouth?" he said.

It seemed wisest to laugh it off. "Ha-ha, fooled you there all right, Grindhusen," I said. But I felt dissatisfied with myself and went straight out of the washhouse.

Anyway, I said to myself, I intend Mademoiselle to acknowledge me when I greet her; she'll soon learn that I have my wits about me. That well and water pipe now—what if I came up with a detailed plan! Not having any surveying instruments to determine the fall from the top of the slope, I set to work improvising one. A wooden pipe would serve, with a couple of lamp chimneys let in as uprights, the joints sealed with putty, and the whole thing filled with water.

More and more jobs kept cropping up at the parsonage: a doorstep to be straightened, a foundation wall to be repaired, the hayloft ramp to be put in order before the corn could be brought in. The priest liked having everything in good order, and since we were paid by the day, it was all the same to us. But as the days went by I enjoyed my workmate's company less and less. I was vexed beyond measure by such things as his habit of holding a loaf against his chest and hacking off chunks with a greasy pocket knife that he was constantly licking; not to mention the fact that he never washed from one Sunday to the next. Then there was the glistening dewdrop which, before sunrise and after sunset, invariably hung from his nose. And the state of his nails! And those misshapen ears!

Whereas I, alas, was an upstart with elegant ways picked up in cafés. Unable after a while to refrain any longer from censur-

ing my companion's filthy habits, I caused such bad blood between us that I feared we would sooner or later have to split up.
Meanwhile, we spoke no more than was strictly necessary.

The well remained as undug as ever. Sunday came around
again, and Grindhusen went home.

My surveying gadget was ready by now, and in the afternoon
I went up on the roof of the main building and set it up. I saw
at once that the line of the "sights" cut the slope some fifteen or
twenty feet below its top. Good. Even if I allowed three or four
feet down to the water level in the well, the pressure would be
more than enough.

As I lay there using my "level," I was spotted by the priest's
son—Harold Meltzer was his name. What was I doing up
there? Measuring the slope—what for? Why did I need to
know the height? Please, could he have a look?

Later on I got a thirty-foot line and measured the slope from
foot to summit, Harold helping me. When we came down
again, I presented myself to the priest and outlined my plan.

VI

The priest listened patiently and didn't immediately show me
the door.

"Really?" he said with a smile. "Well, perhaps. But it will
cost a lot of money. And in any case, what's the point?"

"It's seventy yards to the well we've started to dig. Seventy
yards for the maids to walk, no matter what the conditions,
summer and winter."

"Yes, there's that. But it will cost the earth."

"Not counting the well, which you're having in any case, the
actual pipe—material and labor—won't come to more than a
couple of hundred kroner."

The priest sat up.

"Not more?"

"No."

I paused a little over each answer, as if I'd been born with a slow, deliberate nature; but I'd worked it all out a long time ago.

"It would be a great convenience," said the priest thoughtfully. "That tub in the kitchen's certainly a messy business."

"And think of all the water that has to be carried to the bedrooms."

"Ah, the bedrooms would be no better off. They're upstairs."

"We'd run a pipe up there too."

"Can we really do that? All the way upstairs? Will the pressure be sufficient?"

Here I paused even longer over my answer, as if weighed down with the sense of my responsibility.

"I think I can safely promise you a jet that would clear the roof."

"No, really?" exclaimed the priest. "Come, let's see where you propose digging the well."

We went up the slope, the priest, Harold, and I. I let the priest use my gadget and convinced him that the pressure would be more than sufficient.

"I'd better talk to your mate about it," he said.

By way of undermining Grindhusen, I replied, "Why bother? He doesn't understand these things."

The priest looked at me.

"Really?" he said.

We came down again. The priest said, half to himself, "You're right there—it's an endless business fetching water in the winter. In the summer too, for that matter. I'd better discuss it with my family."

And he went indoors.

Ten minutes or so later I was summoned to the front steps, where the whole family was assembled.

"So you're the man who's going to supply us with water pipes?" Madame asked in a friendly tone.

I bowed, slowly and ceremoniously, cap in hand, while the priest answered for me: yes, I was the man.

Mademoiselle looked at me curiously and at once began chatting with Harold. Madame continued to interrogate me: Would it really be the same system they had in the city, you turned on a tap and the water came? And just the same upstairs? A couple of hundred kroner? "Well, I think you should go ahead," she told her husband.

"Ah, you think so? Come on then, let's all go up the hill once again and have a look."

We went up the hill. I set up my "level" and let them look through it.

"Amazing!" said Madame.

Mademoiselle said never a word.

The priest asked, "But is there water here?"

I replied very sagaciously that I couldn't *swear* to it but there were plenty of hopeful signs.

"What signs?" asked Madame.

"The nature of the ground up here. And those willows and alders. Willows need moisture, you know."

The priest nodded and said, "This fellow knows his job all right, Marie."

On the way home Madame reached the fallacious conclusion that she could manage with one maid less if they had running water. To avoid letting her down, I remarked, "Especially in the summer, perhaps. You could water the garden with a hose from the cellar window."

"Fantastic!" she exclaimed.

I didn't venture even to suggest a pipe to the barn. I had realized all along that a well twice the size, with an extension pipe to the barn, would lighten the dairymaid's work as much as it would the kitchen maid's. But this would just about double the cost. To suggest such a grandiose plan was inadvisable.

Even as it was, I had agreed to wait until Grindhusen returned. The priest said he wanted to sleep on it.

VII

I now had the job of breaking it to my mate that the well was to be dug on the plateau; and to avoid arousing his suspicions, I laid all the blame on the priest, making out that it was his idea, which I had merely supported. Grindhusen was quite happy: he saw at once that it would mean more work for us, since we would have to dig a trench for the pipe.

As good luck would have it, on Monday morning the priest began by saying to Grindhusen, half in jest, "Your mate and I have decided to dig the well up on the plateau and run a pipe down—how's that for a crazy idea?"

Grindhusen thought it was a mighty fine idea.

But when we talked it over and went, the three of us, to inspect the site for the well, Grindhusen began to suspect that I'd had more to do with the plan than I was willing to let on. The trench for the pipe, he pointed out, would have to be very deep, because of the frost—

"Four foot six at the most," I interrupted.

—and that would be an expensive affair.

"Your mate figures a couple of hundred kroner in all," answered the priest.

Grindhusen was all at sea where estimates were concerned and could only say, "Yes, well, two hundred kroner is still a tidy sum."

I said, "There'll be less for his reverence to pay in dilapidations when he moves."

The priest started.

"Dilapidations? But I've no intention of moving."

"Then I sincerely hope that your reverence will enjoy the blessings of running water into a ripe old age."

At this the priest stared at me and asked, "What's your name?"

"Knut Pedersen." *

"And where do you come from?"

"From the north."

I knew what these questions were getting at, and resolved never again to talk in that novelettish way.

However, the well and the pipe were decided on, and we set to work . . .

The days that followed were mainly cheerful ones. At first I was very anxious about whether we would find water, and for several nights I slept badly; but once this anxiety was removed, there remained only a plain, straightforward job of work. There was water aplenty: after a day or two we had to bail it out in bucketfuls each morning. The bottom was of clay, and we got in a fine old mess as we squelched around in the well. After a week of digging, we turned to quarrying stones to line the well—a job we both knew inside out from our Skreia days. Then we dug for another week until the well was deep enough. The bottom was now so wet that we had to start lining at once if the clay walls were not to collapse and bury us.

And so we dug and quarried and lined, while week after week went by. It was a big well and a fine job; the priest was quite pleased. Grindhusen and I began to hit it off better again; and when he learned that I wanted no more than a fair laborer's wage, even if on this job it was often I who took command, he was anxious to do something in return, with the result that his table manners became more appetizing. My lot was now perfect: no one was ever going to lure me to the city again!

In the evenings I would wander about the forest, or the churchyard, reading the inscriptions on the tombstones and thinking of this and that. Also, I was looking for a thumbnail,

* Hamsun's real name.—Trans.

from a dead body. I needed this nail for a whim I had, a caprice. I had found a splendid piece of birch root, from which I intended to carve a pipe bowl in the shape of a clenched fist. The thumb was to form a lid, and I wanted to cut a nail into it, to make it really lifelike. The ring finger was to be encircled by a little gold ring.

With such trivialities as these, my mind was soothed and salved. My life was free from hurry, I could daydream without neglecting some duty, the evenings were my own. If possible, I wanted also to work up a little feeling for the sanctity of the church, and terror of the dead. I recalled from long, long ago a profound and luxurious sense of mystery, and it was this that I wished to partake of again. When I found that nail, maybe a cry would arise from the tombs: "That is mine!" Whereupon I would drop the thing in terror and take to my heels.

"How that weathervane creaks!" Grindhusen would say from time to time.

"Are you scared?"

"Not scared exactly—but it gives me the creeps of a night time when I think of all those dead bodies lying so near."

Happy Grindhusen!

One day Harold taught me how to plant fir cones and shrubs. This was a skill I knew nothing about—it wasn't yet taught when I went to school. But once I had learned the technique I became an assiduous Sunday planter. In return I taught young Harold one or two things that were new to him, and we became good friends.

VIII

All might now have been well but for the young lady, of whom I found myself growing daily more fond. Her name was Elischeba, Elizabeth. She was no real beauty, I suppose, but her red lips and blue, girlish glance made her lovely. Elischeba, Elizabeth, you are in the first flush of dawn, and your eyes hold the world in their gaze. When you spoke with young Eric from the neighboring farm one evening, those eyes were all ripeness and sweetness.

It was easy enough for Grindhusen. In his younger days he had been after the girls like a wolf, and he still, from long habit, swaggered around with his hat at a rakish angle. But by now he was well and truly tamed, as was to be expected; such is the course of nature. Still, not everyone follows the course of nature, not everyone is tamed—and what is to become of those others? And now there was little Elizabeth—who, by the way, was far from little, being as tall as her mother. And with her mother's high bosom.

Since that first Sunday I had received no more invitations to coffee in the kitchen; I myself wanted none, shamefaced as I still was, and made it easy for none to be offered. But finally, in mid-week, one of the maids brought me a message: I was not to bury myself in the woods every Sunday afternoon but was to come in for a cup of coffee. Madame had said so.

Good.

Should I dress in my Sunday best? No harm, perhaps, in giving the young lady a hint of who I was: a man who had of his own free will renounced the life of the city and assumed the badge of servitude, but for all that a man with technical flair who knew how to install running water. But by the time I was dressed, I sensed for myself that my workaday clothes suited me better; so I took off my Sunday things and hid them in my bag.

In the event, it was not Mademoiselle who greeted me in the kitchen but Madame. She chatted with me for some time, and she had placed a small white cloth under my coffee cup.

"It looks like that trick with the egg will turn out expensive for us," she said with a good-humored laugh. "The boy's used up half a dozen eggs already."

The trick I had taught Harold was the one of forcing a

shelled boiled egg down through the neck of a decanter by
rarefying the air in the latter. It was about the only physics I
knew.

"But that experiment with the stick, breaking it in those two
loops of paper—that was really instructive," Madame went on.
"I don't understand these things, but . . . When will the well
be ready?"

"The well *is* ready. Tomorrow we start on the trench."

"How long will that take?"

"About a week. Then the plumber can come."

"Fancy that!"

I thanked her and left. Madame had the habit—retained, no
doubt, from earlier years—of giving you an occasional sidelong
glance. Yet her words were quite devoid of guile.

And now the leaves on the trees were yellowing one by one,
and earth and air were fragrant with autumn. Only the fungus
family was out in full display, shooting up everywhere, growing
thick and good on chubby stems: cepes, fairy-ring champignons,
milk fungus. Here and there a fly agaric flaunted its scarlet cap
and flecks of white. That singular fungus! It grows alongside
the edible kinds, nourished by the same earth, receiving the sun
and rain from heaven on the same terms; it is fat and firm and
good to eat—except that it is full of pungent muscarine. I once
thought of inventing a magnificent old legend about the fly
agaric and saying I had read it in a book.*

I have always enjoyed observing flowers and insects in their
struggle for survival. When the sun was hot they would come to
life again and abandon themselves for a few hours to their
former joy; the big, strong flies were as fully alive as they had
been at midsummer. There was a peculiar kind of flea beetle
here which I hadn't seen before—little yellow things, no bigger
than an 8-point comma, but capable of jumping several thou-

---

* The Vikings are believed to have been in the habit of eating fly agaric
before a battle, with the object of going berserk.—Trans.

sand times their own length. What enormous strength such a creature has in relation to its size! Here comes a little spider with a hindpart like a pale-yellow pearl—a pearl so heavy that the creature can only climb up a blade of grass by turning its back toward the ground. If it meets with an obstacle over which it cannot drag its pearl, it drops down again and starts on another blade. This pearl spider is no mere spider, period. If I hold out a leaf to help it find its feet on a floor, it fumbles around for a little on the leaf before deciding that no, this is not quite right, and drawing back from any such pitfall as a floor . . .

I hear my name being called from the wood below me. It is Harold, my Sunday-school teacher, who has set me a lesson from Pontoppidan's catechism commentary and wants to test me on it. I am moved when I hear religion proclaimed anew, the way I would have liked to proclaim it in my own childhood.

IX

The well was finished, the trench was dug, the plumber had arrived. He chose Grindhusen to help him lay the pipe, while I was put to work in the house, making ready for the pipes leading up from the cellar.

One day, while I was excavating in the cellar, Madame came down. I called out to her to be careful, but she took it very casually. "There's no hole here, is there?" she asked, pointing. "Or here?" Finally she missed her footing and came slithering down into the trench beside me. There we stood. We had no light, and for her, coming in from the daylight, it must have been pitch dark. She groped about the trench and said, "And now can I get up again?"

I lifted her up. It was easy enough: her figure was still very trim for the mother of a big, strong girl.

"Well, I must say!" she exclaimed, shaking the earth from her dress. "That was a good brisk ride . . . I'd like you to help me with something upstairs one of these days, will you? Only we must wait until my husband is over at the chapel—he hates alterations. When do you expect to finish this job?"

I mentioned a period of a week or so.

"And where are you going from here?"

"To the next farm. Grindhusen has arranged for us to harvest potatoes . . . "

Next I came up to the kitchen and sawed a hole in the floor with a compass saw. Miss Elizabeth inevitably had things to do in the kitchen during the time I was busy there, and she overcame her dislike of me enough to say a few words and stand watching the work for a while.

"Imagine, Oline," she said to the maid, "when all you have to do is turn on a faucet."

But Oline, who was old, looked anything but overjoyed. It was blasphemy, she said, making the water come right into the kitchen. For twenty years she had carried in all the water they needed. What was she expected to do now?

"Rest," I said.

"Rest? I thought mankind was made to work."

"And sew things for your trousseau," said Mademoiselle with a little laugh.

It was girlish chatter, but I was grateful to her for taking part in the general conversation and being in the kitchen for a while. And heavens, how intelligent I became, how aptly I talked, how like a boy I plumed myself! I remember it still. But suddenly Miss Elizabeth seemed to decide that it was not proper for her to stay with us any longer and left the room.

That evening I went, as so often before, up to the church-yard; but on seeing that Mademoiselle was there before me, I took myself off and wandered into the forest. Afterward I thought: Now, surely, she will be touched by my modesty and say, "Poor fellow, he showed real delicacy there!" After that it would only remain for her to follow me into the forest. Taken thus by surprise, I would get up from my stone and bow. Then she would be a little embarrassed and say, "I was just passing— it's a lovely evening—what are you doing here?" "Just sitting here," I reply, returning as if from a great distance with my innocent eyes. And when she hears that I am just sitting here late in the evening, then she realizes that I am a deep soul and a dreamer, and falls in love with me . . .

The next evening she was in the churchyard again, and a presumptuous thought came flitting through my head: it was me she was after! But when I looked more closely, I could see that she was doing something to a grave; so it was not me she was after. I crept away to the great ant hill up in the woods and watched the creatures for as long as I could see; then I sat listening to the thud of the spruce cones and rowanberry clusters. I hummed, whispered, pondered; from time to time I had to get up and walk for a bit to keep warm. The hours passed, night came, I was so much in love that I walked bareheaded and let the stars outstare me.

"How late is it?" Grindhusen was liable to ask when I came up to the hayloft.

"Eleven o'clock," I would answer, though it might be two or even three in the morning.

"Is that your idea of bedtime? Ugh, damnation! Waking people up after they've gone right off to sleep!"

Grindhusen would turn onto his other side, and a moment later fall asleep again. It was easy enough for Grindhusen.

But oh, what a fool a middle-aged man becomes when he falls in love. And was it not I who was going to prove by my example that one *can* find peace and quiet?

X

A man turned up to reclaim his stonemason's tools. What—
so Grindhusen hadn't stolen them! How boring and mediocre
Grindhusen was in all his ways—nothing good and generous
about him!

I said, "It's just eat, sleep, and work with you, eh, Grindhusen. There's a man here come for the tools. Why, you only borrowed them, you poor creature."

"You're a fool," said Grindhusen, taking umbrage.

So once again I appeased him by passing off my words as a
joke.

"What do we do now?" he asked.

"Come off it—*you* know."

"I know?"

"Sure. If I know you, that is."

And Grindhusen was appeased.

But during the midday break, while I was cutting his hair, I
offended him again by suggesting he should give it a good
wash.

"It beats me how a man of your age can be so stupid," he
said.

And God knows, Grindhusen may have been right. Grandfather or not, he still had his crop of red hair intact . . .

Was the hayloft suddenly haunted? Who had been in there
one day and made it nice and tidy? Grindhusen and I each had
our own bed space; I had bought myself a couple of blankets,
whereas Grindhusen bedded down every night fully clothed,
burrowing at random into the hay. And now my pair of blankets had been straightened to give the appearance of a genuine
bed. I had no objection: presumably one of the maids wanted to
teach me a few folkways. It was all one to me.

And now I was due to go upstairs and saw a hole in the floor, but Madame told me to wait: tomorrow the priest would be over at the chapel, at the other end of the parish, and I wouldn't be disturbing him. In the morning there came a further post-ponement: Miss Elizabeth was about to go shopping at the store, and I was to go with her and carry all her purchases.

"You go ahead," I said, "I'll follow."

Strange girl! Had she decided to put up with my company? She said, "But will you find the way on your own?"

"Oh yes—I've been there before; it's where we get our food."

Since I could hardly go wandering all over the parish in my clay-stained working clothes, I put on my best trousers, though without changing my smock. Then I set off in pursuit. It was about four miles; over the last mile I kept catching glimpses of Miss Elizabeth ahead of me, but I took care not to follow too hard on her heels. Once she looked around; whereupon I made myself as small as I could and side-stepped into the forest.

Mademoiselle stayed behind at a friend's house, while I re-turned home with the shopping. I arrived around noon and was invited to eat in the kitchen. The house seemed deserted: Harold was out somewhere, the maids were laundering in the washhouse, only Oline was pottering around in the kitchen.

After dinner I went upstairs and began sawing on the land-ing.

"Come in here and give me a hand for a moment," said Madame, leading the way.

We went past the priest's study and into the bedroom.

"I want my bed moved," said Madame. "It's too near the stove in winter—it gets terribly hot."

We moved the bed over to the window.

"Don't you think it's better here?" she asked. "Cooler?"

I chanced to look at her: that slanting side glance of hers was fixed on me. Wow! And all at once I was mere flesh and blood and foolishness. I heard her say, "Are you crazy? For goodness'

sake—the door—" and then my name whispered again and
again . . .

I sawed through that hole on the landing, and finished off the
job, while Madame never left my side. She wanted so badly to
talk, to explain herself, laughing and crying all the time.

I said, "That picture that was hanging over your bed—hadn't
we better move that too?"

"You've got something there," answered Madame.

XI

And now the pipes were all laid, the faucets were turned on,
and the water came gushing into the sinks. Grindhusen had
found someone else to lend him the necessary tools, so we were
able to plaster up a few holes left here and there. Two days later
we had filled in the trench leading up to the well and our work
at the parsonage was done. The priest was pleased with us, and
offered to put up a notice on the red post describing us as expert
plumbers; but since by now it was so late in the year that the
earth might freeze solid at any moment, this would hardly have
helped us. Instead, we asked him to bear us in mind in the
spring.

We now moved to the neighboring farm to dig up potatoes.
Before leaving we had to promise to look in again at the parsonage whenever we had a chance.

At the new place there was quite an army of workers; we split
up into groups and had a fine old time. But the work was unlikely to last for more than a week, after which we would be
footloose again.

One evening the priest came over and offered me work on the
parsonage farm. The offer was a good one, and I considered it
for a while before finally turning it down. I preferred to rove

around as a free agent, picking up such work as I could, sleeping out, taking myself a little by surprise. In the potato field I had met a man with whom I wanted to join forces when I parted from Grindhusen. This new man was a kindred spirit and, to judge by what I saw and heard of him, a good worker. Christened Lars Falkberget, he had adopted the name of Falkenberg as better-sounding.

The potato harvesting was done under the direction of young Eric, and it was he who carted the crop away. He was a handsome young man of twenty, mature and reliable for his age, with the self-assurance of the farmer's son. There was evidently something between him and Miss Elizabeth from the parsonage, because one day she came over to the field where we were working and chatted with him for quite a while. Before leaving she found a few words for me too, telling me that Oline had begun getting used to running water.

"And yourself?" I asked.

Out of politeness she said something in reply to this also, but I could see that she had no wish to get drawn into conversation with me.

How prettily she was dressed, with a new light-colored coat to offset her blue eyes . . .

The next day Eric had an accident: his horse bolted, dragged him across several fields, and finally dashed him against a fence. He was badly knocked about and spitting blood. Falkenberg was now promoted to driving the cart.

Though I feigned sympathy over the accident, and was silent and somber with the rest, I felt no grief. I had no prospect of winning Miss Elizabeth, to be sure, but he who had stood above me in her favor was now out of the way.

The next evening I went and sat in the churchyard. If only Miss Elizabeth would come now! A quarter of an hour passed and she came. I rose abruptly, artful to the core, looked as if I wanted to escape, but found myself caught and gave up the attempt. Here my artfulness failed me; I became unsure of myself from having her so near, and I started saying something: "Eric—that was bad luck he had yesterday."

"I know."

"He hurt himself badly."

"Yes, of course he hurt himself badly. Why do you talk to me about him?"

"I thought . . . No, I don't know. But in any case he'll recover, of course. Then everything will be all right again."

"Of course, of course."

Pause.

It sounded as if she had been aping my words. Suddenly she said with a smile, "You're a strange one. Why do you come all this way and sit here of an evening?"

"It's just a way I've got into. To while away the hours until bedtime."

"You aren't afraid then?"

Her joke steadied me, I felt myself on solid ground again and answered, "There's another reason: I wanted to learn to shudder in my shoes again."

"Shudder in your shoes? Like the boy in the fairy tale? Where did you read about that?"

"I don't know. In some book or other, I suppose."

Pause.

"Why don't you want to work on our farm?"

"It wouldn't suit me. I'm joining forces with a new man now. We shall pack our bags and go."

"Where will you go?"

"I don't know. East or west. We're wanderers."

Pause.

"That's too bad," she said. "I mean, you shouldn't do that . . . Now, how did you say Eric was? That's what I came about."

"He's not well, he's in a very bad way, I believe, but . . ."

"Does the doctor think he'll pull through?"

"I imagine so. I haven't heard to the contrary."

"Good night then."

O to be young and rich and famous and a man of learning!
. . . There she goes . . .

Before leaving the churchyard I found a serviceable thumbnail, which I pocketed. I waited a moment or two, peering this
way and that and listening, but all was quiet. No one cried:
"That is mine!"

XII

Falkenberg and I set out on our wanderings. It was evening,
the weather cool, the heavens high as the stars lit up. I per-
suaded my companion to go via the churchyard; absurd creature
that I was, I wanted to see if there was a light in a little window
down at the parsonage. O to be young and rich and . . .

We walked for several hours; our loads were not too heavy,
we were a pair of wanderers still fairly new to each other, we
could talk together. We passed one roadside store and came to a
second; we could see the chapel tower in the clear evening light.

From long habit I wanted to go into the churchyard here
also. I said, "Why don't we bed down in here for the night?"

"A fat lot of sense that makes!" retorted Falkenberg—"when
there's hay in every barn now, and if we're turned out of the
barns, we'll be snugger still in the woods."

And Falkenberg resumed command of our wanderings.

He was a man in his thirties, tall and well-built (though
stooping a little), with a long, drooping mustache. He was on
the taciturn side, but quick-witted and intelligent; moreover,
he had the loveliest singing voice—in short, he was a very different character from Grindhusen. He spoke a crazy mixture of
western and eastern dialects, with some Swedish words thrown
in, so that it was quite impossible to say where he hailed from.

We came to a farm where the dogs barked and people were

still up; Falkenberg asked to speak to the man. A mere lad came out.

Had he any work for us?

No.

But the fence along the road was very rickety—couldn't we do something about it?

No. The man himself had nothing else to do at this time of year.

Could we have shelter for the night?

Sorry, but—

In the barn?

No, the farm girls were still sleeping there.

"The bastard!" muttered Falkenberg as we took ourselves off.

We turned in through a little wood, keeping an eye open for somewhere to sleep.

"Why don't we go back to the farm—to the girls? They wouldn't throw us out, would they?"

Falkenberg thought it over.

"The dogs would bark," he answered.

We came out into a field with two horses in it. One had a bell.

"He's a fine master, he is," said Falkenberg, "leaving his horses in the open and his farm girls to sleep in the barn so late in the year. "Let's do these beasts a kindness and ride them for a bit."

He caught the bell horse, stuffed its bell full of moss and grass, and mounted. My horse was more skittish, and I had more trouble catching it.

We rode across the field, found a gate, and emerged onto the road. We each had one of my blankets to sit on, but neither of us had a bridle.

It went well, uncommonly well: we rode for several miles until we reached another village. Suddenly we heard people on the road ahead of us.

"Time we started galloping," said Falkenberg over his shoulder.

But the long-limbed Falkenberg was not much of a rider: first he grasped the bell strap; then he threw himself forward and clung to the horse's neck. I had a glimpse of one leg silhouetted against the sky as he fell off.

Fortunately we were in no danger: it was only a courting couple.

After another half hour's ride, by which time we were both of us stiff and sore, we slithered to the ground and urged the horses home. Then we continued on foot.

There came a distant "gakgak, gakgak." I recognized the cry of the gray goose. As children we were taught to fold our hands and stand quite still so as not to frighten the gray goose as it flew by; I had nothing to lose by doing the same again now. A serene and mystical mood flickered within me; I held my breath and gazed. There it came, the sky trailing behind it like the wake of a ship. "Gakgak!" came the cry from overhead, as the splendid plow glided onward beneath the stars . . .

Finally we found a barn on a farm where all was silent and slept for several hours—so soundly that the people on the farm surprised us there next morning.

Falkenberg at once addressed the man and offered to pay: we had arrived so late last night, he explained, that we hadn't wanted to wake anyone; but we weren't runaways. The man not only refused payment but even gave us coffee in the kitchen. However, he had no work for us: the harvest was in, and he and his boy had nothing to do themselves except repair the fences.

XIII

We wandered for three days without finding work; instead, we had to pay for our food and drink and were growing steadily poorer.

"How much have you got left and how much have I?" asked Falkenberg. "We'll never get anywhere like this." And he suggested we should try a little stealing.

We talked this over and decided to bide our time. Food was no problem; we could always swipe a chicken or two. What we really needed was ready money, and ready money we meant to have, one way or another—after all, we weren't angels.

"I'm no angel descended from heaven," said Falkenberg. "Here I am, sitting in my Sunday clothes—which are no better than the next man's work clothes. I wash them in the stream and wait for them to dry; if they wear out I mend them; and if I earn a bit extra, I buy some more. That's the long and the short of it."

"Didn't young Eric say you drank like a fish?"

"That young cub! Of course I drink. Food by itself is so boring . . . Come, let's find a farm with a piano."

I thought: A piano on a farm means a certain standard of living—so that's where the stealing begins.

It was afternoon when we came to such a farm. Falkenberg had put on my town clothes in advance, and given me his bag to carry, leaving him free as the wind. Without more ado he went up the front steps and disappeared inside for a while. When he emerged he told me casually that he was going to tune the piano.

Going to *what?*

"Be quiet, you," said Falkenberg. "I've done it before, although I don't go around boasting about it."

And when he fished out a tuning key from his bag, I realized he was in earnest.

I was told to remain within earshot while he tuned.

So I wandered around and whiled away the time; every now and again, when I came to the south side of the house, I would hear Falkenberg in the living room, working at the piano with might and main. He couldn't strike up a real tune, but he had a good ear; and whenever he tightened a string he was careful to loosen it again by exactly the same amount, so that the instrument was no worse than before.

I got into conversation with a youngster working on the farm. He told me he earned two hundred kroner a year—plus board. Up at six-thirty every morning to feed the horses; in the busy season, five-thirty. Work all day, supper at eight. But healthy and content with his peaceful life in this little world. I remember his perfect set of teeth and the beauty of his smile when he talked about his girl. He had given her a silver ring with a gold heart set in it.

"What did she say to that?"

"She was kind of surprised, like."

"And what did you say?"

"What I said? I don't rightly know. Hoped it would bring her luck. She should have had a length for a dress too, but . . ."

"Is she young?"

"Ay. Talks just like a little Jew's harp, she's that young."

"Where does she live?"

"Shan't say. Else it would be all over the parish."

I stood there before him like an Alexander, with the world at my feet, a shade contemptuous of his humble life. When we parted I gave him one of my woolen blankets, which I was finding a burden to carry; he at once declared that his girl should have it—she could do with a warm blanket.

And Alexander said, "If I had to be someone else, I'd choose to be you."

When Falkenberg came out after finishing his work, he was so genteel in his gestures and so stilted in his speech that I could barely understand him. He was accompanied by the daughter of the house. "Now we must transfer our location to the next farm," he said, "where there may well be another piano requiring inspection. Adieu, mademoiselle, adieu!"

"Six kroner, boy!" he whispered in my ear. "And six at the next farm makes twelve."

And off we went, with me carrying the bags.

XIV

Falkenberg's hunch was correct: the next farm was not going to be outdone—the piano must be tuned. The daughter of the house was away from home, but the work could be done in her absence as a little surprise. She was always complaining about the untuned piano and how impossible it was to play. At this stage I was again left to my own devices, while Falkenberg occupied the living room. When it grew dark he procured a light and continued tuning. He even had his supper there; after which he came out and demanded his pipe.

"What pipe?"

"You fool—the clenched fist!"

Somewhat reluctantly I handed over my ingenious pipe, which I had just completed, with the nail and the gold ring and a long stem.

"Don't let the nail get too hot," I whispered, "or it may curl up."

Falkenberg lit the pipe and went swaggering in with it. But he took good care of me too, asking on my behalf for food and coffee in the kitchen.

I found myself a place to sleep in the barn.

During the night I was woken by Falkenberg standing in the middle of the barn and calling my name. The moon was full and the night clear; I could see my companion's face.

"What is it?"

"Here's that pipe of yours."

"Pipe?"

"Yes, I'm damned if I'll keep it any longer. Look at it—the nail's working loose."

I took the pipe and saw that the nail had curled up.

Falkenberg said, "It was just as if it was making faces at me in the moonlight. And then I remembered where that nail came from . . ."

Happy Falkenberg!

Next morning we were on the point of leaving, when the daughter of the house came home. We heard her hammering out a waltz on the piano; then she came out and said, "Yes, there's a world of difference. Thank you *so* much."

"Mademoiselle is satisfied?" asked the maestro.

"Yes, indeed: there's quite a different tone to it now."

"And where does Mademoiselle recommend that I go next?"

"To Øvrebø, to the Falkenbergs."

"To the *who?*"

"The Falkenbergs. You follow the road straight on and after a couple of miles or so there's a signpost on the right. That's where you turn off."

Whereupon Falkenberg sat down abruptly on the steps and proceeded to cross-examine Mademoiselle about the Falkenbergs of Øvrebø. Fancy meeting his relatives here—it was almost like coming home! His particular thanks to Mademoiselle: it was a most signal service that she had rendered him.

And off we went again, with me carrying the bags.

Once in the wood we sat down for a council of war. Was it advisable for a Falkenberg with the rank of piano tuner to turn up on the Captain's doorstep at Øvrebø and be his kinsman? I was the timid one, and my doubts infected Falkenberg. All the same, it might be rather amusing.

Had he no papers with his name on them? Testimonials?

"Yes, but bloody hell, all they say is that I'm a capable workman."

We wondered whether to tamper with the references a little; but it seemed better to compose one from scratch. Then it could refer to a piano tuner of genius and be made out in the name, not of Lars, but of Leopold. We had a free hand.

"Can you undertake to write that reference?" he asked.

"Certainly I can."

But now my poor stiff imagination spoiled everything by running away with me. A piano tuner was a cipher; I would make him a mechanical genius, credit him with solving the most complicated problems, give him a factory—

"A factory owner doesn't need references," Falkenberg interrupted, and refused to listen to me any more. No, the whole thing seemed to be fizzling out.

Gloomy and dejected, we continued on our way until we reached the signpost.

"So you're not going?" I said.

"You can go," answered Falkenberg angrily. "Here, take your rags and tatters."

But when we were some way past the signpost, Falkenberg slackened his pace and muttered, "All the same, I can't bear to see it thrown away. A chance like that."

"In that case I think you should pay them a call. After all, it's by no means impossible that you really are related to them."

"I wish I'd thought of asking if he has a nephew in America."

"Would you have talked English in that case?"

"Oh, do shut your trap and keep it shut. I don't know what you've got to be so pleased with yourself about."

Overwrought and out of temper, Falkenberg strode on again. But almost at once he stopped abruptly and said, "I'll do it. Lend me your pipe again. I won't light it."

We walked up the hill. Falkenberg put on a great act, pointing now and then with the pipe and airing his views about the way the manor was situated. Somewhat irritated by the arrogant way he strutted along, while I carried the bags, I said, "So you're a piano tuner again?"

"I think I've proved I can tune a piano," he answered curtly. "And that's that."

"But supposing the lady knows a bit about it? And tries the piano afterward?"

Falkenberg fell silent; I saw him chewing it over. With every step his bearing became less erect, his stoop more pronounced.

"Perhaps it's unwise," he said. "Here, take your pipe. We'll just go up and simply ask for work."

XV

As it happened, we were able to make ourselves useful the moment we arrived at the manor. A new flagpole was being raised, and they were short of hands; we joined in, and raised the pole in triumph. There were women watching from every window.

Was the Captain at home?

No.

Madame?

Madame came out. She was tall and fair, and as friendly as a young foal—how prettily she acknowledged our greeting!

Did she by any chance have work for us?

"I don't know. No, I don't think so. You see, my husband's away."

I got the impression that she found it hard to say no, and I began replacing my cap so as not to worry her. But Falkenberg must have struck her as exotic, with his correct dress and his private porter; she looked curiously at him and asked, "What kind of work?"

"Any kind of outdoor work," answered Falkenberg; "we can do fencing, ditching, masonry—"

"Isn't it a bit late in the year for that kind of work?" put in one of the men by the flagpole.

"Yes, I suppose it is," Madame agreed. "I don't know—but it's dinnertime now; perhaps you'd like to go in and have a bite of food? Whatever we're having."

"I don't mind if I do," said Falkenberg.

I was much put out by this vulgar answer, which did us no credit at all. It was time I got a word in.

"*Mille grâces, madame, vous êtes trop aimable,*" I said gallantly, at the same time taking off my cap.

She turned and looked at me for a moment. Her surprise was comical to see.

We were shown into the kitchen and given an excellent meal.

Madame too went indoors. We had finished eating and were about to leave when Madame came out again. Falkenberg had regained his courage and was eager to take advantage of her friendliness. He asked if he might tune her piano.

"Do you tune pianos too?" she asked, wide-eyed.

"Indeed I do. I've tuned several around here."

"Mine's a grand, and naturally I wouldn't want . . ."

"Madame can rest assured."

"Do you have any . . ."

"I've no references. I'm not in the habit of asking for them. But Madame can hear for herself."

"Well, all right—come this way."

She led the way and he followed. As they went in, I had a glimpse of a room with many pictures on the walls.

The maids were bustling to and fro in the kitchen, eyeing me, the stranger; one of them was very pretty. I sat and thanked my stars that I had shaved that morning.

Ten minutes or so went by; Falkenberg had begun his tuning. Madame came back into the kitchen and said; "Well, well, so you speak French. That's more than I do."

Thank goodness, that was the end of the matter. On my side it would have been almost entirely a matter of letting them eat cake, and looking for the woman, and the state being me.

"Your friend has shown me his testimonials," said Madame. "You seem capable fellows, both of you. I don't know—I could telegraph my husband and find out if we have any work for you."

I wanted to thank her, but couldn't get a word out; I started to swallow.

Nerves.

So I took a little tour of the manor and the surrounding fields. Everything was in good order, the harvest under cover—even the rackloads of potato stalks, which in many places are left in the open until the first snow. I could see nothing for us to do. The people here were evidently rich.

As it drew on toward evening and Falkenberg was still tuning the piano, I took some of my provisions and wandered off, to avoid being invited to supper. The moon and the stars were out, but I chose to grope my way into the densest part of the forest and sit there in the dark. Besides, it was more sheltered there. How peaceful the earth was, and the air too! It was growing chilly, with frost on the ground. From time to time came a faint crackling in the straw, the squeak of a mouse, the flapping of a crow above the treetops—then complete silence again. Have you ever in all your life seen such fair hair? No indeed. Born glorious from top to toe, mouth ripe and lovely beyond words, shimmer of dragonflies in her hair. O to have a diadem to take from one's bag and present to her! I shall go and find a pale-pink shell and carve a nail from it, then I shall give her the pipe as a present for her husband, yes, that is what I shall do . . .

Back at the manor Falkenberg met me outside and hurriedly whispered, "She's heard from her husband: we can fell timber in the forest. Have you ever done any felling?"

"Yes."

"Go into the kitchen, then. She's been asking for you."

I went in, and Madame said, "Where did you get to? Please come and eat. You *have* eaten? Where?"

"We have food in our bags."

"You shouldn't have done that. Won't you have a cup of tea then? Are you sure? . . . I've heard from my husband. Can you fell trees? Ah, that's splendid. Look: TWO LOGGERS NEEDED, PETER WILL SHOW MARKED TREES . . ."

Dear God—she stood beside me, pointing at the telegram, her breath fragrant with young woman.

XVI

In the forest. Peter, who had shown us the way there, was one of the farmhands.

When we talked about it, Falkenberg was by no means overwhelmed with gratitude to Madame for finding us work. "There's no cause to go down on our knees," he said; "workmen are scarce around here." Falkenberg, by the way, was no better than average as a logger, whereas I had gained experience in another part of the world and could, if necessary, take command for the present. And indeed Falkenberg himself agreed that I should do so.

And now I began to busy myself with an invention.

With the ordinary felling saws in use today, you have to lie awkwardly on the ground and pull *sideways*. That is why so little work gets done in a day and why the forests are so full of mutilated stumps. By using a conical transmission system attached firmly to the tree's root, it should be possible to saw in the ordinary back-and-forward way, but with the blade cutting horizontally. I began sketching the various parts of such a machine. What gave me the biggest headache was the gentle pressure that the blade of the saw would need. It might be obtained by a compression spring wound up like a clock, or perhaps by a weight. A weight would be simpler, but would remain constant, and as the saw bit more deeply, it would drag more and more and cancel out this pressure. A steel spring, on the other hand, would unwind as the cut grew deeper and would always give the right amount of pressure. I decided on the spring. You wait and see, I said to myself. You can do it. And it would be the proudest moment of my life.

The days went by, one day much like another: we felled nine inch timber, we lopped and topped. Our fare was rich and good: we took packed lunches and coffee with us into the forest, and had a hot meal when we came home in the evening. Then we washed and tidied ourselves up, in order to be a cut above the farmhands, and sat with the three maids in the kitchen, where a large lamp was burning. Falkenberg and Emma became sweethearts.

And every so often a wave of melodious sounds would reach us from the grand piano in the living room; every so often, also, Madame would look in on us, exuding young-womanhood and blessed friendliness. "How did it go in the forest today?" she would ask. "Did you see the bear?" But one evening she thanked Falkenberg for the good job he had done on the piano. What—really? Falkenberg's weatherbeaten face became handsome with pleasure, and I felt positively proud of him when he answered modestly, "Yes, I was thinking myself it's a little better."

Either his piano tuning had improved with practice or Madame was thankful that he hadn't made her piano any worse.

Every evening Falkenberg dressed himself up in my town clothes. It would never have done for me to claim them back and start wearing them myself; the other would simply have believed that I'd borrowed them from my mate.

"You keep the clothes and I'll have Emma," I said as a joke.

"All right, take Emma" was Falkenberg's reply.

It dawned on me that a coolness had sprung up between Falkenberg and his girl. Poor Falkenberg had followed my example and fallen in love. What a pair of utter boys we were!

Up in the forest, Falkenberg would ask, "Think she'll look in on us again this evening?"

And I might answer, "I don't mind how long the Captain stays away."

"Nor me. Listen, if I hear he's treating her badly, watch out for sparks."

Then one evening Falkenberg chanced to sing a song; and once again I was proud on his behalf. Madame came out, he was asked to repeat that song and then to sing another; his fine voice filled the kitchen, and Madame said, in awestruck tones, "But—I've never heard anything like it!"

That was when I began feeling envious.

"Have you had lessons?" asked Madame. "Do you read music?"

"Yes," answered Falkenberg, "I belonged to a society."

But here, I thought, he should have said no, he had never been lucky enough to have lessons.

"Have you ever sung to an audience? Has anyone heard you?"

"I've sung at dances occasionally. And once at a wedding."

"But has anyone who knows something about music heard you?"

"I couldn't really say. Well, yes, I suppose so."

"Do sing something more!"

Falkenberg sang.

I thought: It will end up with him being invited into the living room one evening, with Madame at the piano. I said, "Excuse me, but isn't the Captain due home soon?"

"Ye-es." Madame's answer was like a question. "Why do you ask?"

"I was thinking about the work."

"Have you felled all the marked trees already?"

"No, not yet, only . . . No, far from it, only . . .."

"Well?" said Madame; then she had an idea. "I don't know—but if it's money . . .."

I clutched at that straw and said; "Well, I would be grateful."

Falkenberg said nothing.

"Dear me, you mustn't be afraid to speak up. Here!" she said, and handed me the money I had asked for. "And you?"

"Nothing, thank you," said Falkenberg.

Dear God, another defeat, another plunge to earth! While the infamous Falkenberg sat there playing the rich man who needed no advance! Before the night was out, I would tear the clothes from off his back, strip him naked!

Which, of course, I never did.

XVII

And the days went by.

"If she looks in this evening," Falkenberg would say up in

the forest, "I'll sing the song about the poppy. I'd forgotten about that one."

"Haven't you forgotten about Emma too?" I asked.

"Emma? Shall I tell you something? You're just the same as ever."

"Am I?"

"Through and through. You'd gladly take Emma in full view of Madame; I couldn't do that."

"You liar!" I answered indignantly. "You won't find *me* chasing after a bit of skirt as long as I'm here."

"No, and from now on I won't be doing any night duties either. Do you think she'll look in this evening? I'd forgotten about the poppy until now. Listen."

Falkenberg sang about the poppy.

"You're a lucky devil with your singing," I said; "but don't imagine that either of us is going to get her."

"Get her, indeed! You really are a prize monkey!"

"Ah, if I was young and rich and handsome, I'd get her all right," I said.

"Ah yes, *if.* In that case I'd get her too. But then what about the Captain?"

"Yes, and what about you? And what about me? And what about herself and the entire world? And what about the pair of us shutting our big, ugly mouths where she's concerned?" I said, furious with myself for my part in this childish chatter. "What sort of rubbish is this for two elderly loggers to be talking?"

We both grew thin and pale, and Falkenberg's suffering face was lined and furrowed; we had lost our former appetite for food. To conceal our respective conditions from each other, I went around whistling cheerful tunes, while Falkenberg boasted at every meal about how he was overeating and getting stiff and ungainly in consequence.

"Why, you're not eating anything," Madame would say when we brought home uneaten the greater part of our packed lunch. "You're a fine pair of loggers."

"It's Falkenberg," I said.

"Huh, it's *him*," said Falkenberg; "he's given up eating entirely."

From time to time, when Madame asked us to do her a favor, some small service or other, we would both rush to perform it; finally we took to bringing water to the kitchen unasked, and fetching in firewood. Once Falkenberg cheated me out of bringing home from the forest a bunch of hazel twigs to beat carpets with, which Madame had expressly asked me and no one else to cut for her.

And still he continued to sing in the evenings.

This was when I hit on my plan for making Madame jealous. Come, come, my good man, are you mad or merely stupid? Madame won't give your scheme as much as a thought!

All the same, I wanted to make her jealous.

Of the three maids, only Emma was worth considering for my experiment; so I began flirting with Emma.

"Emma, I know of someone who's sighing for you."

"Where did you learn that from?"

"From the stars."

"I'd much sooner you'd learned it from someone here on earth."

"I have too. At firsthand."

"He's talking about himself," said Falkenberg, nervous about being dragged in.

"Very well then, I'm talking about myself. *Paratum cor meum.*"

But Emma was disagreeable and showed no inclination to talk to me, for all my ability to outshine Falkenberg at languages. What—couldn't I even get the upper hand over Emma? After that I became extremely silent and proud, and went my own ways, and made more drawings for my machine, and small-scale models. And in the evenings, when Falkenberg sang and Madame listened, I took myself off to the servants' hall and stayed there with the farmhands—a much more dignified line. The only drawback was that Peter was ill in bed and could not endure the noise of an ax or a hammer; so I had to go to the outhouse every time I needed to strike a good hard blow.

But from time to time I fancied that, in spite of everything, perhaps Madame regretted my being lost to the kitchen. It certainly looked that way. One evening while we were having our meal she said to me, "I hear from the men that you're working on a machine."

"It's a new kind of saw he's fooling around with," said Falkenberg; "but it's going to be too heavy."

I let that pass; I was cunning and chose to suffer in silence. Was not lack of recognition the fate of every inventor? Wait a little, my moment had not yet come. At times I could scarce contain the urge to reveal my identity to the girls, how I was really a gentleman's son whom love had led astray and who now sought consolation in the bottle. Ah yes, very true, man proposes, God disposes . . . And in time it might even reach Madame's ears.

"I've a good mind to start joining you in the servants' hall of an evening," said Falkenberg.

And I knew very well why Falkenberg had suddenly taken a fancy to the servants' hall; for whatever reason, he was no longer invited to sing as often as before.

XVIII

The Captain was back.

A big, full-bearded man came up to us in the forest one day and said, "I'm Captain Falkenberg. How's it going, boys?"

We greeted him respectfully, thanked him, and said it was going all right.

We talked for a bit about the trees we had felled and the trees that remained; and the Captain praised us for leaving such

short, neat stumps. Then he calculated how much we had done
per day and said it was about average.

"The Captain is forgetting to allow for Sundays," I said.

"You're right," he replied. "In that case it's above average.
Any damage? Saw all right?"

"Yes."

"No injuries?"

"No."

Pause.

"You shouldn't really be getting your board from me," he
said; "but if you prefer it that way, we can sort it out when we
settle up."

"We'll accept what the Captain decides."

"That's right," added Falkenberg.

The Captain took a quick turn through the forest and came
back.

"You couldn't have better weather," he said. "No snow to
clear away."

"No snow, that's true. But we could do with a bit more
frost."

"What for? Are you too hot?"

"Well, yes, that too. But mainly because the saw goes more
easily in frozen wood."

"You're an old hand at this work?"

"Yes."

"Is it you who sings?"

"No such luck. He's the one."

"Ah, so *you're* the singer? We're namesakes, eh?"

"Well, yes, in a way," answered Falkenberg, a shade embarrassed. "I'm Lars Falkenberg, as my testimonials show."

"Where are you from?"

"Trøndelag."

The Captain returned home. He was friendly but brisk and
decided: never a smile, never a joke. His face was good, if
unremarkable.

From now on Falkenberg sang only in the servants' hall or in the open air; the Captain's arrival put an end to the singing in the kitchen. Falkenberg chafed over this and spoke dark words to the effect that life was hell and that one might just as well choose a day and hang oneself. But his despair was short-lived. One Sunday he went back to the two farms where he had tuned pianos and asked for testimonials. On his return he showed me the documents and said, "They'll do to keep body and soul together at a pinch."

"So you're not going to hang yourself?"

"You've more cause for that than I have," answered Falkenberg.

But I too was feeling less despondent. As soon as the Captain heard about my machine, he wanted to know more. He saw at a glance that my drawings were inadequate, having been made on absurdly small bits of paper and without even a pair of compasses; he lent me a handsome set of drawing instruments and taught me a bit about constructional calculation. He, too, was afraid my saw would prove too cumbersome. "But carry on," he added; "get it all drawn up on a fixed scale, then we shall see."

However, I knew that a reasonably accurate model would give a better idea of the thing, and when I had completed the drawings, I set about making a model in wood. Having no lathe, I had to cut the two cylinders and the various wheels and screws by hand. I was so absorbed in this that I failed to hear the bell for Sunday dinner. The Captain came and shouted, "Dinner!" Then he saw what I was up to, and offered to drive over to the blacksmith the very next day and get everything I needed turned on a lathe. "Just give me the measurements," he said. "Don't you need some tools as well? A backsaw. Good. Drills. Screws. A small chisel. Anything else?"

He noted it all down. You couldn't have had a better man to work for.

But that evening, when I had eaten and was on my way to

the servants' hall, I heard Madame calling to me. She was standing in the courtyard, in the shadow between the kitchen windows; but now she stepped forward.

"My husband noticed that—well, that you're rather thinly
clad," she said. "I don't know if—here, take these!"

And she thrust a complete suit into my arms.

I mumbled and stammered some thanks: I would soon be
able to afford a suit for myself, there was no hurry, I didn't need
any—

"Oh, I know you can afford it, of course, but your friend has
such good clothes, and you—oh, go on, take them."

She fled indoors, exactly like a young girl who's afraid of
being caught showing too much kindness. I was obliged to call
after her with my final thanks.

The next evening, when the Captain came with my cylinders
and wheels, I seized the opportunity of thanking him for the
clothes.

"Oh—er—yes," he answered. "It was my wife who thought
. . . Do they fit you?"

"Oh yes, they fit."

"That's good. Yes, it was my wife who . . . Well, here are
the wheels. And the tools. Good night."

Evidently they were both equally given to good deeds. And
when they had done one, each blamed the other. This must be,
here on earth, the marriage that dreamers have dreamed of.

XIX

And now the forest is bare of leaves and bereft of bird song;
only the crows rasp out their cries at five in the morning, as
they spread out over the fields. We see them, Falkenberg and I,

as we make our way to the forest; the fledgling birds, which have not yet learned to fear the world, hop at our feet in the path.

We meet the finch, that sparrow of the woods. He has already made a tour of the forest, and now he is on his way back to the humans he likes being with and getting to know from every angle. The strange little finch! He is a bird of passage, really; but his parents have taught him that one *can* survive a winter in the north; and now he in turn will teach his children that one can *only* survive it there. But he still has the migrant blood in his veins, he is still a wanderer. So one day he gathers with his flock and journeys the length of many a parish, to a quite different set of human beings whom likewise he means to get to know—and suddenly the aspen groves are empty of finches. And a whole long week may pass before another flock of these flying creatures settles once more in the aspen groves . . . Dear God, the times I have watched the finch, the entertainment he has given me!

Falkenberg tells me one day that he is right side up with the world again. This winter he intends, by felling timber and tuning pianos, to put aside a hundred kroner, and to make it up with Emma. I too, he adds, should stop sighing after ladies of high degree and go back to my equals.

He is right.

On Saturday evening we knocked off rather earlier than usual, in order to make some purchases. We needed shirts, tobacco, and wine.

Standing in the village store, I caught sight of a little shell-studded sewing box, such as sailors used to buy in Amsterdam in the old days, and bring home for their sweethearts; now the Germans make them in thousands. I bought the box, meaning to make the thumbnail for my pipe from one of the shells. "What do you want with that sewing box?" asked Falkenberg. "Is it for Emma?" His jealousy was aroused, and not to be outdone, he bought Emma a silk handkerchief.

On the way home we started drinking the wine and became talkative. Falkenberg was still jealous. So I selected the shell I needed, broke it off, and gave him the box. After that we were friends again.

It began to grow dark and there was no moon. Suddenly we heard accordion music from a house up on the hill. We figured there must be a dance going on—the light came and went like a lighthouse beam. "Come on, up we go," said Falkenberg.

We were in high spirits.

Outside the house we came upon a group of boys and girls standing in the cool night air; Emma was among them.

"Why, there's Emma!" cried Falkenberg cheerfully; he was not at all put out by her having gone there without him. "Emma, come here, I've got something for you."

He thought a civil word was all she needed; but Emma turned on her heel and went indoors. When Falkenberg tried to follow, he found his way blocked, and it was made clear to him that he had no business there.

"But Emma's there, don't you see? Tell her to come out."

"She's not coming out. She's with Mark, the shoemaker."

Falkenberg was beaten. He had gone around for so long showing his indifference to Emma that she had given him up. While he lingered there as if struck by a thunderbolt, some of the girls began making fun of him: had the poor little kitten lost his mitten, and did he begin to cry?

In full view of everyone Falkenberg put his bottle to his lips and drank; then he wiped it dry with his hand and passed it to his neighbor. Feelings toward us improved: we were good sorts, we had bottles in our pockets, we were ready to pass them around; besides, we were newcomers to the place, we added a touch of variety. And Falkenberg cracked all manner of jokes about Mark, the shoemaker, whom he insisted on calling Luke.

The dance was still going on indoors, but none of the girls chose to desert us for it. "I bet Emma's wishing she was out here with us now," said Falkenberg boastfully. Instead, there was Helene and Rønnaug and Sara, each of whom shook hands in the pretty, traditional way after a swig from the bottle; while others, more sophisticated, merely said, "Your very good health." Helene became Falkenberg's girl: he put his arm around her waist and claimed her for his night duty. When they edged farther and farther away from the rest of us, no one called them to heel; one after another, we paired off and went our ways into the forest. I had acquired Sara.

When we emerged from the forest again, Rønnaug still stood there, in the cool night air. What a strange girl—had she remained standing there throughout? I took her hand and chatted to her a little; she merely giggled at everything I said and made no answer. When we began moving toward the forest, we heard Sara calling after us in the darkness, "Come, Rønnaug, we'd better be going home now!" But Rønnaug made no answer; a girl of few words. She was large and placid, with skin the color of milk.

XX

The first snow had fallen; it melted immediately, but winter could not be far away. And our work in the forest for the Captain was drawing to an end; we had perhaps two weeks left. What should we turn our hands to then? There was work to be had on the mountain railway, or we might pick up more logging somewhere else. Falkenberg favored the railway.

But my machine would not yet be ready. We each had our problems. In addition to the machine, I needed to complete that thumbnail for the pipe, and the evenings were going to be too short for me; while Falkenberg had to make it up with Emma—a slow and difficult business. She had been seeing Mark, the shoemaker, granted; but then Falkenberg had, in an emotional moment, evened the score by presenting the girl

Helene with a shell-studded sewing box and a silk handkerchief.

Falkenberg was in a fix. He said, "Whichever way you turn, it's nothing but trials and tribulations and stupidity."

"Really?"

"That's my view, if you really want to know. She won't be coming with me to the mountains."

"Is it Mark, the shoemaker, who's keeping her back?"

Falkenberg glowered in silence.

"I never went on with my singing either," he said by and by.

We started talking about the Captain and Madame. Falkenberg had a nasty feeling that things were not right between them.

The gossipmonger! I said, "Excuse my saying so, but you don't know the first thing about it."

"Is that so?" he answered angrily. And getting more and more heated, he said, "Have you ever seen them following each other around, or billing and cooing to each other? I've never once heard them exchange two words together."

The idiot! The loud-mouthed idiot!

"What's the matter with your sawing today?" I jeered. "Just look at that cut you've made!"

"*I*'ve made? There are two of us, aren't there?"

"Ah well, perhaps the wood's thawed out too much. Let's try the ax again."

For a long time we chopped away on our own, speaking only in angry monosyllables. What was that lie he had had the impudence to utter—that they never said a word to each other? But, by God, he was right! Falkenberg had a nose for such things, he understood people.

"Well, at least they speak nicely about each other to us," I said.

Falkenberg continued chopping.

I considered it further.

"Well, you may be partly right, it may not be the marriage that dreamers have dreamed of; still . . ."

This was wasted on Falkenberg; he had no idea what I was

talking about. During the midday break I resumed the conversation. "Didn't you say that if he treated her badly I was to watch out for sparks?"

"I did indeed."

"And have there been any sparks?"

"Have I ever said he treats her badly?" asked Falkenberg indignantly. "No, they're bored with each other, that's what. When one comes in, the other goes out. If he starts saying anything in the kitchen, her eyes glaze over and she doesn't take in a word."

We did another long spell of chopping, each of us immersed in his own thoughts.

"I may have no option but to beat him up," said Falkenberg.

"Who?"

"Luke . . ."

I completed the pipe and sent it to the Captain via Emma. The thumbnail looked completely natural, and the excellent tools I had acquired enabled me to inlay it in the thumb and fasten it from below without the two tiny copper nails being visible. I was pleased with my work.

While we were eating our evening meal, the Captain came out into the kitchen to thank me for it. Falkenberg's shrewdness was instantly confirmed: no sooner had the Captain entered the room than his wife left it.

The Captain congratulated me on the pipe and asked how I had fastened the thumbnail; he said I was an artist, a real master. The entire kitchen stood listening to this; and when the Captain called someone a master, his words carried some weight. I believe that at that moment I could have had Emma.

That night I succeeded in learning how to shudder.

A female corpse visited me up in the loft and held out her left hand to show me: the thumbnail was missing. I shook my head: I had had a nail once upon a time, but I had thrown it away and used a shell instead. But the corpse continued to stand there, and I continued to lie there, ice-cold with terror. Finally I managed to say that I was sorry, but there was nothing more that I could do about it; she had best be on her way, in God's name. And our Father, which art in Heaven . . . . The corpse came right up to me; I thrust out my two clenched fists, gave a chilling scream—and found myself crushing Falkenberg flat against the wall.

"What is it?" Falkenberg yelled. "For the love of Christ!"

I woke up, bathed in sweat, opened my eyes, and lay watching the corpse slowly fade into the darkness of the room.

"It's the corpse," I groaned. "She wants her nail back." Falkenberg sat up in bed with a jerk; he too was wide awake.

"I saw her!" he said.

"You too? Did you see her thumb? Ugh!"

"I wouldn't be in your shoes for anything."

"Let me go next to the wall!" I implored him.

"Where am I to go, then?"

"You're not in any danger, you can safely go on the outside."

"So she can come and get me first? No, thank you."

And with that Falkenberg lay down again and pulled the blanket over his eyes.

I toyed with the idea of going down and sleeping with Peter; he was on the mend by now and couldn't infect me with his illness. But I was afraid to face going down the steps.

I had a dreadful night.

In the morning I searched high and low for the nail, and found it on the floor among the sawdust and shavings. I buried it on the way to the forest.

"The question is whether you don't have to return the nail to where you took it from," said Falkenberg.

"But that's miles away, a full-scale journey . . ."

"You may be required to make it, all the same. She may not want to have a thumb in one place and a thumbnail in another."

But I felt so well again, the daylight had given me so much bravado, that I laughed at Falkenberg for being so superstitious and told him his outlook had been rendered obsolete by science.

XXI

One evening a carriage drew up at the manor, and since Peter was still unwell and the other farmhand only a boy, it fell to me to look after the horses. A lady got out of the carriage. "The Captain and his wife are at home, I believe?" she said. The clatter of wheels brought faces to the windows, lamps were lit in rooms and on landings, Madame came to the door and called, "Is that you, Elizabeth? I've been waiting and waiting for you. Welcome!"

It was Miss Elizabeth from the parsonage.

"Is *he* here?" she asked in surprise.

"Who?"

It was me she meant. She had recognized me . . .

Next day the two young ladies came out to us in the forest. At first I was afraid that word might have reached the parsonage about a certain ride on borrowed horses, but when I heard no mention of the subject I relaxed.

"The water pipe is working well," said Miss Elizabeth.

That was good to hear.

"Water pipe?" asked Madame.

"He's fixed up a water pipe for us. Into the kitchen and up the stairs. We just turn on a tap. You ought to have one too."

"I see. Could it be done here?"

I answered, yes, it could certainly be done.

"Why haven't you told my husband?"

"I mentioned it to him. He wanted to discuss it with Madame."

An embarrassing silence. He had never even mentioned to her a topic which concerned her as closely as this.

To break the silence I blurted out, "In any case, it's too late in the year now. Winter would be on us before we could finish the job. But maybe in the spring."

Madame returned as if from a great distance.

"Come to think of it, I do remember him mentioning it once," she said. "And our talking it over and deciding it was too late in the year . . . Elizabeth, isn't it fun watching trees come down like this?"

We sometimes used a rope to guide the tree when it fell, and Falkenberg had just fastened this rope high up on a tree, which was already swaying.

"Why do you do that?"

"To guide the tree in the right direction . . ." I started to explain.

But Madame cut me short, repeating her question point-blank to Falkenberg, and adding, "Aren't all directions the same?"

So Falkenberg was obliged to step in.

"Oh no, we have to guide it. To prevent it from crushing too many saplings as it comes down."

"Did you hear," Madame asked her friend, "did you hear that voice of his? He's the one who sings."

I could have bitten my tongue off for talking so much and not sensing her wishes! Well, I would show her that her reprimand was not lost on me. Besides, it was Miss Elizabeth and no one else that I loved; she wasn't temperamental, and she was every bit as pretty as the other, yes, a thousand times prettier. I would sign on at her father's place . . . Meanwhile, I made it a rule, whenever Madame addressed me, to look first at Falkenberg and then at her, and to hesitate over my answer as if nervous of speaking out of turn. I think this behavior of mine was beginning to worry her; and once she said with a timid smile, "Goodness me, it was you I asked."

That smile and those words . . . My heart raced for joy, I began chopping with all the strength and skill I had acquired, I made some splendid cuts; the work seemed more like play. I caught only occasional snatches of what was being said.

"I'm to sing for them this evening," said Falkenberg when we were alone.

Evening came.

I stood in the courtyard and exchanged a few words with the Captain. We had about three or four days' work left in the forest.

"Where do you go next?"

"To work on the railway."

"Perhaps I can make use of you here," said the Captain. "I'm going to rebuild the drive down to the main road—it's too steep as it is. Come with me and I'll show you."

He led me to the south side of the house and began pointing, although it was already quite dark.

"And by the time the road's finished, and one or two other things, it should be spring," he said. "And then there'll be the water pipe. Not to mention Peter being ill; we can't go on like this, I must have more help."

Suddenly we heard Falkenberg singing. The living room was lit up, and Falkenberg was in there, being accompanied on the grand piano. A wealth of melodious sounds floated out to us from that remarkable voice; against my will, I found myself trembling.

The Captain started and looked up at the windows.

"Still"—he said suddenly—"maybe the road too had best wait till the spring. How many days' work did you say you had left in the forest?"

"About three or four."

"Right, let's say those three or four days and then finish for this year."

That was a remarkably quick decision, thought I to myself. Aloud I said, "There's nothing against making a road in the winter; in some ways it's better then. There's blasting to be done, crushed stone to be laid in—"

"Yes, I know, but . . . No, I'd better go in and listen to the singing."

The Captain went indoors.

I thought: He did that from politeness, of course; he wanted to help do the honors when Falkenberg had been invited into the living room. But if the truth were known, he was happier chatting with me.

How conceited I was, and how mistaken!

XXII

The main parts of my saw were now completed and I could assemble them for testing. Near the ramp to the hayloft stood the stump of a wind-felled aspen. I fastened my gadget to this stump and straightway satisfied myself that the saw could cut. Now then, hearken ye, my people, the problem is solved! For a saw blade I had bought myself an outsize backsaw and equipped it with teeth along the full extent of its back; when you sawed, these teeth engaged a small cogwheel which was driven forward by the compression spring. The spring itself I had originally made from a broad corset busk that Emma had given me, but this had proved in earlier experiments to be too slack; and so I had made myself a new spring from a saw blade only six millimeters across, having first removed its teeth. This time the spring proved too powerful: I had to manage as best I could by winding it only halfway and repeating this process each time it unwound.

My trouble was lack of theoretical knowledge: I had, nearly all the time, to proceed by trial and error, and this made the work very slow. For example, the conical transmission system had proved too cumbersome, and I had had to abandon it entirely in favor of a simpler system.

It was a Sunday when I fastened my machine to the aspen stump; the fresh white woodwork and gleaming saw blade sparkled in the sun. Soon there were faces at the windows, and the Captain came out. He never answered my greeting; he was too intent on the saw as he approached.

"How's it going?"

I started to saw.

"Why, I do believe . . ."

Madame and Miss Elizabeth came out, all the maids came out, Falkenberg came out. And I kept the saw going. Now then, just hearken ye, all my people!

The Captain said, "Won't it take too long fastening the thing to every single tree?"

"Some of the time lost will be made up by the work being much easier. This way you'll never need to stop for a breather."

"Why not?"

"Because the *lateral pressure* comes from the spring. That's the pressure that tires you out most."

"And the rest of the lost time?"

"I intend to discard this screw-on arrangement and to use instead a clamp operated by a sharp depression of the foot. The clamp will have a series of notches and will fit any size tree."

I showed him my drawing of this clamp, which I hadn't had time to complete.

The Captain now had a go at the saw, to see for himself how much strength it needed. He said, "I wonder whether it won't be too heavy, pulling a saw twice the width of an ordinary felling saw?"

"Well, of course," said Falkenberg. "That's obvious."

Everybody looked first at Falkenberg and then at me. Now it was my turn.

"One man can push a fully loaded goods wagon along a railroad track," I answered. "Here you'll have two men to push and pull a saw that slides over two rollers, which in turn run on two steel wires lubricated with oil. This saw will be considerably easier to handle than the old kind; at a pinch it could be worked by one man."

"I figure that's hardly possible."

"We shall see."

Miss Elizabeth asked, half in jest, "But can you explain to an ignorant person like me what's wrong with sawing a tree straight across in the old-fashioned way?"

"He wants to eliminate the lateral pressure for the men sawing," explained the Captain. "With this saw you can actually make a horizontal cut with the same kind of pressure you need for a saw that cuts vertically downward. Look: you press down and produce a sideways cut." He turned to me. "Tell me, don't you think there's a danger of depressing the blade at the ends and making a convex cut?"

"In the first place, the two rollers that the saw rests on will prevent that."

"Yes, they should help. And in the second place?"

"In the second place, you couldn't make a convex cut with this saw if you tried. Because the blade has a T-shaped back which makes it virtually impossible to bend."

I fancied that some of the Captain's objections were made against his own better judgment: with his knowledge, he himself could have answered them better than I. However, there were other points, not raised by the Captain, which worried me. A machine which was going to be carted around in the forest must not have too delicate a mechanism. For example, I was afraid of the two steel wires taking a knock and either breaking altogether or getting bent so that the rollers would jam. I would have to do without the wires and set the rollers under the back of the saw. My machine was still far from ready . . .

The Captain went up to Falkenberg and said, "I imagine you've no objection to taking the ladies on a long drive tomorrow? Peter's not well enough yet."

"Lord, no, I've no objection."

"It's to take the young lady back to the parsonage," the Captain explained as he turned to go. "You'll need to be on the road by six o'clock."

Falkenberg was delighted at this mark of confidence, and

amused himself by accusing me of envy. I was not, in point of fact, the least bit envious. For a moment, perhaps, I was slightly hurt at my mate being preferred to myself, but beyond question I would sooner be on my own in the quiet of the forest than sit shivering on a coachman's box.

Falkenberg, who was in high spirits, said, "You're turning so green with envy, you'd better take some castor oil for it."

He spent the whole morning messing around with preparations for the journey: washing the carriage, oiling the wheels, checking the harness. And I helped him.

"I don't believe you're capable of driving a coach and pair," I said to tease him. "Never mind, I'll teach you the essentials before you set out tomorrow."

"It's too bad you're in such a state, and all for the want of a little castor oil," he retorted.

We continued in this merry, joking vein.

In the evening the Captain came to me and said, "I wanted to spare you and send your mate with the ladies, but Miss Elizabeth insists on having you."

"Me?"

"Because she knows you already."

"But she'd be quite safe with my mate too."

"Do you object to going?"

"No."

"Good. You go, then."

My immediate thought was: Aha, so it's me the ladies prefer after all, because I'm an inventor and a saw owner, and quite good-looking when I'm all spruced up—fantastically good-looking, in fact.

But to Falkenberg the Captain had given an explanation which shattered my vanity at a blow: Miss Elizabeth was to bring me back to the parsonage so that her father could have another shot at engaging me as a farmhand. It had all been arranged between her father and herself.

I pondered and pondered over this explanation.

"But if you sign on at the parsonage, that puts an end to our working on the railway," said Falkenberg.

I answered, "I'm not signing on."

XXIII

Early next morning I set out with the two ladies in the closed carriage. At first it was bitterly cold, and I made good use of my woolen blanket, draping it alternately around my knees and over my shoulders as a shawl.

I followed the road along which I had wandered here with Falkenberg and recognized one landmark after another: here a piano that Falkenberg had tuned, there another; that was where we had heard the gray goose . . . The sun rose, it grew warm, the hours passed. At a crossroads the ladies knocked on the carriage window, saying it was time for lunch.

I could tell from the sun that it was much too early for the ladies' lunch, although well enough on for mine, accustomed as I was to eating with Falkenberg at noon. So I drove on.

"Aren't you going to stop?" the ladies shouted.

"You're used to eating at three, you know . . . and I thought . . ."

"But we're hungry."

I drove to the side of the road, unharnessed the horses, gave them their fodder, and fetched them water. Had these strange people adjusted their mealtime to mine?

"Luncheon is served!" one of them called.

Feeling I couldn't very well join the others for this meal, I remained standing by the horses.

"Well?" said Madame.

"If you'd be kind enough to give me a bite," I said.

The pair of them plied me with food and feared I wasn't get-

ting enough; and when I had opened the bottles, I got my full
share of beer, too; it was a regular roadside banquet, a small
fairy tale in my life. Madame I hardly dared to look at, lest she
should have occasion to feel hurt.

They talked and joked together, and showed their friendliness
by drawing me into it all. Miss Elizabeth said, "Oh, I *do* think
it's fun eating out of doors. Don't you?"

"It's nothing new for him, of course," said Madame. "He has
a meal in the forest every day."

Ah, that voice, those eyes, that tender womanly expression in
the hand holding out the glass toward me . . . And now I,
too, might have said something for myself, entertained them
with a tale or two from the great wide world, or set them right
when they chattered away and showed their ignorance of how
one rides a camel or harvests grapes . . .

I hastened to finish my meal and retire again. I took the
buckets and went, quite unnecessarily, to fetch more water for
the horses; then I sat down beside the stream.

After an interval Madame called for my services.

"You must come back to the carriage. We're going to see if
we can find some wild hops or something."

But as I reached the carriage they were agreeing that the hop
season was over and that there were no rowanberries around
here, or gaily colored leaves.

"There's nothing to be found in the woods," said Mademoiselle. Then she asked me another direct question: "Tell me,
you've no churchyard here to wander about in, have you?"

"No."

"How do you manage without?" And she explained to Madame what a strange fellow I was, wandering around the
churchyard at night in company with the dead, and how that
was where I invented my machines.

For the sake of saying something, I asked her about young
Eric. Hadn't his horse bolted, hadn't he been spitting
blood . . . ?

"He's on the mend," answered Mademoiselle sharply. "Shouldn't we be on our way again, Louise?"

"Yes, can't we be off?"

"Whenever you wish," I replied.

And we drove on again.

The hours passed, the sun sank, the air turned chilly again, and raw; later on we had wind and wet—half rain, half snow. We passed the chapel, a roadside store or two, and farm after farm.

A tap on the carriage window.

"Wasn't it here you went riding on borrowed horses one night?" Mademoiselle asked with a laugh. "We heard all about that, you know."

The two ladies had a good laugh over it.

I hit on a retort.

"And yet your father still wants to take me on as one of his hands, I believe."

"Yes."

"While we're on the subject, miss, how did your father know I was working for Captain Falkenberg? When you yourself were surprised to see me there?"

She thought quickly, then answered, with a glance at Madame, "I wrote and told them."

Madame lowered her eyes.

I had the impression that the girl was lying; but her admirable answer silenced me. There was nothing improbable about her saying to her parents, in one of those letters full of rural gossip, something like: "And guess who I've met here? The man who laid our water pipe, he's here cutting timber for the Captain . . ."

But when we arrived at the parsonage the new hand had already been engaged—had been working there, in fact, for the last three weeks. It was he who took charge of our horses.

So I pondered and pondered once again: why had I been chosen as coachman? Perhaps it was meant as a small consolation for Falkenberg's being invited to sing in the living room. If so, did these people not realize who I was—a man on the point of perfecting an invention, a man who had gone beyond the need for charity?

I was short and sharp with everyone, and weary of myself. I ate in the kitchen, received Oline's blessing for the running water, and went to look after my horses. At twilight I retired to the hayloft with my blanket . . .

I was awakened by fumbling hands.

"But you mustn't sleep here, you know, you'll freeze to death," said the priest's wife. "Come, I'll show you."

We discussed it for a little. I had no desire to move and got her to sit down instead. A creature of fire she was, a daughter of nature. And her inmost being re-echoed still to the strains of a ravishing waltz.

XXIV

Next morning I was in a better frame of mind: calm again, and reasonable, and resigned. If only I had known what was best for me and never left this place; I could have been taken on here and put in charge of all the other hands. Yes, and dug myself nicely into a peaceful rural life.

Mrs. Falkenberg was standing in the yard: a human column, light in color, standing free in the spacious courtyard, without a hat.

I bade her good morning.

"Good morning!" she called back, and advanced slowly toward me. Then she said, very quietly, "I wanted to see where they put you last night, but I couldn't get away. Or rather, I got away, but . . . you didn't sleep in the hayloft, did you?"

I heard the last words as if in a dream and couldn't answer.

"Why don't you answer?"

"You mean, whether I slept in the hayloft? Yes, I did."

"Did you really? Was it all right?"

"Yes."

"I see. Yes, of course. We're going home later today."

She turned and went, her face one crimson glow.

Harold came and asked me to make him a kite.

"Very well, I'll make you a kite," I answered in my confusion, "an enormous kite that will sail right up into the clouds. I promise you that."

We worked for a couple of hours, Harold and I, he so kind and innocent in his eagerness, I for my part thinking of anything but the kite. We gave it a tail several yards long; we pasted and knotted and lashed. Twice Miss Elizabeth came and watched. She may have been as sweet and lively as ever, but I was indifferent to what she was and never gave her a thought.

I was told to harness the horses—an order which I should have obeyed at once, for the way home was a long one; instead, I sent Harold in to ask for another half hour, and we went on working until the kite was ready. Tomorrow, when the paste was dry, Harold could fly his kite, following it with his eyes and feeling an unfamiliar excitement, as I did now.

The horses were harnessed.

Madame appeared at the door; the priest and his family too. Both the priest and his wife knew me again, returned my greeting, and said a few words; but I heard nothing about my signing on as one of their hands. And the wife's blue eyes were fixed on me in that slanting side glance of hers as she knew me again, although she had also known me the night before.

Miss Elizabeth brought food for the journey and wrapped her friend up well.

"Are you sure you've got enough over you?" she asked for the last time.

"Thank you, I've more than enough. Goodbye, goodbye."

"Now, see you drive as nicely as you did yesterday," said Mademoiselle, and nodded to me also.

We drove off.

The weather was cold and raw, and I realized at once that Madame was none too well protected by the blanket she had.

We drove for hour after hour; the horses knew they were homeward bound and trotted unasked. I had no mittens, so my hands grew stiff around the reins. As we passed a cottage set back a little from the road, Madame knocked on the window to announce it was time for lunch. When she got out she was pale from the cold.

"We'll have our lunch up in that cottage," she said. "Follow me when you're ready, and bring the basket with you."

And with that she wandered off up the slope.

It must have been the cold that made her want to eat in a stranger's cottage, I thought; surely she wasn't afraid of me . . . I tethered the horses, fed them, and, since it looked like rain or snow, fastened their oilskins over them. Then I patted them and took the basket up to the cottage.

An old woman living in the cottage welcomed me in, and continued making coffee. Madame unpacked the basket and said, without looking at me, "I suppose you'd like me to fill your plate again today?"

"That would be most kind."

We ate in silence. I sat on a little bench near the door, with my plate beside me; Madame sat at the table, looking out of the window for the most part and eating scarcely a thing. From time to time she would exchange a few words with the old woman, or glance at my plate to make sure it wasn't empty. The little room was so cramped that I was no more than two paces from the window; which meant that we sat together, willy-nilly.

When the coffee arrived, there was no room for my cup on the bench, so I sat holding it in my hand. Then Madame, slowly turning her face toward me, said with downcast eyes, "There's room here, you know."

I heard my heart beat violently and muttered something in reply. "Thank you, I'm fine . . . I'd just as soon . . ."

Beyond doubt, she was uneasy, afraid of my saying something, doing something; once more she sat with her face averted, but I saw how her breast was heaving. "Relax!" I wanted to say; not a word would escape my wretched lips.

I needed to put the empty plate and cup back on the table but feared my approach would frighten her, since she continued to sit with her face averted. I rattled my cup a little to catch her attention, then brought her my things and thanked her.

She tried to put on her hostess voice. "Won't you have some more? Why, you've hardly . . ."

"No, thank you very much . . . Shall I start packing up? If I can, that is."

I had chanced to look at my hands: in the warmth of the cottage they had swollen up hideously, and were now so shapeless and clumsy that I was scarcely capable of packing up. She followed my train of thought, looked first at my hands and then at the floor, and said with a smile, "Have you no mittens?"

"No, I don't need them."

I went back to my seat and waited for her to pack up, so that I could carry the basket. Suddenly she turned her face toward me again and asked, still without looking up, "Where do you come from?"

"From the north."

Pause.

I ventured to ask in turn, "Has Madame been there?"

"Yes, as a child."

As she said this, she glanced at her watch as if to preclude further questions, and also to remind me of the time.

I rose at once and went out to the horses.

It was already growing dark; the sky was overcast and sleet had started to fall. I quietly pulled my blanket down from the box and hid it under the front seat inside. That done, I watered and harnessed the horses. Shortly afterward Madame came walking down the slope; I walked toward her, intending to go for the basket.

"Where are you going?"

"For the basket."

"You needn't bother, thank you. It's not worth taking."

We came to the carriage; she got in, and I made as if to help her wrap herself up. Thus I found the blanket under the front seat; I kept the border well out of sight, to prevent her from recognizing it.

"Well, this is a stroke of luck!" she exclaimed. "Where did you find it?"

"Here."

"I could have got more blankets at the parsonage, but the poor people would never have got them back . . . Thank you, I can manage for myself . . . No, thank you, I can manage . . . Get ready to start."

I closed the carriage door and mounted the box.

If she knocks on the window again, I thought, it will be about the blanket this time; and I'm not stopping.

Hour after hour went by, it grew pitch-dark, the rain and snow fell with increasing violence, the going became worse and worse. Once or twice I jumped down from the box and ran alongside the horses to get warm; the moisture poured off my clothes.

We were nearing home.

I thought: As long as there aren't too many lights blazing, so that she recognizes the blanket . . .

The whole place was lit up, worse luck; Madame was expected.

In desperation I pulled up the horses some way short of the entrance and opened the carriage door.

"What's the matter?"

"I wondered if you'd be kind enough to get out here. The going is so bad . . . the wheels . . ."

She must have thought I was trying to lure her out into heaven knows what. She said, "For goodness' sake, drive on!"

The horses moved on and drew up exactly where the lights were most dazzling. Emma came out to receive her mistress—

who handed her the blankets, having folded them in readiness
while she sat in the carriage.

"Thank you for driving!" she said to me. "Heavens above,
how wet you are!"

XXV

A surprising piece of news awaited me: Falkenberg had
signed on as one of the Captain's hands.

This nullified our agreement and left me on a limb. I
couldn't understand it at all. Ah well, time to think about that
in the morning. By now it was two o'clock, and still I lay
awake, shivering and brooding. All these hours I had been unable to get warm; now suddenly I found myself too hot and lay
there with a high fever . . . How frightened she had been yesterday: hadn't dared to eat with me by the roadside, had never
once looked me in the face . . .

In a lucid moment it occurred to me that I might wake
Falkenberg with my restless turning, and perhaps talk de-
liriously. Clenching my teeth, I leaped out of bed, pulled on
my clothes again, tumbled downstairs, and bounded away over
the fields. After a while my clothes began to warm me, and I
headed for our forest work place, with sweat and rain streaming
down my face. If only I could find the saw and work the fever
out of my limbs—my tried and tested cure from of old. I
couldn't find the saw, but I found the ax where I had hidden it
on Saturday evening and started to chop. It was so dark I could
hardly see a thing; but I kept feeling the cut with my hand and
felled several trees. I was drenched in sweat.

When I felt sufficiently exhausted, I hid the ax in the same
place and ran home at the first glimmering of day.

"Where have you been?" asked Falkenberg.

I didn't want him to know about my catching cold yesterday,

and maybe gossip about it in the kitchen, so I mumbled something to the effect that I hardly knew where I'd been.

"I suppose you've been with Rønnaug," he said.

I said yes, I'd been with Rønnaug, since he'd guessed already.

"It was hardly a guessing matter," he said. "As for me, I don't go out visiting any more."

"You've got Emma now, I suppose?"

"Looks like it. It's a shame you can't stay on here too. Then you might have had one of the others."

Falkenberg enlarged on this theme, how I might have had my pick of the other girls, only the Captain had no more need for my services. I wasn't even to go to the forest today . . . His words came to me from far away, across an approaching ocean of sleep.

By the time morning had fully arrived, my fever had gone; I was a little faint, but began all the same preparing to work in the forest.

"You don't need to wear your woodcutting outfit any more," said Falkenberg. "I've told you once already."

Why, so he had! Nevertheless, I put my forest clothes on, simply because the others were so wet. Falkenberg was a little shy with me because he had broken up our partnership; his excuse was that he had thought I was going to sign on at the parsonage.

"So you're not coming with me to the mountains after all?" I asked.

"Hm. No, I suppose not. But surely you understand. I'm tired of bumming around. And I couldn't find a better place than this."

I pretended it made little difference to me, I took a sudden interest in Peter: it was worst for him, poor man, being thrown out and made homeless.

"Homeless indeed!" retorted Falkenberg. "He'll stay here for the full quota of weeks he's allowed to be sick by law, and then he'll go home. His father's got a farm of his own."

Then Falkenberg declared that our splitting up made him feel as if he were only half a man. If it wasn't for Emma, he would sell the Captain down the river.

"Here," he said, "you can have these."

"What are they?"

"They're the references. I won't need them now, and they may help you out of a tight spot—if you ever feel like tuning a piano."

And he handed me not only the documents but the tuning key as well.

But without Falkenberg's keen ear, I had no use for these items, and I told him I could as easily tune a grindstone as a piano.

At which he exploded with laughter and felt better, because I continued clowning to the end . . .

Falkenberg had gone. Since I could afford to be idle now, I lay down fully dressed on the bed, resting a little more and reflecting. Ah well, we had finished our work, we would have had to leave in any case, I could hardly expect to stay here forever. The only factor outside all our reckoning was Falkenberg's remaining behind. If only I had been the one taken on, I would have worked hard enough for two! Couldn't I buy Falkenberg off? Come to think of it, I had even seemed to detect in the Captain distaste at this workman going around the place with *his* name. But perhaps I had been mistaken.

I brooded and brooded. To the best of my knowledge I had, after all, been a good worker, and I had never stolen one second of the Captain's time in order to work on my invention . . .

I fell asleep again and was awakened by footsteps on the stairs. Before I could get myself properly out of bed, the Captain stood at the door.

"That's all right, don't get up," he said pleasantly and started to leave. "Still, now that I've woken you, perhaps we could settle up?"

"Thank you. As the Captain wishes."

"I ought to tell you that your mate and I both thought you were going to sign on at the parsonage, and so . . . And now the good weather's over, there's no more felling to be done—not that there was in any case. What was I going to say? I've settled up with your mate, I don't know if . . ."

"I'm content to accept the same, naturally."

"Your mate and I agreed you should have slightly more per day."

Falkenberg had mentioned no such thing to me; it must be the Captain's idea.

"I agreed with him to share and share alike," I said.

"Ah, but you were the foreman. Naturally you should have an extra fifty øre per day."

Seeing my disclaimer had not been appreciated, I let him work it out as he pleased and took the money. I remarked that it was more than I had expected.

"Glad to hear it," said the Captain. "And I'd like to give you this testimonial for work well done."

He handed me the paper.

He was a straightforward, upright man. If he said nothing about installing a water pipe in the spring, he doubtless had his reasons, and I shrank from bothering him.

"So you're going to work on the railway?" he asked.

"I don't honestly know."

"Ah well, it's been nice having you here."

He went to the door.

Wretch that I am, I could contain myself no longer. I asked, "Mightn't the Captain have some work for me later on, in the spring?"

"I don't know, we'll have to see. I . . . It all depends. If you find yourself in these parts, then . . . What do you intend doing with your machine?"

"If I may be so bold as to ask if it can stay here—"

"Of course."

When the Captain had gone, I sat down on the bed. Well, that was that; yes, and God be with us all! . . . Nine o'clock—she is up; there she is, walking about in the building that I can see from my window. Let me clear out and have done with it.

I got out my sack and packed it, put the wet jacket on over my smock, and was ready to go. But then I sat down again.

Emma came and said, "Breakfast is ready—come and eat!"

To my horror she had my blanket over her arm.

"And Madame said I was to ask if this blanket is yours."

"Mine? No—I've got mine here in this sack."

Emma went out with the blanket.

How could I possibly admit it was mine? Devil take the blanket! . . . Perhaps I should go down and have something to eat. Then I could say goodbye and thank you at the same time. That would not be too conspicuous.

Emma returned with the blanket and placed it, neatly folded, on a stool.

"If you don't come now, your coffee will be cold," she said.

"Why are you putting that blanket there?"

"Madame said I was to do so."

"Well, I suppose it could be Falkenberg's," I muttered.

"Are you leaving now?" Emma asked.

"Yes, since you won't have anything to do with me."

"Oh, you're impossible!" she exclaimed, with a toss of her head.

I followed Emma down into the kitchen; as I sat at the table, I saw the Captain on his way to the forest. I was glad to see him gone; now, perhaps, Madame would show her face.

I finished my meal and got up. Should I go now without more ado? Of course. So I said goodbye to the girls, with a few words and a joke for each.

"I should have said goodbye to Madame also, but . . ."

"Madame is in, I'll . . ."

Emma was gone for a moment; then she was back again.

"Madame has a headache and has gone to lie down on the sofa. But she sends her best wishes."

"Come again!" said all the girls as I left.

I tucked my sack under my arm and set out on my way. Suddenly I remembered the ax: Falkenberg might be looking for it and not finding it. So I went back, knocked on the kitchen window, and left a message about the ax.

As I walked down the road, I turned around once or twice and looked back toward the windows of the house. Finally the whole place disappeared from view.

XXVI

I circled round Øvrebø all day long, in and out of farms in search of work, a roving, aimless outcast. The weather was cold and raw; only my restless wandering kept me warm.

Toward evening I made for my former place of work among the Captain's timber. No ax blows reached my ears; Falkenberg had gone home. I found the trees I had felled in the night and roared with laughter at the appalling stumps I had left. Falkenberg must have seen the wanton destruction and speculated on who its perpetrator might be. Perhaps the good Falkenberg had concluded it was a ghost, and this was why he had fled back home while the daylight lasted. Ha-ha-ha!

My merriment was not, of course, the healthy kind, being the result of my fever in the night and subsequent faintness; and very soon I was feeling sad again. Here on this very spot she had stood one day with her friend; they had come out to us in the forest and had chatted with us . . .

When it was well and truly dark, I set off for the manor. Perhaps I could spend one more night in the loft, and tomorrow when her headache was gone, she would come out. I came near enough to see the lights of the farm and then turned back. Perhaps it was still too early.

For two hours, I reckon, I wandered and sat, wandered and sat; then I approached the manor again. I could perfectly well go up in the loft and sleep there—let the miserable Falkenberg grumble if he dare! Ah, now I knew what to do: I would hide my sack in the forest before showing up, so as to look as if I had merely come back for some small item I had forgotten.

I went back to the forest.

Only when I had hidden the sack did I realize that Falkenberg and the loft and the bed there were no concern of mine. I was an ass and a simpleton: for me it was not a question of finding a place for the night but of seeing one particular person and then putting the manor and the entire parish behind me. My dear sir, I said to myself, weren't you the one who was going to seek out the quiet life and healthy people, and regain your peace of mind?

I drew the sack from its hiding place again, slung it on my back, and for the third time advanced on the manor. I skirted the servants' hall and reached the south side of the main building. There was a light in the living room.

And now, although it was dark, I lowered the sack from my shoulder so as not to be taken for a beggar, tucked it under my arm like a parcel, and cautiously approached the house. When I had come near enough I stopped. I stood, erect and strong, in front of the living-room windows, took off my cap, and remained standing there. There was no one to be seen indoors, not even a shadow. The dining room was dark, the evening meal was over. It must be quite late in the evening, I told myself.

Suddenly the lamp in the living room went out, and the whole house looked deserted. I waited for a while; then a solitary light appeared in an upstairs room. It was *her* room! Or so I thought. The light burned for half an hour or so and then went out. Now she had gone to bed. Good night.

Good night forever.

For of course I had no intention of returning here in the spring. Not on your life.

On coming down to the main road, I heaved the sack up on my shoulder again and set out on my wanderings . . .

Next morning I continued on my way. I had lain in a barn, frozen stiff for want of bedclothes; moreover, I had had to leave at the coldest hour of dawn, to avoid being discovered.

I walked and walked. The forest was sometimes evergreens and sometimes birch. Seeing a cluster of fine, straight-stemmed junipers, I cut myself a staff from one and sat by the edge of the forest whittling it down. A few yellow leaves still clung to the trees; but the birches were one mass of male catkins hung with pearls of rain. From time to time half a dozen small birds would swoop down on one of these birches and peck at the catkins, then look for a stone or a rough tree trunk and rub the gum from off their beaks. No give-and-take among these birds: there were a million catkins to plunder, but still they pursued each other and chased each other away. And the one pursued had no recourse but to flee. If a small bird bore down on a larger bird, the latter was forced away; even a large thrush never thought of resisting a sparrow, but merely swerved to one side. I supposed it must have been the attacker's speed that made him dangerous.

Gradually my early-morning shivers and malaise wore off, and I amused myself observing the various things I met with on my way and thinking random thoughts about each one. The birds entertained me most. It exhilarated me, also, to think that my pockets were full of money.

The previous morning Falkenberg had chanced to mention where Peter's home was; and now I headed in that direction. It was a small farm, where I was unlikely to find work; but now that I was rich, work no longer had pride of place in my thoughts. Peter should be coming home very soon and might have something to tell me.

I arranged things so as to reach Peter's home in the evening. I

brought tidings from the son of the house: he was very much
better and would soon be coming home. And could they give
me a roof for the night?

XXVII

I had been there a couple of days; Peter had come home, but
could tell me nothing.

"Everything all right at Øvrebø?"

"I heard nothing to the contrary."

"Did you see them all before you left? The Captain, Madame?"

"Yes."

"Nobody sick?"

"No. Who did you have in mind?"

"Falkenberg," I said. "He was complaining about an injury
to his hand; seems like it must be all right again."

It was a cheerless home, though prosperous enough. The
master of the house was a deputy member of the Storting, and
had taken to sitting and reading the newspapers of an evening. The
whole household wilted under this infernal reading, and the
daughters were bored to death. When Peter arrived home, the
entire family set to work calculating whether he had been paid in
full and whether he had been lying sick at the Captain's expense for
the full permitted period—the full *statutory* period, said the
politician. And when I was unlucky enough to break a paltry little
windowpane, there were whisperings and black looks in my
direction from every quarter. The next day I went to the local store,
bought a new pane, and fixed it in neatly with putty—whereupon
the politician said, "You really shouldn't have gone to all that
trouble for the sake of a windowpane."

But it wasn't only for the sake of the windowpane that I went
to the store: I bought in addition two or three bottles of wine,

to show I wasn't fussed over the price of a windowpane or two, and likewise a sewing machine, as a present for the girls when I left. We could drink the wine that evening, since tomorrow was Sunday, when we would all have time to sleep late. But on Monday morning I meant to resume my wanderings.

In the event, things turned out rather differently. The two girls had been up in the loft, poking around in my sack; both the sewing machine and the bottles had put ideas in their heads; they formed their conclusions about these objects and began dropping hints. Take it easy, girls, all in my own good time!

That evening I was sitting in the living room chatting with the family. We had just had supper, and the master of the house had put on his spectacles and addressed himself to the newspapers. From outside came the sound of a throat being cleared. "There's someone there," I said. The girls looked at each other and went out. A moment later they threw the door open and ushered in two young men. "Come in and sit down," said the wife.

It dawned on me at once that these two young yokels had been sent for apropos my wine and that they were the two girls' beaux. Such promising fillies—eighteen, nineteen, and already as clever as they come! But wine was simply not on the menu, no, not one drop . . .

The talk was about the weather, how it was no good looking for better weather at this time of year; still, it was bad luck they couldn't go on with the plowing because of the wet. The chit-chat had no life in it, and one of the girls turned to me and asked why I was so quiet.

"I dare say it's because I'm leaving," I replied. "By Monday morning I shall be a dozen miles from here."

"So perhaps we should have a farewell drink tonight?"

There was tittering at this suggestion, as a shrewd thrust at myself, sitting there and hoarding my wine like a miser. But I neither knew nor cared for these girls, or it would have been another story.

"What farewell drink?" I asked. "I've bought three bottles of wine to take where I'm going, that's all."

"Are you really carrying the wine twelve miles?" asked one girl amid loud laughter. "There are plenty of stores on the way, surely?"

"The young lady is forgetting that tomorrow is Sunday," I answered, "when all shops and stores are closed."

The laughter died away, but they liked me no better for telling them where they got off. I turned to the lady of the house and asked resentfully how much I owed.

No hurry, was there? Wouldn't tomorrow be time enough?

Yes, there was a hurry. I had been there two days; better consider the price.

She thought for a long time; finally she left the room, with her husband in tow, for the necessary deliberations.

They were away so long that I went up to the loft, got my sack ready, and carried it down to the entrance. I decided to be even more resentful and to leave that very evening. It would be a good way of making my escape.

When I re-entered the living room, Peter said, "You're not proposing to walk out into the night, are you?"

"That's exactly what I'm proposing to do."

"You shouldn't be so stupid as to care what these wenches say."

"For heaven's sake, let the old man go!" said his sister.

At last the politician and his wife returned. They maintained a stubborn, cautious silence.

Well, how much did I owe?

Hm. It was for me to decide.

The whole brood was trash, and here was I suffocating in the midst of it all. I flung her the first bank note that came to hand.

Was that enough?

Hm. It certainly went some way toward, but. And then again it might be enough, but.

How much was it I had given her?

A five.

Well, perhaps that was a bit on the skimpy side. I felt for more money.

"No, Mother, it was a *ten*," said Peter. "And that's far too much—you must give him some change."

The old girl opened her fist, looked at the note, and was instantly all astonishment. "Well goodness, gracious me, if it isn't a ten! I didn't look at it properly. In that case, thank you very much."

In his extremity the politician began telling the two boys about what he'd been reading in the newspaper: a nasty accident, hand crushed in a threshing machine. The girls carried on as if they never saw me, though truth to tell they sat like two cats with necks contracted and knife-narrow eyes. Nothing to wait for here—goodbye to the place.

The wife followed me out to the entrance and tried to butter me up. "Be a dear and lend us a bottle of wine. It's so embarrassing with the two boys sitting there."

"Good—bye!" was all I would say: I was not to be spoken to.

I had my sack over my shoulder and the sewing machine in one hand; it weighed a ton and the road had turned to mud, but my heart was light as I walked. It was a tiresome business I had got mixed up in, and I might as well admit that I had shown up as somewhat stingy. Stingy? Not at all. I formed myself into a small committee and pointed out that those confounded girls had tried to entertain their beaux with *my* wine. But wasn't my resentment at bottom merely a symptom of male blood? If the guests had been two strange girls instead of the two boys, would the wine not then have flowed? Surely! And "the old man," she had said. But was she not right? I must indeed have become old to make such an issue of being pushed aside in favor of a plowboy . . .

But as I trudged along my resentment wore off, the committee was dissolved, and I walked for hour after hour with my ridiculous burden: three bottles of wine and a sewing machine.

The weather was mild and misty, so that I saw farmhouse lights only when I was already quite near; then, usually, the dogs would rush out at me and prevent me from sneaking into a barn. The hour grew later and later; I was weary and woebegone and beset with anxieties about the future. Why, oh why, had I squandered so much of my money, and all to no purpose? I had better sell the sewing machine and convert it back into cash.

At long last I came to a cottage with no dog. There was still a light in the window, and without more ado I went in and asked for shelter.

XXVIII

The only person in the living room was a girl of fifteen or so who sat at a table sewing. When I asked for shelter she replied, in the most trustful possible way, that she would ask; then she disappeared into a small adjoining room. I called after her that I could manage very nicely just sitting here by the stove until the morning.

After a short interval the girl came back with her mother, who was still fastening and buttoning her clothes. Good evening! Well, they hadn't the space to make me really comfortable, but I was welcome to sleep in the other little room.

Where would they sleep themselves, then?

Oh, it would soon be morning now. Besides, the girl was going to sit up and sew for quite a while yet.

What was she sewing? A dress?

No, only a dressy skirt. She was to wear it for church tomorrow, but hadn't wanted to let her mother help her.

I produced my sewing machine and said jokingly that one dressy skirt more or less meant nothing to a fellow like this! Just let me show her!

Was I a tailor by any chance?

No. But I sold sewing machines.

I picked up the directions and read aloud what we had to do, while the girl listened attentively; she was only a child, with slender fingers all blue from the dye coming off. These blue fingers were so pitiful to see that I brought out the wine and poured some for each of us. Then we continued sewing, I with the directions in my hand, the girl turning away on the machine. "It's going splendidly," she said, and her eyes glowed.

How old was she?

Sixteen. Confirmed last year.

What was her name?

Olga.

Her mother stood watching us and wanting to have a go on the machine; but every time she came near it, Olga said, "Careful, Mother, you mustn't mantreat it!" And when the spool needed filling and her mother got hold of the shuttle for a moment, Olga was again afraid of its being mantreated.

The mother put on the coffeepot and made up the fire, the room grew nice and warm; these lonely people were at ease and full of trust, and Olga laughed whenever I thought up a joke about the machine. Although it was for sale, I noticed that neither of them asked how much it cost; it lay far, far beyond their reach. But what a joy to see it in operation!

She should have had a machine like that, should Olga; she had an excellent way with it.

Her mother replied that Olga would have to wait until she had been in service for a while.

Was Olga going into service?

Yes, she hoped so. Both her other daughters were in service—never gave a spot of bother, praise God. Olga was to meet them at church tomorrow.

On one wall hung a little cracked mirror, on the other some cheap prints of soldiers on horseback and royal couples in full regalia. One of the pictures was old and tattered, and showed the Empress Eugénie; hardly a recent purchase. I asked where it had come from.

Couldn't rightly remember. Husband must have picked it up one time or another.

In these parts?

Had an idea it might have been at Hersæt—husband had been in service there in his younger days. Could be thirty years ago.

I had a little plan in my head. I said, "That picture's worth a lot of money."

The woman thought I was making fun of her; so I examined it closely and declared unwaveringly that this was no cheap picture—most certainly not.

The woman was no fool, and only said, Really, did I think so? It had hung there ever since the cottage was built. Anyway, it was Olga's picture; she had regarded it as hers from the time she was little.

I put on a mysterious, knowing manner and asked, as if to get to the bottom of the matter, "And where's Hersæt?"

Hersæt was in the next parish, about twelve miles away. The Sheriff lived there . . .

The coffee was ready, and Olga and I stopped for a break. Only the hooks remained to be put in. I asked if I might see the blouse that went with the skirt; but it seemed there was no real blouse, only a knitted kerchief. But one of her sisters had given her a cast-off jacket, and this jacket was to go outside everything and hide everything.

"Olga's growing so fast at present, it would be madness to think of buying her a proper blouse for a year to come," I was informed.

Olga sat putting in the hooks; and soon the job was done. By now she could hardly keep her eyes open, so I assumed an air of authority and ordered her to bed. Her mother felt obliged to sit up and keep me company, even though I begged her, too, to go back to bed.

"But now," she said to her daughter, "you must thank the kind gentleman properly for all his help."

Whereupon Olga came and took my hand and curtseyed. I saw my chance and shooed her off into the little bedroom.

"And now you'd better go too," I said to her mother. "I won't talk any more now, in any case, because I'm tired."

When she saw me pitching camp by the stove and arranging my sack as a pillow, she laughed, shook her head, and left me to my devices.

XXIX

I am happy and comfortable here; it is morning, the sun shines in through the window, and both Olga and her mother are a joy to behold, with their hair all wet and smoothed.

They shared their breakfast with me, and we drank large quantities of coffee; after which Olga dressed herself up in her new skirt, her knitted kerchief, and her jacket. That marvelous jacket! It had lasting all around the edges, and two rows of buttons of the same material, while the neck and sleeves were trimmed with braid; and it was far, far too big for little Olga, who was thin and bony as a young calf.

"Shall we shorten the jacket a little?" I suggested. "We've time if we're quick."

But mother and daughter glanced at each other, meaning it was Sunday, when needles and knives are things prohibited. I knew well what they were thinking—in my childhood I used to think like that myself—and I tried to save the situation with a little freethinking: ah, but the sewing would be done by a machine and that was different—no worse than when an innocent carriage rolls along the highway on a Sunday.

But no: this they could not follow. Besides, the jacket was meant for growing into; in a year or two it would fit nicely.

I tried to think of something I could slip into Olga's hand as she left, but I had nothing; so I gave her a krone instead. She shook hands and curtseyed again; then she showed the coin to her mother and whispered, her eyes sparkling, that she would give it to her sister at church. And her mother, almost equally moved, agreed that perhaps she should.

So Olga went to church in her overlong jacket, shambling down the slope with her feet turned in and out as chance might take them. Dear God, how sweet and amusing she was . . .

Was Hersæt a big manor?

A big manor, yes.

I sat for a while, blinking my sleepy eyes and playing the etymologist. Hersæt could mean *herresæte:* gentleman's seat. Or a *herse*—a local chieftain—may have ruled there. And the chieftain's daughter is the haughtiest maiden for many a mile, and the jarl himself comes and asks for her hand. And the year after she bears him a son, who becomes king . . .

In short, I planned to go to Hersæt. It was all the same where I went; so I would go there. I might get work from the Sheriff, I might stumble on something or other; at the very least there would be new faces. And having thus decided on Hersæt, I felt I had an aim and an object.

I was drowsy and stupid from lack of sleep; so I got permission to lie down on the mother's bed. A beautiful blue-cross spider wandered slowly up over the wall, and I lay there following it with my eyes until I fell asleep.

I slept for a couple of hours, then suddenly woke, feeling rested and fit. My hostess was cooking the midday dinner. I packed my sack, paid for my bed and board, and ended by saying I'd like to do a swap with Olga: her picture for my sewing machine.

Sheer disbelief again.

It was all one, I said; if she was satisfied, so was I. The picture had its value; I knew what I was doing.

I took the picture down from the wall, blew the dust from it, and rolled it up carefully; it left a rectangle of lighter color on the timber wall. Then I said goodbye.

The woman followed me out: couldn't I wait until Olga came home, so that she could thank me in person? Oh, if only I would!

But I couldn't spare the time. "Tell her, if there's anything she's uncertain about, to look in the directions."

She stood for a long time following me with her eyes. I swaggered along the road, whistling with satisfaction at what I had done. Now I had only the sack to carry, I was rested, the sun shone, and the road had dried out somewhat. Soon I burst out singing with satisfaction at what I had done.

Nerves . . .

I reached Hersæt the following day. It looked such a big and splendid place that at first I felt like walking straight past; but after talking for a while with one of the farmhands, I decided to present myself to the Sheriff. I had worked for rich people before—the Captain at Øvrebø, for example . . .

The Sheriff was a short, broad-shouldered man, with a long white beard and dark eyebrows. His voice was gruff but his eyes were kindly. Later, I found he was a jovial man who enjoyed the occasional joke and a good hearty laugh. At other times he could be self-important about his wealth and position; and he was something of a climber.

"Afraid I've no work for you here. Where have you come from?"

I mentioned some places along my route.

"You've no money, so you go around begging, eh?"

I was *not* begging, and I *had* money.

"Well, you'd better be on your way. Sorry, but I've no work for you here, the plowing season's over. Can you cut stakes for a fence?"

"Yes."

"I see. Well, I don't have wooden fences any more, I've switched to wire. Can you do masonry work?"

"Yes."

"Pity. I've had bricklayers all autumn, you could have lent a hand."

He stood poking the ground with his stick.

"What made you come to me?"

"Everyone said, If you want work, go to the Sheriff."

"Is that so? Well, yes, I'm constantly having all kinds of people in; this autumn it's been the bricklayers. Can you put up a fence that's proof against hens? Because I've yet to meet a living soul who can, ha-ha! Did you say you'd been with Captain Falkenberg at Øvrebø?"

"Yes."

"What were you doing there?"

"Felling timber."

"Don't know the man—his place is a fair distance from here. Still, I've heard of him. Have you got papers from him?"

I handed him the testimonial.

"Right, come with me," said the Sheriff without more ado.

He led me around the house and into the kitchen.

"Give this man a first-rate meal," he said; "he's come a long way." . . .

I sat in the big, bright kitchen and had my best meal for many a day. I had just finished eating when the Sheriff returned.

"You, there," he began—

I rose at once and stood like a sentry—a small courtesy which he evidently did not despise.

"No, go on eating, finish your meal. Finished already? I thought perhaps . . . Come with me."

The Sheriff led me to the woodshed.

"You could do a stint of chopping down firewood, what do you say to that? I've got a couple of men, but I'm using one of them on official business at present, so you'd better go wood-cutting with the other. I've plenty of firewood, as you can see, but there's room for more—one can never have too much of the stuff. You said you had money; let me see."

I showed him my bank notes.

"Good. You see, I represent the government, which means I have to keep tabs on my own men. Still, it's obvious you've nothing on your conscience or you wouldn't have come to the Sheriff, ha-ha-ha! Well, as I was saying, you can take it easy today and start chopping down firewood tomorrow."

I began busying myself with preparations for the morrow: getting my clothes in order, sharpening the saw and the ax. I had no mittens, but it was not yet the weather for mittens; otherwise I lacked for nothing.

Several times the Sheriff came out and talked of this and that; he enjoyed talking to me, no doubt, stranger and wanderer that I was. "Come here, Margaret!" he called to his wife as she crossed the courtyard. "This is the new man—I'm getting him to chop down firewood."

XXX

We had no detailed instructions, so we used our intelligence and began by felling only dead trees; and in the evening the Sheriff told us we had done right. The remaining timber he would select for us in the morning.

I soon saw that our present work was not going to last until Christmas. With the weather we were having—light frost at night but no snow—and the ground as it was, there was noth-ing to hold us up, and we felled a mass of timber every day; as the Sheriff himself put it, we were cutting down trees like a pair of maniacs, ha-ha-ha! The old man was easy to work for; he visited us frequently in the forest, always in a good humor, and since I seldom answered in the same joking vein, he doubtless concluded I was a dull dog, though a reliable one. After a while he started sending me to the post office, fetching and carrying official letters.

There were no children about the place, and no young people except for the maids and one of the hands, so the evenings tended to drag. I amused myself by getting hold of some tin and some acids, and tin-plating a number of old kettles in the kitchen. But this didn't last me for long. Then one evening I sat down and wrote the following letter:

> If only I were where you are, I would work hard enough for two!

The next day, when I had to go to the post office for the Sheriff, I took my letter too and posted it. I was in a great state of agitation; the letter even had a slightly uncouth appearance, the result of my borrowing stationery from the Sheriff and having to plaster a whole string of stamps over his name printed on the envelope. What on earth would she say when she got it? The letter was unsigned and gave no return address.

Well, we worked in the woods, the lad and I, exchanged small talk, labored with might and main, and were the best of friends. The days went by, and the end of the work, alas, was already in sight; but I still nursed a faint hope that the Sheriff might find something else for me to do when the woodcutting was finished. Something was sure to turn up. I had no desire to start wandering again before Christmas.

Then one day, while visiting the post office again, I was handed a letter. I could not grasp that it was for me and stood there irresolutely, turning it over and over; but the postmaster, who knew me by now, glanced at the envelope again and confirmed that it was addressed to me, care of the Sheriff. A sudden thought struck me and I clutched the letter. Yet, it was for me, I was forgetting . . . yes, it was true . . .

Bells began ringing in my ears, I hurried out into the road, opened the letter, and read:

Don't *write* to me—

No name, no address, but crystal-clear and lovely. The second word was underlined.

How I got home I don't know. I remember sitting by the side of the road on a guardstone, reading the letter, sticking it in my pocket, and then walking on to another guardstone and repeating the process. Don't *write.* Could I, then, come and maybe talk with her? This exquisite little paper, this flowing, elegant hand! Her fingers had encircled this letter, it had lain before her eyes, it was perfumed with her breath. And then at the end a dash: there could be a world of meaning in that dash.

I came home, delivered the mail, and went into the forest. I was lost in dreams, and doubtless incomprehensible to my companion as he saw me, time and time again, reading a letter and then putting it safely away with my money.

How clever of her to find me! She must have held the envelope up to the light and read the Sheriff's name under the stamps; then tilted her beautiful head on one side for a moment, blinked her eyes, and thought, So now he is working for the Sheriff at Hersæt . . .

When we were back home that evening, the Sheriff came out to us, talked about this and that, then asked, "Wasn't it Captain Falkenberg at Øvrebø you said you'd worked for?"

"Yes."

"I see he's invented a machine."

"A machine?"

"A felling saw. It's in the papers."

I gave a start. Surely he hadn't invented *my* felling saw?

"There must be some mistake," I said; "it wasn't the Captain who invented the saw."

"No?"

"No, indeed. Though the saw was left with him."

I told the Sheriff everything. He went in to get the paper, and we read together: "New invention . . . our special correspondent . . . sawing technique of great potential importance to owners of forest land . . . principle of the mechanism is as follows . . ."

"You're not telling me it's you who invented it?"

"I most certainly am."

"And the Captain's trying to steal it, eh? That will make a jolly little case, an extraordinarily jolly little case. Leave it to me. Did anyone see you working on the invention?"

"Yes, everyone in the place."

"Damned if it isn't the most brazen thing I ever heard! Stealing your invention! Think of the money—it could reach the million mark!"

I had to confess that I couldn't understand the Captain.

"I understand him all right; I'm not Sheriff for nothing. I've had my eye on that man for a long time now—he's not so deucedly rich as he makes out. Now he's going to get a little letter from *me*, quite a short little letter—what do you say to that? Ha-ha-ha! Leave it to me."

But now I became uneasy: the Sheriff was too hasty—the Captain could well be innocent, the reporter could have been inaccurate. I begged the Sheriff to let me write myself.

"And agree to go halves with the scoundrel? Never! You leave the whole thing in my hands. Besides, if you write, you won't do it in style, the way I would."

But I coaxed and coaxed, until finally it was agreed that I should write the first letter and that he should step in at a later stage. I got some more of his writing paper.

There was no writing done that evening; the excitements of the day had left me in a state of inner turmoil. I brooded and reflected; for Madame's sake I would avoid writing direct to the Captain, which might make things awkward for her; instead, I would drop a line to my mate Falkenberg, asking him to keep an eye on the machine.

That night I had another visit from the corpse, from this miserable shrouded woman who gave me no peace over her thumbnail. After the prolonged agitation of the day, she made sure to visit me in the night. Chilled to the bone with terror, I saw her come gliding in, stop in the middle of the floor, and hold out her hand. By the other wall, directly opposite, my workmate lay in his bed, and it was with a strange sense of relief that I heard him groaning and tossing about; that meant there were two of us in danger. I shook my head, meaning that I had buried the nail in a peaceful spot and could do no more. But the corpse continued to stand there. I begged her to forgive me; but suddenly I was seized with anger and told her furiously that I would put up with her nonsense no longer. I had only borrowed her nail in an emergency, and it was months since I had done what I could and buried it again . . . At this she came gliding sideways over to my pillow and tried to get behind me. I flung myself forward and up, and let out a shriek.

"What is it?" asked the lad in the other bed.

I rubbed my eyes and said it was only a dream.

"Who was that in here?" asked the boy.

"I don't know. Was anyone in here?"

"I saw someone go . . . ."

XXXI

I let two days go by; then I sat down calmly and loftily to write to Falkenberg. I had left a little sawing device behind at Øvrebø, I wrote; it might one day acquire a certain importance for owners of forest land, and I intended to come and collect it in the near future. Please keep an eye on it and see that nothing happens to it.

Such a mild letter—the most dignified line to take. In case Falkenberg should mention it in the kitchen, as well he might, and perhaps even show it around, it must be the soul of delicacy. But it was not just mildness and more mildness and nothing but mildness, for, to show I was in earnest, I added a definite date: I would collect the machine on Monday the eleventh of December.

I thought: This deadline makes it clear and explicit: if on that Monday the machine is not there, then something is going to be done about it.

I posted the letter myself, and again plastered the envelope with a string of stamps . . .

I was still in a state of delicious ecstasy: I had received the loveliest letter in the world, I carried it here in my breast pocket, it was to *me*. Don't *write*. No, indeed, but I could come. And the letter ended with a dash.

Surely there was nothing wrong about that underlining—it could not, for example, merely be intended to emphasize the prohibition in a general way? Ladies were terrors for underlining every possible word and sprinkling dashes here, there, and everywhere. But not her, never her!

A few days more and the work at the Sheriff's would be finished; it all fitted nicely, everything worked out, on the eleventh I should be at Øvrebø! And perhaps not a moment too soon: if it was really the case that the Captain had designs on my machine, I needed to move fast. Was a stranger to steal my hard-earned million? Had I not toiled for it? I began almost to regret the mildness of my letter to Falkenberg: it could have been considerably sharper: now he might not believe that I was any kind of tough guy. Who knows, he might even have the nerve to bear witness against me and deny that I'd invented the machine. Ho-ho, my good friend Falkenberg, just you try! If you do, you will forfeit your eternal salvation for a start; and in case that isn't enough, I shall tell on you for perjury, to my friend and patron the Sheriff. And you know what will happen then.

"But of course you must go," said the Sheriff when I talked to him. "And by all means bring the machine back here. You have to look after your own interests—there may be large sums involved."

Next day the post brought an item of news which transformed the situation at a stroke: a letter in the newspaper from Captain Falkenberg himself, saying that the attribution to himself of the construction of a new felling saw rested on a misunderstanding. Credit for the invention was due, on the contrary, to a man who had worked for a time on his estate. About the machine itself he wished to express no opinion. Captain Falkenberg.

The Sheriff and I looked at each other.

"What do you make of that?" he asked.

"That the Captain, at all events, is innocent."

"So. Do you know what I think?"

Pause. The Sheriff a sheriff from top to toe, a man who recognizes an intrigue when he sees one.

"He is *not* innocent," he said.

"Do you really think so?"

"I'm used to this sort of thing. Now he's drawing in his horns; your letter has given him warning. Ha-ha-ha!"

So I had to confess to the Sheriff that, far from addressing myself to the Captain, I had merely dropped a line to one of the hands at Øvrebø, and that not even this letter could have arrived yet, since it had been posted only the evening before.

This struck the Sheriff speechless, and he gave up trying to recognize intrigues. On the other hand, he seemed from this moment to have doubts about the value of the entire invention.

"It may well be that the machine's a dud," he said, adding good-naturedly, "I mean, it may need modifying and improving. You must have noticed how they're constantly having to change the design of warships and flying machines . . . Are you still set on going?"

After this I heard no more about my coming back and bringing the machine with me; but the Sheriff gave me a good testimonial. He would gladly have kept me on longer, it said, but the work was interrupted by my having private interests elsewhere to look after . . .

Next morning, just as I was leaving, I found a young girl standing outside in the courtyard waiting for me. It was Olga. Was there ever such a child? She must have been on her feet since midnight to get here so early. There she stood in her blue skirt and her jacket.

"Hello, Olga! Where are you off to?"

She had come to see me.

How did she know I was here?

She had asked here and there. Was it true, please, that she was to have the sewing machine? Surely it couldn't—

Yes, indeed the machine was hers; I had got her picture in exchange. Was it working well?

Yes, it was working well.

We exchanged only a few words; I wanted to get rid of her before the Sheriff came out and started asking questions.

"And now you must go home, child. You've a long way to go."

Olga gave me her hand; it was completely buried in mine, and lay there as long as I chose to keep it. Then she thanked me and shambled cheerfully away, her toes turned in and out as chance might take them.

XXXII

I had nearly reached my goal.

That Sunday night I slept at a little cottage near Øvrebø in order to arrive at the manor early on Monday morning. By nine they would all be up—when, surely, I must be lucky enough to meet the one I sought!

By now I was a bundle of nerves and kept picturing to myself all manner of evils: my letter to Falkenberg had been perfectly proper and free from abuse, but the Captain might, nevertheless, have taken umbrage over that accursed date, that deadline I had set him. Would to God I had never sent any letter!

As I approached the place, I stooped more and more and shrank into myself, even though I had committed no offense. I left the road and made a detour so as to reach the outbuildings first—and there I met Falkenberg. He stood washing down the carriage. We greeted each other and were the same good friends as before.

Was he taking the carriage out somewhere?

No, he had only just got back last night. Been to the station to catch a train.

Who was catching the train?

Madame.

Madame?

Madame.

Pause.

Well, well. Where was Madame going?

Spending a few days in town.

Pause.

"A stranger's been here and written about your machine in the papers," said Falkenberg.

"Has the Captain gone too?"

"No, the Captain's at home. He really looked down his nose when your letter came."

I lured Falkenberg up to our old loft. My sack still contained two bottles of wine, which I now brought out and opened. Aha! These bottles, which I had carried to and fro for mile after mile, and which had needed such careful handling, were now proving their worth. But for them Falkenberg would not have said nearly so much.

"Why did the Captain look down his nose about my letter? Did he see it?"

"It all started," said Falkenberg, "with Madame being in the kitchen when I brought the post. 'What's that letter with all those stamps on?' she asked. I opened it and said it was from you and you'd be here on the eleventh."

"What did she say to that?"

"She didn't say anything. Just asked again, 'Coming on the eleventh, is he?' 'That's right,' I said."

"And two days later you were told to drive her to the station?"

"Yes, it must have been about two days later. So then I said to myself: Since Madame knows about the letter, I suppose the Captain ought to know about it too. Do you know what he said when I showed it to him?"

I didn't answer; I was thinking and thinking. Was there something behind all this? Was she running away from me? I must be mad—the Captain's wife at Øvrebø doesn't go running away from one of her workmen. But it looked very strange to me. I had hoped to be allowed to talk to her since I was forbidden to write.

Falkenberg continued a shade uneasily, "I showed the Captain your letter, you see, even though you hadn't said I should. Was that wrong of me?"

"Oh, never mind. What did he say, then?"

" 'Well, you'd better take good care of the machine, hadn't you?' he said, pulling a bit of a face. 'So that nobody comes and takes it,' he said."

"Is the Captain angry with me now, then?"

"Oh no. No, I can't believe that. And I've heard no more about it since."

Never mind about the Captain. When Falkenberg had drunk a fair quantity of wine, I asked him if he knew Madame's address in town. No, but Emma might. We got hold of Emma, gave her some wine, talked of this and that, circled around the question, getting nearer and nearer, and finally asked it in the discreetest possible way. No, Emma didn't know the address.

But Madame was doing her Christmas shopping and had traveled with Miss Elizabeth from the parsonage, so the people there would probably know the address. What did I want it for, in any case?

I had picked up an old filigree brooch and thought I might ask if she'd care to buy it from me.

"Let's have a look."

Fortunately I was able to show Emma the brooch, a beautiful old piece of work which I had bought from one of the maids at Hersæt.

"Madame won't want that," said Emma. "And no more would I."

"Oh yes, you would, Emma, if you got me in the bargain," I said with forced jocularity.

Exit Emma. I pumped Falkenberg again. Falkenberg had a good nose for such things, there were times when he understood people.

Did he still sing for Madame?

No, he did not. And Falkenberg was sorry he had signed on; there seemed to be more and more weeping and sorrow about the place.

Weeping and sorrow? Were the Captain and Madame not on good terms, then?

Lord, yes, they were on good terms—as they'd always been. Last Saturday she was in tears all day.

"I can't make that out—they're always so civil and straight with each other," I said, and waited for his reply.

"Yes, and so bored," said Falkenberg. "She's lost a lot of weight too, even in the time since you left—gone terribly thin and pale."

I sat for a couple of hours in the loft, keeping an eye on the main building from my window, but the Captain never showed up. Why did he stay indoors? It was hopeless waiting any longer; I would have to go, without making my excuses to the Captain. There were plenty of good excuses I could have made: I

could have blamed the newspaper article, with some justifica-
tion, for making me mildly megalomaniac. Now it only remained to bundle the machine together, cover it up with my
sack as best I could, and set out on my wanderings again.

Emma went into the kitchen and stole some food for me
before I left.

I had another long trek ahead of me: first to the parsonage—
which, as it happened, lay almost directly on my path—and
then to the railroad station. A little light snow was falling,
which made the going none too easy; moreover, instead of daw-
dling as I would have liked, I was obliged to make a forced
march: the ladies were only going to town for their Christmas
shopping, and they had a head start already.

On the following afternoon I arrived at the parsonage. I had
worked out that my best chance was to get talking with the
priest's wife.

"I'm on my way into town," I told her. "And here I am, carrying a machine around with me—may I leave the heaviest of
the woodwork here?"

"Going into town, are you?" she asked. "But surely you'll
stay here for tonight?"

"No, thank you kindly. I have to be in town by tomorrow."

She pondered awhile and said, "Elizabeth's in town. You
could take her a parcel, something she's forgotten."

I thought: Aha, the address!

"But there's something I'd need to get ready first."

"In that case, mightn't Miss Elizabeth have left before I arrive?"

"No, no, she's with Mrs. Falkenberg, they're staying there a
week."

This was a pleasant piece of news, a glorious piece of news.
Now I had both the address and the length of stay.

Madame stood there, gave me a sidelong glance, and said,
"You'll stay for the night, won't you? Because there really is
something I need to put in order . . ."

I was given a room in the house, since it was now too cold for the hayloft. And when the household had settled down for the night and everything was quiet, Madame came to my room with the parcel and said, "Excuse my coming at this hour. But you may want to leave first thing in the morning, before I'm up."

XXXIII

So here I was, back in the city, with its noise and bustle and newspapers and people; finding, after all these months, that I had nothing really against it. I spent a morning collecting my scattered wits, picked up some different clothes, and set off to call on Miss Elizabeth. She was staying with relatives.

Would I be lucky enough this time to meet the other? I was as nervous as a kitten, and so boorishly unused to gloves that I pulled them off; but as I climbed the steps I saw that my hands did not match my clothes and pulled the gloves on again. Then I rang the bell.

"Miss Elizabeth? Yes, if you wouldn't mind waiting a moment."

Miss Elizabeth came out. "Good afternoon. Was it me you wanted . . . ? Why, it's *you!*"

I had a parcel for her from her mother. Here.

She ripped the parcel open and peered inside. "No! Mother really is unique! The opera glasses. We've been to the theater already . . . I didn't recognize you at first."

"Really? And yet it's not all that long."

"No, only . . . Tell me, isn't there someone else you'd like to ask about? Ha-ha-ha!"

"Yes."

"She's not here. It's only me staying here, with some of my family. She's at the Victoria."

"Well, it was you I brought the parcel for," I said, trying to master my disappointment.

"Wait a bit, I'm just going out again, we can go together."

Miss Elizabeth wrapped herself up, stuck her head in at a door, called out, "Goodbye for now," and followed me out. We took a cab and drove to a quiet café. Miss Elizabeth thought it was *such* fun going to cafés. But this one was no fun at all.

Would she rather go somewhere else?

Yes. To the Grand.

I feared I would be unsafe there; I had been away so long that I might be dragged into saying hello to my acquaintances. But Mademoiselle insisted on the Grand. After only a few days' practice she was already full of self-confidence. But I had been so fond of her before.

We drove off again to the Grand. It was getting on toward evening. Mademoiselle sat herself down where the lights were most dazzling; radiant, herself, over what fun it all was. I ordered wine.

She laughed and said, "Why, how smart you've become!"

"I could hardly come in here in my smock."

"No, of course not. Though, to be honest, that smock . . . Shall I tell you what I think?"

"Please do."

"The smock suited you better."

There now, devil take these town clothes! I sat there, my head afire with other things, and snapped my fingers at this chatter.

"Are you staying in town for long?" I asked.

"It's up to Louise; we've done what we came to do. Oh dear, it's much too short . . ." Then she cheered up again and asked with a laugh, "Did you enjoy being with us in the country?"

"Yes, it was a good time, that."

"Are you coming again soon? Ha-ha-ha!"

It seemed to me she was just sitting there making fun of me: showing that she saw through me, that I hadn't properly learned my lines for my rustic role. The chit! I who could teach a workman his job and was master of several trades! Although in my true calling only my second-best dreams came true.

"Shall I ask Papa to put up a notice in the spring, saying you undertake all kinds of plumbing work?"

She closed her eyes and laughed her ringing laugh.

I was tense, agitated, and pained by this jocularity, however kindly intentioned. I looked around the café to collect myself, saw hats raised here and there, and raised my own, but felt miles away from it all. It was my attractive young companion who drew people's attention.

"You know these people, then?"

"Oh, one or two . . . Have you had a good time in town?"

"Fabulous. I've got two cousins, both boys, and they have various friends."

"Poor young Eric, back home!" I said as a joke.

"You and your young Eric. No, here it's somebody called Bewer. Only I've just fallen out with him."

"That will soon pass."

"Do you think so? Anyway, it's quite serious. Do you know, I'm half expecting him to come here now."

"If he does, you must point him out to me."

"I thought, as we were driving here, you and I could sit here and make him jealous."

"Good, let's do that."

"Yes, but. Well, you ought really to be a bit younger for that. I mean—"

I forced a laugh. "Oh, we'll manage all right. Don't despise us old fogeys, us Methuselahs, we're a match for anyone at times. Just let me sit with you on the banquette, so he doesn't see my bald patch."

Ah, how hard it is to manage the fateful transition to old age gracefully and calmly! Instead, convulsions, writhings, grimaces, strife with the younger generation, envy.

"Please, Miss Elizabeth," I began, and implored her with all my heart, "couldn't you go to the telephone and get Mrs. Falkenberg to come here now?"

She considered the request.

"Yes, let's do that," she said, taking pity on me.

We went to the telephone, rang the Victoria, and were connected with Madame.

"Is that you, Louise? You'll never guess who I'm with—can you come and join us? That's good. We're at the Grand. No, I won't tell you. Yes, of course, it's a man, only he's a gentleman now—I won't say more. Are you coming, then? What's that, you're having second thoughts? Family? Yes yes, you must do as you please, only—yes, he's right beside me now. You *are* in a hurry, aren't you? Well, goodbye then."

Miss Elizabeth rang off and said tersely, "Going to a family gathering."

We went back to our places and had some more wine; I tried to strike a festive note and suggested champagne. Yes, please.

As we sat there, Mademoiselle said, "There's Bewer. Our drinking champagne now couldn't be better."

Engrossed as I was with one subject, and asked now to show my paces and captivate the young lady to another's advantage, I started saying one thing and meaning another—a ploy certain to misfire. I was incapable of getting that telephone conversation out of my head: she must have smelled a rat, guessed it was me waiting for her. But what crime had I committed? Why on earth had I been discharged so abruptly from Øvrebø and Falkenberg taken on in my place? Maybe the Captain and Madame were not always the best of friends, but the husband had scented danger in my presence there and wanted to save his wife from quite so ludicrous a fall. And so now she went around feeling ashamed that I had worked at her place, that she had used me as her coachman and shared two picnic lunches with me. Ashamed, too, of my advancing years . . .

"This won't do at all," said Miss Elizabeth.

So I exerted myself again and said so many crazy things that she started laughing. I drank liberally and grew bolder in my flights of fancy, until finally she seemed to imagine I was genuinely making up to her, with no one else in mind. She began eyeing me.

"Really and truly, you find me rather attractive?"

"Now listen, please—it's Mrs. Falkenberg I'm talking about."

"Sh!" she said. "Of course, it's Mrs. Falkenberg, I've known that all along, only you don't need to say so. I do believe it's beginning to have some effect on that fellow over there. Keep it up, don't let's lose interest."

So she had never imagined I was making up to her with no one else in mind. I was too old for that sort of thing, damn and blast it all.

"But you can't have Mrs. Falkenberg, you know," she began again. "It's hopeless."

"No, I can't have her, and I can't have you either."

"Are you talking to Mrs. Falkenberg again?"

"No, I'm talking to you now."

Pause.

"Did you know I was in love with you once? Yes, I was, back at home."

"This is getting amusing," I said, shifting up on the banquette. "Yes, now we're really going to give it to Bewer."

"Fancy, I used to go up to the churchyard in the evenings just to meet you. But you were too stupid to understand a thing."

"I take it you're talking to Bewer now," I said.

"No, it's the honest truth I'm telling you. And once I came

over to see you in the potato field. It wasn't your young Eric I
came to see."

"Fancy its being me!" I said, and made a great show of melancholy.

"Yes, I'm sure you find it strange. But don't forget, we
country folks too need someone to get fond of."

"Does Mrs. Falkenberg say that too?"

"Mrs. Falkenberg—no, she says she never wants to get fond
of anyone, she only wants to play the piano and that sort of
thing. But I was speaking for myself. Do you know what I did
once? No, I'm darned if I'll tell you. Do you want to hear?"

"I'm dying to hear."

"Yes, because after all I'm just a little girl in relation to you,
so it doesn't matter: it was when you were sleeping in the
hayloft at home; I crept up there once and straightened your
blankets and made them into a proper bed."

"So it was you who did that!" I exclaimed spontaneously; I
was forgetting my lines.

"You ought to have seen me creeping in, ha-ha-ha!"

But the girl was not yet practiced enough: she changed color
over her little confession and tried to cover up with a forced
laugh.

To help her out I said, "All the same now, you're a splendid
creature. Mrs. Falkenberg could never had done a thing like
that."

"No, but then she's older. Or did you think we were the
same age?"

"And Mrs. Falkenberg says she never wants to get fond of
anyone?"

"Yes. Oof, no really, I don't know. Mrs. Falkenberg's married, you see, she doesn't say anything. Now, talk to me a bit
again . . . Yes, and then there was the time we were to go to
the store together, do you remember? I kept walking slower and
slower so that you would catch up with me . . ."

"That was nice of you. And now I want to make you happy in return."

. I got up, went over to young Bewer, and asked him if he would care to have a glass with us, at our table. I fetched him along, while Miss Elizabeth turned red as a beet root. Next I chatted the two youngsters well and truly together; after which I remembered that I had some business to see to and would have to leave them—very reluctantly, ladies and gentlemen. "You indeed, Miss Elizabeth, have completely bewitched me; but I can see I stand no chance. And in any case, it's a mystery now to me . . ."

XXXIV

I drifted along to the town hall square and stood for a while among the cab drivers, watching the entrance to the Victoria. But it was true, of course: she was at a family gathering that evening. So I wandered into the hotel and spoke to the porter.

"Yes, the lady is in. Room number 12, second floor."

"She hasn't gone out, then?"

"No."

"Is she leaving soon?"

"She hasn't said anything."

I came out again, and the cab drivers all sat up and called out, "Cab, sir?" I chose a cab and got in.

"Where to?"

"We'll stay here. I'll pay you by the hour."

The cab drivers began forming little groups and whispering their various opinions: he's watching the hotel, bet you it's his wife in there with a traveling salesman.

Yes, I was watching the hotel. There were scattered lights in the rooms, and it suddenly struck me that she might be up there and see me from a window. "Wait a bit," I said to the cab driver, and went back into the hotel.

"Which floor is number 12?"

"Second floor."

"And does it face the square?"

"Yes."

"Ah, so it *was* my sister who was waving," I said, lying in order to get past the porter.

I went up the stairs, and to give myself no time for second thoughts, I knocked on the door the moment I found the number. No answer. I knocked again.

"Is that the chambermaid?" came from inside.

I could hardly say yes; my voice would have given me away. I tried the door; it was locked. She must have feared my coming; she might even have seen me outside.

"No, it's not the chambermaid," I said, and heard how strangely my words vibrated.

After that I waited for a long time, listening; I could hear someone rustling about inside, but the door remained locked. Then there came two short, sharp rings down to the hall from one of the rooms. It's her, I thought to myself, she's uneasy and has rung for the maid. I moved away from the door so as not to make things awkward for her, and when the maid appeared, I walked past her as if on my way down. I heard the maid say, "Yes, it's the chambermaid." And then the door being opened.

"No, madame," the maid said next, "it was only a gentleman on his way down."

I thought of taking a room in the hotel, but the idea repelled me: she wasn't a married woman on an assignation with a traveling salesman. When I arrived downstairs I simply said to the porter as I passed that the lady seemed to be resting.

Then I went out and sat in the cab again. The time passed, the hour was up, the driver asked if I wasn't cold. Well, yes, a little. Was I waiting for someone? Yes . . . He gave me his blanket from the box, and to reward his kindness I handed him the price of a highball.

The time passed. Hour after hour passed. The cab drivers lost their inhibitions and started saying to each other that I was letting the horses freeze to death.

Oh, what was the use? I paid the driver, went home, and wrote the following letter:

> Since I mustn't *write* to you, may I simply see you again? I will ask for you at the hotel tomorrow afternoon at five o'clock.

Should I make it an earlier hour? But the light in the earlier part of the day was so white, and if I became agitated and my mouth started twitching, I would look ghastly.

I delivered the letter to the Victoria myself and went home again.

A long, long night made up of long, long hours. Just when I needed to sleep and wake up strong and fresh again, I was unable to do so. At dawn I got up, roamed the streets for a long time, drifted back home, lay down, and slept.

The hours passed. On waking and coming to my senses, I hurried straight to the telephone in my anxiety and asked if the lady had left.

No, she had not left.

Thank God, so she didn't mean to run away from me—for she must have had my letter hours ago. No, I had merely chosen an unlucky moment last night, that was all.

I ate some food, lay down, and fell asleep again. When I woke it was long past midday. I stumbled to the telephone again and rang.

No, the lady had not left. But she was packed. She was out at the moment.

I got ready immediately, rushed straight down to the town hall square, and began keeping watch. In the course of half an hour a great many people passed through the hotel doors, but none of them was her. Five o'clock came, and I went in to the porter.

The lady had left.

Left?

"Was it you who telephoned? She came that very moment and took her luggage. But she gave me a letter."

I took the letter and, without opening it, asked about the train.

"The train left at four-forty-five," said the porter, looking at his watch. "It's five o'clock now."

I had squandered half an hour keeping watch outside.

I sat down on one of the steps and stared at my feet. The porter went on talking. He must have known full well that the lady was not my sister.

"I said to the lady that there had just been a gentleman on the telephone. All she said was that she hadn't got time and would I give you this letter."

"Was there another lady with her when she left?"

"No."

I got up and went. Out in the street, I opened the letter and read:

You *must* not follow me about any more—

I stuck it listlessly in my pocket. It held no surprises for me, conveyed no new impressions. Real feminine stuff, words written in haste and on impulse, underlinings and dashes . . .

Then it occurred to me to go to Miss Elizabeth's door and ring; there was still this last faint hope. I heard the bell buzzing inside as I pressed the button and stood listening as if in a whirling wilderness.

Miss Elizabeth had left an hour ago.

So then came more wine, and then came whisky. And then came gallons of whisky. In short, a three-week binge during which a curtain descended on my earthly consciousness. In this condition I had an idea one day: of sending a mirror, with a gay gilt frame, to a certain cottage in the country. It was to go to a little girl by the name of Olga, who was as kind and amusing as a young calf.

Because, you see, I still suffer from nerves.

In my room lies the machine. I can't set it up properly, because most of the woodwork remains in a country parsonage. No matter, my affection for it has grown dim. My fellow neurasthenics, we are poor human beings and not much use, either, as any kind of beast.

One day, I suppose, I shall weary of staying unconscious any longer; then I shall make my way once more to an island.

On Muted Strings

Prologue

It looked like being a good year for berries: red whortleberries, crowberries, and cloudberries. Not that one can live on berries. But it is good that they should grow there in the meadows and be so inviting to the eye. And they are refreshing things to find when you are thirsty and hungry.

Such had been my thoughts the night before.

I knew, of course, that it was several months before the late-autumn berries would be ripe. But the woods and the fields give other joys than berries. In spring and summer the berries are mere blossoms as yet; but there are bluebells and babies'-slippers, deep windless forests, the scent of trees, stillness. The roar of a distant torrent descends on the ear as if from heaven— the most long-drawn-out sound in time or eternity. And if a song thrush sings so that his voice soars God-how-high, and if while poised up there on the topmost note he suddenly makes a right angle in the pitch, the line as clear and as clean as if cut with a diamond; then he sings down the scale again, softly and beautifully. Along the shore, too, there is life: guillemots and oyster catchers and terns are running about; the wagtail is out finding food, moving in little spurts, bobbing his tail, sharp-beaked and elegant; then he flies up on a fence, and he too sings. But when the sun has gone down, then sometimes a grebe strikes up his melancholy *hurra* from a remote mountain lake. He is the last. Now there is only the grasshopper, about whom there is nothing to say, he is so invisible and insignifi-cant. He lies there, as if rubbing himself in resin.

All this I had sat and pondered: how summer too had its joys for the wanderer, so there was no need to wait until the fall.

Now, however, I reflect on how I sit writing calm words about these peaceful things—for all the world as if I were not coming, later, to violent and dangerous events. It is just a trick I learned from a man in the Southern Hemisphere, from Rough, a Mexican. Brass spangles tinkled around the brim of his enor-mous hat; that alone brings him vividly to mind. But I remem-ber, above all, how calmly he spoke of his first murder. "I once had a sweetheart called María," Rough recalled with his air of resignation. "Come to think of it, she was only sixteen at the time, and I was nineteen. Her hands were so tiny that when it came to thanking me for something or saying hello, all you could feel were her bony fingers; that's the kind she was. One evening the boss called her in from the fields to do some sewing for him. There was nothing to stop him, and a day or two later he called her in again from the fields to sew. It went on like this for several weeks, then it stopped. Seven months later María died and was buried in the ground, tiny hands and all. I went to her brother Inez and said, 'At six o'clock tomorrow morning the boss is riding into town, and he'll be alone.' 'I know,' he said. 'You might lend me that little rifle of yours to shoot him with tomorrow,' I said. 'I shall be using it myself,' he said. So we talked for a bit about other things, about the harvest and about a big well we'd dug; when I left I took down his rifle from the wall and took it with me. In the forest Inez was at my heels and shouted to me to stop. We sat down and talked some more about this and that, and after a bit Inez snatched the rifle from me and went back home. Early next morning I was waiting by the gate to open it for the boss, and Inez was there too, in the bushes. I said to him, 'You'd better start walking on ahead, so we're not two against one.' 'He's got pistols in his belt,' said Inez; 'what have you got?' 'I've got nothing like that,' I said, 'but I've got a lump of lead in my hand, and that makes no noise.' Inez had a look at the lead and thought for a bit; then he nodded and went home. Then the boss came riding up; he was old and gray, sixty at least. 'Open the gate!' he shouted. But I never opened the gate. I suppose he thought I'd gone mad. He cracked his whip at me, but I took no notice. So he had to get off himself and open the gate. Then I gave him the first blow, it got him in the eye and cracked a hole open. 'Ah-ur-gh!' he said and went sprawling. I said a few words to him, but he didn't understand, and after a few more blows he was dead. He had stacks of money in his pocket, I took what I needed for the journey, then I mounted and rode off. Inez was standing by the door as I passed. 'You can make the border in three and a half days,' he said."

That was how Rough told his story, gazing calmly in front of him when he had finished.

I have no murders to tell about, but I have joys and sufferings and love. And love is every bit as violent and dangerous as murder.

It is green now in every wood, I thought to myself that morning as I dressed. The snow is melting on the mountains, everywhere now the cattle are standing in the barns, chafing to be let out, and in human habitations windows are thrown wide open. I unbuttoned my shirt, let the wind blow in on me, and became a star-struck, seething mass of unruliness within—ah, for a moment I was back in old times, when I was younger and more tempestuous than I am now. If there should chance to be a forest east or west of here, I thought, where an old man can thrive as well as a young, that is where I shall go!

Rain and sun and wind in alternation. I had already been walking for many days; it was still too cold to sleep out at night, but I had no trouble finding shelter on the farms. One man marveled at my walking and walking without apparent purpose. I must be someone in disguise, acting the eccentric—a poet, perhaps. The man knew nothing of my plans: that I was en route for familiar places where lived certain people I wanted to see again. But his intellect was good, and I involuntarily nodded, as if to say there was something in what he said. There's a large theatrical element in all of us; we feel flattered at being taken for more than we are. But then his wife and daughter joined in, maundering away at us in their everyday language of the heart: "But he hasn't been begging at all," they said; "he paid for his evening meal!" Now I turned cowardly and crafty to the core, said nothing to this, and allowed the man to make further accusations, to which likewise I offered no reply. And we three people of the heart defeated the man with his intellect: he had to explain that he was joking, surely we were capable of seeing a joke! I stayed on this farm for a night and a day, greasing my shoes with special care and mending my clothes.

But then the man became suspicious of me again. "When you leave you'll be giving my daughter a handsome tip," he said. I affected nonchalance and answered with a laugh, "Will I really?"

"Yes," he replied, "and then we'll sit back and think what a very superior person you must have been."

How unspeakably offensive he was! I did the only thing possible: ignored his taunts, and asked for work. I liked it here, I said; he could do with my help for the season, I could turn my hand to anything he cared to mention. "I'd rather see you clear right off," the man retorted; "you fool, you!"

It was clear that he had made me the object of his hatred; and none of the womenfolk were at hand to take my part. I looked at him, unable to make him out. His gaze was steady, and suddenly it seemed to me that I had never seen such intelligent eyes in anyone. But he carried his malignity too far and went off the rails. "What shall we say your name was?" he asked. "You don't need to say it was anything," I answered. "A wandering John Wesley?" he hazarded. I entered into the joke and said, "Yes, why not?" But this answer acted on the man like a goad; he became more and more saucy and said, "I feel sorry for Mrs. Wesley, then!" At which I shrugged my shoulders and replied, "You're mistaken; I'm not married." And with that I turned to go. But with unnatural quickness of wit he shouted after me, "It's you who's mistaken: I was referring to the mother who bore you!"

Down in the road, I turned and saw that the man had been taken in hand by his wife and daughter. And I thought to myself: No, it's not exactly roses, roses all the way when you go wandering.

At the next farm I learned that the man was a former quartermaster sergeant; then for a time he had been in a lunatic asylum, through losing a case in the Supreme Court. This spring his illness had broken out again; perhaps it was my coming that had given him the final push over the edge. But the lightning flashes of insight he had shown at the very moment when the madness closed over him! I remember him from time to time, and he certainly taught me a lesson: how hard it is to judge people correctly, who is mad and who is wise. And may God preserve us all from being seen through!

That day I came past a house where a youngster sat on the doorstep playing a mouth organ. He was no great performer, but he must have been a happy soul to sit there playing to himself. I just touched my cap so as not to disturb him, and remained standing at a distance. He took no notice of me; instead, he wiped his mouth organ dry, put it to his mouth, and started playing again. This went on for some time, until I took advantage of another wiping session and coughed. "Is that you, Ingeborg?" he asked. I thought he was talking over his shoulder to some woman in the house and made no answer. "You standing there," he said. I asked in some confusion, "Me? Can't you see me?" To this he made no reply, but fumbled a little all around him, as if to get up. Then I realized he was blind. "Sit still, don't let me frighten you," I said, and sat down beside him.

We chatted about one thing and another; he was about eighteen, blind from his fourteenth year, tall and strong, the lower half of his face downy with an incipient beard. Thank God, he said, his health was good. But his eyesight, I said—did he still remember what the world looked like? Oh yes, he had many nice memories from the time when he saw. All in all, he was contented and happy. He was going to Christiania this spring, to a professor who would operate on him and perhaps even give him back part of his sight! Ah yes, one day all would be well! His wits were limited, he looked like a heavy eater: stout, and strong as a beast. But there was something unhealthy-looking about him, something of the idiot; his devotion to his destiny was more than a little foolish. Surely such optimism argued stupidity; there must be a certain lack of gray matter in a man who could go around in permanent contentment with life, and even expect something new and good from it.

But I was in the mood to learn something from all I met on my wanderings; even this poor lad who sat here on his doorstep had made me wiser in one small respect. How had he managed to mistake me for the woman called Ingeborg, whose name he had called? I must have been walking too quietly, I had forgotten my cart-horse role, my shoes were too light. I had been corrupted by the refinements of many years, I must take a refresher course in being a peasant.

Three more days now to the goal which my curiosity had set itself: to Øvrebø, to Captain Falkenberg's place. It made excellent sense to arrive there on foot just now and ask for work: in the long spring season there was plenty to do on such a large estate. It was six years since I had been there last; the time had gone by, and for several weeks I had let my beard grow, so that no one would recognize me.

It was now midweek; I must arrange things so that I arrived on Saturday evening. Then the Captain would let me stay there over Sunday while he considered my request, and on Monday he would come and say yes or no.

Strangely enough, I felt no excitement, no unrest, at the thought of what was looming up ahead; at a good, leisurely pace I came wandering past farms and woods and meadows. I thought to myself: And yet this same Øvrebø was once the scene of some eventful weeks in my life; I was even in love with Madame, with the Captain's wife, Louise. Most certainly I was. She had fair hair and dark-gray eyes, and she was like a young girl. It was six years ago, an eternity ago; would she be greatly changed? For myself, time had made heavy inroads on me, I had grown dull and withered and indifferent—I looked at a woman now the way I looked at literature. The end had come. So what? Everything must have an end. In the early stages of this condition I felt as if I had lost something, as if some benevolent pickpocket had been at work. Then I set myself to find out whether I could endure my own company any longer, whether I could put up with myself. Oh yes. Nothing was the same as before, but it had all happened silently, peacefully, inevitably. Everything must have an end.

In old age we no longer live our lives; we merely keep on our feet with the aid of memories. We are like a batch of letters that someone has sent: we are no longer in the post, we have arrived. The same is true whether our contents have stirred up joys and sorrows, or whether they have made no impression at all. Thank you for life, it was fun to live!

As for woman, she was what all wise men have always known her to be: a pauper in talents, but rich in irresponsibility, in vanity, in wantonness; with much of the child but nothing of its innocence.

I stood by the signpost where the side road leads up to Øvrebø. I felt no emotion. The day lay broad and bright over meadows and woods, here and there the fields were being plowed and harrowed, but it was high noon and hot sun, and progress was so slow as to be almost imperceptible. I continued past the signpost, to fill in time before arriving at the manor. After an hour or so I turned off into the forest and wandered around for a while, amid the berry blossoms and the scent of small green leaves. Scores of thrushes were chasing a crow before them across the sky, kicking up an unholy din, like a babel of faulty castanets. I lay down on my back, with my sack under my head, and fell asleep.

On waking, I walked over to the nearest plowman, to make a few inquiries about the Falkenbergs of Øvrebø, whether they were still alive, whether they were flourishing. The man I encountered gave me cautious answers, standing there with his small, cunning eyes and saying, "Depends whether the Captain's at home." "Is he often away?" "No, he's at home, like as not." "Has he finished his plowing and sowing?" The man smiled. "No, I wouldn't say that." "Has he enough help?" "That I can't tell you—yes, belike he has. And the plowing and sowing's done—leastways, the manure's been carted out. Oh ay."

Then the man geed to his horses and continued plowing, while I walked beside him. There was not much to be learned from this man. The next time the horses stopped for a breather, I wormed out of him a few more contradictions about the people at Øvrebø. The Captain was with his regiment right through every summer, see, and then his lady was on her own. Oh yes, they always had lots of visitors, needless to say; but the Captain was away. That's to say, he liked it best at home, see, but he had to be with his regiment too. No; no children as yet, didn't look like she'd have any children, the lady, that was. "What am I saying, she could have lots of children yet, dozens of children, for that matter. Gee up!"

We plowed and paused for another breather. Not wanting to arrive at Øvrebø at an awkward moment, I asked the man if he thought they had company at the Captain's today. He thought not. Mind you, they often had company, but. And there was music and games and guests there all the time nowadays, but. That's to say, they were gentry, up at the Captain's, and they could afford it, no doubt, with all their riches and finery.

That plowman was a real pill. I tried, next, to find out something about another Falkenberg: Lars Falkenberg, my former mate in the timber felling, he who tuned pianos in a pinch. And now the man's information became much more definite: Lars? Sure, he was here. Should just think he did know Lars! He had finished working for the Captain, but the Captain had given him a small clearing to build on and live on; he had married Emma, one of the maids, and had two children. Good, hardworking people, who already had two cows on their clearing.

Here he reached the end of his furrow and turned the horses around, so I said goodbye and went.

As I stood in the courtyard at Øvrebø, I recognized all the buildings; but they needed painting. I noticed that the flagpole which I had helped to raise six years ago was still standing; but there was no halyard, and the knob at the top was missing.

I had arrived. It was four o'clock on the afternoon of the twenty-sixth of April.

Old people remember dates.

I

*I*t turned out differently from what I had imagined. Captain Falkenberg came out, heard my request, and turned it down then and there. He had all the help he needed, and the plowing and sowing were almost finished.

All right. Might I sit in the servants' hall and rest for a while?

By all means.

Without inviting me to stay over Sunday, the Captain turned on his heel and went back into the house. It seemed I had got him out of bed: he was still in his nightshirt and had no waistcoat on, having merely thrown on a jacket without buttoning it up. He had gone gray around the temples, and his beard was grizzled.

I sat in the servants' hall and waited for the farmhands to come in for their afternoon meal. There was only a man and a boy, and when I got talking to them, it appeared to be a misunderstanding on the Captain's part about the plowing and sowing being almost finished. Ah well, that was his pigeon! I made no secret of the fact that I was looking for work; as for my capabilities, I let them read the excellent testimonial given me by the Sheriff at Hersæt in the old days. When it was time for the men to go, I shouldered my sack and went out with them, ready to leave. I had a quick look in at the stables (where there were a surprising number of horses), the barn, the poultry, and the pigs; in the bin I saw manure from last year which had not yet been carted out.

"How can that be?"

"Well, what can one do?" answered the older of the hands. "I was carting manure from late winter onward, all on my own. Now there are two of us, after a fashion, but there's the plowing and harrowing to do."

His pigeon!

"Well, goodbye," I said, and went. I intended to call on my good comrade Lars Falkenberg, but this I kept quiet about. I had glimpsed a cluster of snall new buildings far up in the forest and reckoned that must be Lars's place.

The foreman must have been inwardly grieved at the loss to Øvrebø of a man to help with the seasonal work; as I set off I saw him tramp across the yard and enter the house.

I had gone a hundred yards or so when the foreman came running after me with the news that I had been taken on after all; he had spoken with the Captain and been given a free hand to employ me. "There's nothing for you to do until Monday; but come in and have some food!"

The foreman was a good, straightforward fellow; he came with me into the kitchen to break the news. "Give this man something to eat—he's going to work here!"

New cook, new maids. I had my meal and went out again. No sign of the master or the mistress.

I got bored with sitting idle in the servants' room all evening, so I followed the farmhands out into the field and chatted with them. The foreman came from a farm a little to the north, but since he wasn't the oldest son and had no farm of his own to manage, he had made up his mind to serve at Øvrebø for a time. And indeed he could have done a lot worse. The Captain concerned himself steadily less and less with the estate—not to mention his long absences; so the foreman had often to use his own judgment. Last autumn he had turned over large expanses of marshy land which he intended to sow. And he pointed with his finger. Here he had plowed, here he would let well enough alone; look at that field he'd reclaimed last year, wasn't it a lovely sight already?

It was good to hear how well the young man knew his job, and his sensible talk put me in good heart. He had also attended the county high school, where he had learned to keep farming accounts, entering hayloads in one column and calves' birthdays in another. His pigeon! In earlier days a peasant kept such accounts in his head, and his womenfolk knew to the day when each and every one of their twenty or fifty cows was due to calve.

But the foreman had his wits about him, nevertheless, and was not afraid of hard work—though recently he had been somewhat overwhelmed by the sheer insuperable volume of work on the Captain's estate. It was an obvious encouragement that now he was getting an extra pair of hands. Starting on Monday, he decided, I was to take the horse from the harrowing and use it to cart manure, while the boy used one of the Captain's two carriage horses for the harrowing; the foreman himself would stick to the plowing. Ah yes, we would get this year's seed sown yet!

Sunday.

I had to be careful not to know anything from my previous stay here: for example, how far the Captain's woods stretched, where the various buildings and outbuildings were situated, or the well, or the roads. I busied myself getting ready for the morning, greasing the cart and the harness, giving my horse a little extra attention. After dinner I spent four or five hours wandering around in the Captain's woods, passed Lars's cottage without going in, and went as far as the parish boundary before turning back. I was amazed to see how many trees had been felled.

When I got back the foreman asked, "Did you hear the singing and carrying on last night?"

"Yes. Who was it?"

"The visitors." He laughed.

The visitors, to be sure. The place was always full of them these days.

They included an exceedingly fat but lively gentleman with a cavalry mustache who was a captain in the same regiment as Captain Falkenberg; in the course of the evening I saw him and the other guests come trickling out of the house. There was also a man they addressed as Engineer; he was young, early twenties, medium height, dark-complexioned, and clean-shaven. And there was Elizabeth from the parsonage. I had vivid memories of Elizabeth, so I had no difficulty in recognizing her now, even though she was six years older and more mature. Little Elizabeth of the old days was no longer a girl; her breast stood out strongly and gave an impression of exaggeratedly good health. The foreman told me she had married: she had accepted young Eric after all—a young farmer's son she had been fond of since childhood days. She was still friendly with Mrs. Falkenberg and a frequent visitor at Øvrebø. But her husband never came with her.

And now Captain Falkenberg came and joined Elizabeth, who was standing by the flagpole. They chatted away, engrossed in their conversation; the Captain glanced around him each time before he spoke, so perhaps it was not trivialities he was talking but some topic demanding caution.

Next came the fat, jolly captain; his laughter reached us over in the servants' hall. He called to Falkenberg to join him but received only a short answer, delivered slantwise. There were some stone steps leading down to a lilac grove; and there the fat captain proceeded, followed by a maid with wine and glasses, and the engineer bringing up the rear.

The foreman burst out laughing and said, "Really, that captain!"

"What's his name?"

"They all just call him Brother; they called him that last year too. I don't know what his real name is."

"And the engineer?"

"His name's Lassen, I believe. He's only been here once before in my time."

Then Mrs. Falkenberg came out onto the front steps; she stopped for a moment and stood looking at the couple over by the flagpole. Her figure was still neat and elegant, but her features were sagging; her cheeks seemed to have shrunk, compared with her former fullness. She too made her way to the lilac grove, and I recognized her walk, which was as easy and supple as ever. It was only to be expected that after all these years she should have lost much of her good looks.

More people came out from the house: a middle-aged lady with a shawl around her, accompanied by two gentlemen.

The foreman told me there were not always quite so many visitors about the place; but two days ago it had been the Captain's birthday, when two carriageloads of people had come dashing up; the four strange horses were in the stable yet.

And now they were shouting in earnest for the two by the flagpole. "Coming!" called the Captain impatiently; but he still lingered on. Now he was flicking a speck of dust from Elizabeth's shoulder, now he was having a good look around before laying a hand on her arm as he impressed some point upon her.

The foreman said, "They always have so much to talk about, those two. She never comes here without their taking long walks together."

"Doesn't Mrs. Falkenberg mind?"

"Not that I know of."

"And hasn't Elizabeth got any children either?"

"Oh yes, she's got several."

"How does she manage to get away so often from her children and that big farm?"

"As long as Eric's mother's alive there's no problem; she can easily get away."

The foreman went out, leaving me alone in the servants' hall. Here I had sat, once upon a time, constructing a remarkable felling saw. How absorbed in it I had been! One of the farmhands, Peter, lay sick in the little adjoining bedroom; but I was agog with eagerness and would run out into the passage whenever I wanted to chop or hammer. Now I thought of that felling saw the way I thought about literature. That is what time does to us all.

The foreman came in again.

"If the visitors are still here tomorrow, I'm taking two of their horses for plowing with," he said, engrossed in his own concerns.

I looked out of the window. The couple by the flagpole had moved away at last.

As the evening went on, things became more and more lively down in the lilac grove; the maids went to and fro carrying trays—of food as well as of drink, for the gentry were having supper under the bushes. Suddenly there were shouts of "Brother! Brother!" with Brother himself laughing and shouting louder than anyone. His chair had broken under that enormous weight; and now came a request to the servants' hall for a really good, solid, wooden chair capable of supporting him. Oh yes, they were enjoying themselves down in the grove all right. From time to time Captain Falkenberg came up to the courtyard to show that he could still walk straight and was thoroughly in command of the situation.

"I put my money on him," said the foreman. "He's not the

man to pack it in first. Once last year, when I was driving him, he never stopped drinking the whole way, but it didn't make the slightest difference to him."

The sun went down. It must have turned chilly in the grove, because the gentry moved indoors. But the great living-room windows were thrown wide open, and waves of melodious sound from Mrs. Falkenberg's piano surged out to us. Later on there was dance music—played, I guess, by fat Captain Brother.

"What a crew!" the foreman muttered. "Dancing and playing all night, sleeping all day. I'm turning in now."

I remained sitting by the window, and saw my old comrade Lars Falkenberg cross the yard and enter the house; he had been sent for to sing to the gentry. After a while, Captain Brother and a few more started helping out with their voices, until the rafters fairly rang with the merriment. In an hour or so Lars Falkenberg came to the servants' hall, in his pocket a half bottle they had given him for his pains. Finding only me, a stranger, in the hall, he went into the bedroom and had a drop or two with the foreman; after a while I was invited to join them. I took care not to say too much and so give myself away; but when Lars left to go home he asked me to accompany him for part of the way. Then it appeared that I had already been seen through; that Lars knew I was his mate from the timber-felling days.

The Captain had told him.

Good, I thought: in that case there was no point in my taking further precautions. In short, I was far from displeased at this turn of events: it meant the Captain was supremely indifferent to my sauntering about the place as I pleased.

I walked all the way home with Lars Falkenberg, chatting with him about the old days, about his clearing, and about the people down on the manor. The Captain was no longer held in the same high regard; he had ceased to be the spokesman for the district, and people no longer came as they used to, both men and women, to seek his advice. Take the drive down to the main road: rebuilding that had been the last thing he did—and that was five years ago. The buildings needed painting, but he let them be. The farmland had been misused, the woods too heavily plundered. Did he drink? Well, so it was said, but it wasn't strictly true—devil take all gossips and slanderers! He drank a little; and apart from that he would drive off from time to time and stay away for a while; but when he did come home again, he had no go in him then either—that was the tragedy. It was as if an evil spirit had got into him, said Lars.

And Madame?

Madame! She went around as before, playing her piano and looking as pretty as a picture. "And they keep open house, with visitors all the time. But they pay heavy taxes of one kind and another, and it costs a mint just to keep all those great buildings. But it's a real judgment on the pair of them how dead weary they are of each other—you wouldn't believe it. If they do ever say a word to each other, they look some other way and hardly open their lips. They don't speak for anyone to notice, except to other people, for months on end. And in the summer the Captain's with his regiment and never comes home or gives a thought to his wife or the place. Ah, but they've no children—that's the trouble!" said Lars.

Emma came out from the cottage and joined us. She looked extremely well and as pretty as ever, and I told her so. "Oh, Emma's well enough," Lars agreed; "but she never stops having children, the monster!" With which he handed her his half bottle and forced her to drink what was left. Emma wanted us all to go in. "We might just as well be sitting in comfort indoors as standing here." "Ah, but it's summertime now," replied Lars, who was by no means anxious to invite me in. When I left, he came with me again for a little way, pointing out to me where he had dug and ditched and fenced on his little clearing. He had made a good, intelligent job of his miniature farm, and I was filled with a strange delight as I stood outside this snug little home in the forest. Behind the cottage and the barn the wind soughed gently through the pine forest; beside them grew deciduous trees, with aspen leaves rustling like silk.

I walked home. The evening wore on, the birds were all silent, the air mild, the twilight soft and blue.

"Let us be young tonight!" came loud and clear in a man's voice from behind the lilacs. "Let us dance in the calf pen tonight!"

"Do you remember what you were like last year?" came Mrs. Falkenberg's voice in reply. "You were young and sweet then, and didn't say such things."

"No, then I didn't say such things. To think that you still remember! But last year too you scolded me one night. 'You're very beautiful tonight,' I said. 'No,' you answered, 'I'm not beautiful any more; and you're a child, and you mustn't drink so much,' you said."

"Yes, that's what I said," answered Mrs. Falkenberg with a laugh.

"Yes, that's what you said. But surely I ought to have known whether you were beautiful, since I was sitting there looking at you."

"You child, you child!"

"And tonight you're even more beautiful."

"There's someone coming."

Two figures stood erect behind the lilacs: Mrs. Falkenberg and the visiting engineer. When they saw it was only me, they breathed more easily again and went on talking as if I didn't exist. And—such is human nature—although I had only wanted to be left in peace by everyone, yet now I was offended because these two held me in such small esteem. What if my hair and beard are gray, I asked myself; should they not honor me therefore?

"Yes, and tonight you're even more beautiful," repeated the engineer.

I walked right past them, touched my cap casually, and continued on my way.

"All I can say is that it won't do you any good," answered Madame. "You've lost something!" she called after me.

Lost? My handkerchief lay on the path, where I had deliberately dropped it; now I turned and picked it up, murmured some thanks, and went on my way again.

"What a sharp eye you've got for irrelevant objects!" said the engineer. "A peasant's rag with red flowers on it! Come, let's go into the summerhouse!"

"It's locked at night," answered Madame. "Perhaps there's someone in there."

After that I heard no more.

My sleeping quarters were in the loft over the servants' hall, and I had left open a window facing the grove. When I came up there, I could still hear voices behind the bushes, but not the actual words. I thought to myself: Why is the summerhouse locked at night, and whose idea was that? Perhaps some crafty character's who thought that if this door was always kept locked, it would be less risky to slip away one night in good company, take the key, and stay there.

Some distance down the path I had just taken I saw two people approaching: the fat Captain Brother and the middle-aged lady with the shawl. They must have been sitting somewhere in the grove as I passed; and now I began to wonder whether I might have been talking aloud to myself and said anything in their hearing.

Suddenly I saw the engineer get up from behind the bushes and hurry across to the summerhouse. Finding the door locked, he put his shoulder to it and broke it open. There was a splintering sound.

"Come on, there's no one here!" he called.

Mrs. Falkenberg stood up and said in great indignation, "What are you up to, you madman?"

However, even as she spoke, she was moving toward him.

"Up to?" he answered. "Love isn't glycerine, it's nitroglycerine."

Then he took Mrs. Falkenberg by the arm and led her in.

Their pigeon.

But now the fat captain and his lady came strolling along—quite unbeknownst, probably, to the pair in the summerhouse. Mrs. Falkenberg would hardly be best pleased at being discovered alone with a man in such a secluded spot. I looked around my room for some means of warning them, and found an empty bottle; I positioned myself by the window and hurled it with all my strength toward the summerhouse. There was a crash of breaking glass and tiles, followed by the clatter of fragments down the roof; at the same moment there was a cry of terror from the summerhouse, and Mrs. Falkenberg came storming out, followed by the engineer, who still had hold of her clothes. They stopped for a moment to peer around. "Brother! Brother!" exclaimed Mrs. Falkenberg, and sped away down through the grove. "No, don't come with me!" she called back over her shoulder, "you're *not* to come with me."

Undeterred, the engineer ran in pursuit. He was marvelously young and utterly relentless.

But now came the fat captain and his lady, conducting a priceless conversation, as if it was only love that made the world go round. The fat gentleman must have been close on sixty, the woman he was with around forty; their tender affection was a sight for sore eyes.

The fat captain said, "Until tonight it has been just within the bounds of endurance, but now it taxes a man beyond his strength— Madame, you have utterly bewitched me."

"I didn't realize it was so serious," she answered, speaking kindly to him and helping him along.

"But it is," he retorted. "And now I must put an end to it, I tell you. We have just come from the grove; there I thought I could bear it for one more night, so I didn't say much. But now I beg you to come back to the grove with me."

She shook her head.

"No; I do so much want to be your . . . do what you—"

"*Thank* you!" he exclaimed.

And he threw his arms around her in the middle of the path,

and pressed his round belly against hers. They looked like two refractory combatants. That scamp of a captain!

"Let me go!" she begged.

He relaxed his grip a little, then tightened it again. And again it looked as if they were locked in combat.

"Come back with me to the grove!" he said again and again.

"Out of the question," she answered. "Especially now, with all this dew."

But the captain was full of amorous words, and now he let them overflow.

"Ah, time was I harbored churlish thoughts about eyes. Blue eyes—bah! Gray eyes—bah! A gaze of any color, be it ever so intense—again and yet again, bah! But then came you with your brown eyes!"

"Yes, they are brown," the lady conceded.

"You are burning me with them, you are roasting me the same color."

"In fact, you're not the first person to praise my eyes. My husband—"

"But what about me?" cried the captain. "I tell you, purely and simply, that if I had met you twenty years ago, I would not have answered for my reason. Come with me now, there really isn't all that much dew in the grove."

"Let's go indoors, rather," she suggested.

"Indoors! There's not one single corner where we can be alone."

"I think we'll find a place," she replied.

"Yes, because I must put an end to this tonight," said the captain.

And they went.

I asked myself: was it really to warn someone that I had thrown that empty bottle?

At three in the morning I heard the foreman go out and feed the horses. At four he knocked on the ceiling below where I slept.

He was welcome to the privilege of being the first man astir, though I could have woken him at any hour of the night; for I had not slept. It was no great matter to go without sleep for a night or two in this fine, light air, which did not make for drowsiness.

The foreman set out for the fields, driving a new plow team. He had inspected the visiting horses and chosen Elizabeth's. They were good farm horses, with coarse legs.

II

More visitors arrived at Øvrebø; the merriment never let up. Meanwhile, we farmhands manured and plowed and sowed. Some of the fields were already sprouting green in our wake—a sight which filled us with joy.

But from time to time we had to overcome opposition from Captain Falkenberg himself. "He's given up using his wits or caring about his interests," said the foreman. Yes, an evil spirit had indeed got into him: he went around half drunk, half listless, preoccupied with his role of incomparable host; for nearly a week now he had joined his guests in turning day into night and night into day. And the racket at night was such that the beasts in the stables and barns could get no rest; nor could the maids sleep at the proper time, for the young gentlemen even came into their quarters at night and sat on their beds chatting with them, for the pleasure of seeing them undressed.

We working folk took no part in this, of course; but many a time we felt more sad than proud to be serving on the Captain's estate. The foreman got hold of a temperance badge and wore it outside his smock.

One day the Captain came to me in the fields and ordered me to get out the carriage and fetch two new visitors from the station. It was mid-afternoon, and he had doubtless just got up. He had me in a tight spot; and why had he not gone to the foreman? Was he beginning to get embarrassed by that temperance badge? The Captain must have seen that I was hanging back; he smiled and said, "Afraid of what Nils might say? In that case I'd better speak to him first."

Nils was the name of the foreman.

But I just didn't dare let the Captain go over to Nils at that moment—he was still plowing with the visitors' horses and had asked me to tip him off if there was any danger of discovery. I took out my handkerchief, wiped my face, and waved a little; the foreman saw me and at once unhitched the horses from the plow. What will he do now? I wondered. Aha! The admirable Nils would manage all right: although it was much too early for knocking off, he started taking the horses home.

If only I could now delay the Captain a little! The foreman realized what was up: he pressed on, and he already, while still on the way home, started undoing the harness.

The Captain looked at me suddenly and said, "Well, have you lost your tongue?"

"Nils seems to be in trouble of some kind," I said; "he's unhitched the horses."

"Well? And?"

"Well, I just thought . . ."

But to hell with standing there dissembling! I could help Nils a little now; the coming storm he would have to weather for himself. I went straight to the point and said, "Well, it's like this: it's the sowing season now, and over there it's already starting to grow where we've been; but we've still got a lot of ground to—"

"All right, let it grow, let it grow."

"There's three acres of arable here, and another three and a half where Nils is working, and I thought perhaps the Captain might reconsider his order."

The Captain turned on his heel and left me without more words.

I'll have to walk the plank, I thought. But I obeyed orders and followed him home with the horse and cart.

By now I felt easy about the foreman; he had almost reached the outbuildings. The Captain beckoned to him, but without avail. Then he called "Halt!" in his best officer's voice; but the foreman heard nothing.

By the time we reached the stables, the foreman had the horses back in their stalls. The Captain's manner was stiff in the extreme; but he had evidently been having second thoughts during his walk.

"Why have you brought the horses in?" he asked.

"The plow broke down," answered the foreman. "I'm stabling the horses while I fix it—it won't take long."

The Captain gave his order: "One of you is to take the carriage to the station."

The foreman glanced at me and mumbled, "Hm. I see. But is this really the right time for it?"

"What's that you're muttering about?"

"We're two and a half men," answered the foreman, "for the entire spring work. It's none too many."

But the Captain must have become suspicious about those chestnuts that the foreman had driven home in such a hurry. He went up to each animal in turn, to find which were warm, then he drew himself up in front of us, wiped his hands with his handkerchief, and said, "Are you plowing with other people's horses, Nils?"

Pause.

"I won't have it."

"Hm. No, I see," answered the foreman. But suddenly he flared up and went on, "We've more need of horses at Øvrebø this spring than any previous spring, we're breaking more soil than ever before. And these visitors' horses stood here day after

day, eating and eating, not even earning the water they drank.
So I took them out for a little spell now and again and loosened
up their joints for them."

The Captain repeated, speaking very clearly, "I won't have it
any more. Do you hear, Nils?"

Pause.

"Didn't you say one of the Captain's plow horses was unwell
yesterday?" I put in.

The foreman seized on this. "Yes, that's right. Stood shivering in its stall. So I couldn't take it out."

The Captain measured me from top to toe. Then he said,
"What are you standing there for?"

"The Captain ordered me to drive to the station."

"Then go and get ready."

But Nils took him up on the instant.

"No, it's no use."

Bravo, Nils! I said to myself. He was absolutely right, and he
looked it too, as he stuck firmly and steadfastly to his guns. As
for the horses, our own animals had been worked to exhaustion
during the long spring season, while the visitors' horses stood
there doing nothing but eat, and spoiling for want of exercise.

"No use?" asked the Captain, thunderstruck.

"If the Captain takes away my help, then I've finished here,"
said Nils.

The Captain went to the stable door and stood there, staring
ahead of him, biting his mustache, and thinking. Then he said
over his shoulder, "Can't you spare the lad either?"

"No, he's on the harrowing."

It was the first time we had collided head-on with the Captain and come out best. Later we had a few small tussles, but he
soon gave in.

"There's a crate to come up from the station," he said one
day; "can the boy fetch it?"

"The boy's as valuable as a man to us at present; he's doing the harrowing. If he drives to the station now, he won't be back till tomorrow evening—that's a day and a half lost."

Bravo! I said to myself again. Nils had told me earlier about this crate at the station: it contained fresh supplies of liquor. The maids had heard about it.

They exchanged a few more words; the Captain wrinkled his brow and opined that never before had the spring season lasted so long. Finally the foreman said in exasperation, "If you take the boy away from the field, I quit!" Then he went further, as we had agreed beforehand, and asked me, "Do you quit too?"

"Yes," I replied.

At this the Captain yielded and said with a smile, "A conspiracy, I see. Still, I have to admit you're right in a way. And you have green thumbs."

But our green thumbs were something which the Captain was hardly qualified to judge, and which gave him little pleasure. He probably cast an eye over the fields from time to time and formed the impression that plenty of plowing and sowing had taken place, but that was all. As for us farmhands, we worked and worked, and served our master and mistress to the uttermost. That was our way.

That, I suppose, was our way.

And yet there were times when our immense zeal came under suspicion: was it, perhaps, not quite so exalted after all? The foreman was a local man who wanted to get through his season's work at least as quickly as other local men; his honor was at stake. And I shared his feeling. Then again, when the foreman took to wearing a temperance badge, his main motive may well have been to get the Captain sober enough to notice our splendid efforts. And in this respect too I felt as he did. Perhaps, moreover, I entertained the hope that Madame—well, that Mrs. Falkenberg should understand what good souls we were. I doubt if I was above such considerations.

The first time I saw Mrs. Falkenberg at close quarters was one afternoon when I was coming out of the kitchen and she was crossing the courtyard, slender and bareheaded. I raised my peaked cap and looked at her; her face was strangely young and innocent. With perfect indifference she answered, "Good day!" and walked past.

It could not be that everything was finished between the Captain and his wife. Or so I reasoned, on the strength of the following events:

Ragnhild, the parlormaid, was her mistress's friend and spy. She kept watch on her account, was last into bed, and stood on the stairs examining her hands and listening; if, when outside a door, she was suddenly called for, she would perform three or four silent leaps. She was an attractive girl, with particularly bright eyes, and, for good measure, admirably warm-blooded. One evening I caught her standing right outside the summerhouse, sniffing at the lilacs. She started at my coming, pointed warningly at the summerhouse, and ran off with her tongue between her teeth.

The Captain was well aware of Ragnhild's activities, and on one occasion said to his wife in everyone's hearing—he was drunk, no doubt, and irritated about something or other—"That Ragnhild's a devious creature. Can't think why we keep her on."

Madame answered, "It's not the first time you've wanted to get rid of Ragnhild; goodness only knows why—she's the best maid we've ever had."

"For a certain purpose, maybe" was the Captain's parting shot.

This gave me food for thought. Such might be Madame's cunning that she kept this spy merely to make it look as if she cared what the Captain got up to. The world would then conclude that Madame, poor thing, went around secretly longing for her husband, and being perpetually disappointed and wronged by him. And would she not then be fully justified in paying him back in his own coin? In heaven's name, might not this be the position?

But I was to change my opinion.

The following day the Captain altered his tactics. Having failed to get rid of Ragnhild, and of the vigilance she exercised when he lurked in some dark corner with Elizabeth or planned a late-evening tête-à-tête in the summerhouse, he now veered around and started paying court to the girl. Oho! That device was surely one which some woman, which Elizabeth, had helped him to hit on.

We farmhands were sitting at the long kitchen table; the maids were about their business, and Madame herself was there. Enter the Captain, with a brush in his hand.

"Give my coat a quick brush-down, will you?" he said to Ragnhild.

She did as she was asked. When she had finished, the Captain said, "Thank you, my dear!"

Madame looked a little surprised, and at once sent her maid on an errand up to the loft. The Captain watched her leave the room and said, "What wonderfully bright eyes that girl's got!"

I glanced across at Madame. Her eyes blazed, she flushed crimson, she moved toward the door. But then she turned, and now her face was pale. She had evidently made a quick decision. Speaking over her shoulder, she said to her husband, "I wonder if Ragnhild's eyes aren't just a shade too bright."

The Captain asked in surprise, "How so?"

Madame gave a little laugh, glanced toward where we sat at the table, and went on, "Well, she's started getting very friendly with the farmhands."

Silence in the kitchen.

"So perhaps it's best if she goes," said Madame.

There was a superb impudence in this performance of Madame's, but there was nothing we could do—we realized that she had simply used us as a stalking-horse.

As we left the kitchen, the foreman said indignantly, "I've a good mind to go in again and say a thing or two."

But it was not worth worrying about, and I dissuaded him.

Two or three days later, the Captain again found an opportunity to pay Ragnhild a crude compliment in his wife's hearing: "with a young body like yours" were the words in question.

Dear me, the conversational tone at Øvrebø nowadays! Every year it must have gone down and down, with drunken guests and idleness and indifference and childlessness all playing their part.

That evening Ragnhild came to me and told me she had been given notice. Madame hadn't bothered to give reasons, beyond making an insinuation about myself.

This, again, was disingenuous. Madame knew very well that I was not staying much longer in any case, so why make me a scapegoat? She wanted to put a spoke in her husband's wheel, that was the fact of the matter.

Ragnhild was duly distressed, and cried a little, and dabbed her eyes. But after a while she comforted herself with the notion that once I had gone Madame would withdraw her notice. Which I, in my heart of hearts, was convinced she would not do.

The Captain and Elizabeth might well be pleased: the tiresome parlormaid would soon be safely out of the way.

But how was one to know? There could easily be a mistake in my balance sheet of the situation. Certain new developments made me change my opinion once again. How hard it is to judge people correctly!

It became clear to me that Mrs. Falkenberg was really and truly jealous of her husband, not merely pretending jealousy in order to be free to go her own crooked ways. Not a bit of it. On the other hand, she could hardly have believed for one moment that her husband had his eye on the parlormaid. That was merely a trick and a pretense; she would use any and every means that suited her purpose. She had gone red in the kitchen, admittedly; but that was just a sudden, natural expression of injury over her husband's unseemly words, not real jealousy.

Her husband, however, was welcome to think she was jealous of the girl. That was precisely her intention. She was saying in plain language: "Yes, I am indeed jealous again; you see, all is as it used to be; I am yours for the taking!" Mrs. Falkenberg was better than I had thought. For years husband and wife had drifted further and further apart, indifferently, perhaps of late defiantly; now she wished to take the first step and show her love anew. That was it. But toward the one she feared most of all she would not show her jealousy for worlds: toward Eliza-beth, that dangerous friend, so many years younger than herself.

That was it.

And the Captain? Did anything stir in him when he saw his wife turn red that day in the kitchen? Perhaps a faint memory of other days may possibly have flickered through his head, a sense of mild surprise, of gladness even. But not a trace of emotion did he show. Over the years his arrogance and defiance must have grown too strong. That was the way it looked.

But then came the developments I mentioned.

III

Mrs. Falkenberg had for some time been playing a game with her husband. She had feigned indifference to his indifference, consoling herself now and then with flirtatious attentions from the guests in their house. Now these guests were leaving one by one. However, fat Captain Brother and the lady with the shawl remained; and so did the engineer, Lassen. Captain Falkenberg's reaction to this seemed to be: "By all means, my friend! Stay on for as long as you feel inclined!" Nor did he seem concerned by his wife's growing familiarity with the engineer, whom she had taken to calling Hugo, as he did. "Hugo!" she would call from the steps. And the Captain's voice would answer helpfully, "Hugo's gone down the drive!"

One day, however, I heard the Captain answer with a sarcastic smile and a gesture toward the lilac grove, "Little King Hugo is awaiting you in his kingdom." I saw Mrs. Falkenberg jump; then she gave an embarrassed laugh to cover her confusion and went down to join the engineer.

At last she had struck a spark from her husband. Now she would try to strike some more.

This was on a Sunday.

Later in the day Madame was unusually restless. She spoke a few words to me and commented on the good work that Nils and I had been doing.

"Lars has been to the post office for me today, to collect an important letter I'm expecting. Will you do me a service and go up to his cottage for it?"

I said I would do so with pleasure.

"Lars won't get back till about eleven o'clock this evening. So you don't need to go for a long time yet."

"Very good."

"And when you get back you're to give the letter to Ragnhild."

This was the first time during my present stay at Øvrebø that Mrs. Falkenberg had spoken to me. The experience was so new that I went back to my bedroom and sat there, feeling like one restored to a semblance of life. One or two thoughts occurred to me also. It was sheer tomfoolery, I said to myself, pretending to be here incognito any longer—so why, in warm weather, be bothered with a long gray beard that made me look like a patriarch? I took a razor and shaved it right off.

Around ten o'clock I went up to the cottage. Lars was not yet back, and only arrived after I had been there a while with Emma. I took the letter and returned home. It was close on midnight.

Ragnhild was nowhere to be seen, and the other maids had gone to bed. I glanced at the lilac grove, where Captain Falkenberg and Elizabeth were sitting at the round stone table talking; they took no notice of me. Then I saw a light in Madame's room upstairs and had the inspired thought that tonight I looked as I had done six years ago, being clean-shaven now as then. I took the letter from my pocket and went in by the main door, to deliver the letter in person.

At the top of the stairs Ragnhild came bounding noiselessly up to me and took the letter. She was evidently in a state of intense excitement, and I felt the heat of her breath as she pointed across the landing—to where I could hear voices.

I got the impression that Ragnhild had stationed herself there, or been stationed there by others; either way, it was no concern of mine. And when she whispered to me, "Don't say a word, just go quietly down again!" I obeyed, and went to my room.

I had left my window open. I could hear the couple down in the grove, where they sat drinking wine at the stone table; and I could still see the light in Madame's room.

Ten minutes passed; then the light went out.

A moment later I heard hurried footsteps going up the stairs in the house, and involuntarily I looked to see if it was the Captain who had gone up. But the Captain still sat as before.

Next I heard the same footsteps descending the stairs, followed by others. I kept my eye on the front door. The first to emerge was Ragnhild, who came dashing out as if in flight from someone, and headed for the servants' hall. Next came Mrs. Falkenberg with the letter in her hand showing white in the dusk, and her hair down; after her came the engineer. They both sauntered down the drive toward the main road.

Ragnhild burst into my room and flung herself down on a stool, panting with eagerness to tell her story. The strange goings-on she'd been mixed up in that evening, she whispered. Shut the window! Madame and that engineer of hers— no precautions whatsoever—they'd been no more than a hair's breadth away from doing it. He never even let go of Madame when Ragnhild came in with the letter. Ooh! In Madame's own room, with the lamp blown out!

"You're crazy!" I said.

But the sly girl—there was evidently nothing wrong with her eyes or ears. Spying had become such a habit with her that she couldn't leave off even where Madame was concerned. She really was an extraordinary girl.

At first I was virtue incarnate and refused to listen to her slanders. What, had she stood there eavesdropping? Shame on her!

What else could she do? she retorted. Her orders were to come in with the letter as soon as her mistress put out the light, and not before. But Madame's windows faced the grove, where the Captain was sitting with Elizabeth from the parsonage. No chance of waiting there. Better to stay on the landing and squint through the keyhole every so often, to see if the light was out.

It no longer sounded so unreasonable.

Suddenly Ragnhild shook her head and said admiringly, "Really, that young dog—nearly getting Madame to . . . they were only a hair's breadth away!"

What had he nearly got Madame to do? I was pierced by jealousy, I stopped being virtuous, I asked penetrating questions about it all. "What did you say they were doing? How did it all start?"

Ragnhild didn't know how it had started. Madame had told her that a letter was being collected from the cottage, and when it arrived she was to wait until the light in Madame's room went out and then bring it straight up. "Very good," said Ragnhild. "Not until I put out the light, you understand," repeated Madame. And Ragnhild had settled down to wait for the letter. But it took ages to come, and she had started thinking, mulling the whole thing over; it was all very strange. Meanwhile, she went up on the landing, hoping to pick up a clue. She could hear Madame and the engineer talking freely together within, and she started listening. Then she squinted through the keyhole and saw Madame was taking down her hair, while the engineer kept saying how lovely she was. Really, that engineer—and then he kissed her!

"On the mouth? Never!"

Ragnhild saw my gross excitement and tried to soothe me.

"On the mouth? Well, perhaps not exactly, but. And the engineer's mouth's nothing to speak of, in my opinion. Why, haven't you shaved beautifully—let's have a look!"

"But what did Madame say to that? Didn't she wriggle free?"

"Yes, I think so. Yes, that's right. And then she screamed."

"Screamed?"

"Yes, right out loud. And the engineer said, 'Sh!' And every time Madame raised her voice he shut her up again. 'Oh, they're welcome to hear us' was all she'd say; 'there they are themselves, flirting away down in the bushes,' she says—meaning the Captain and Elizabeth from the parsonage. 'Look, there they are!' she says and goes to the window. 'All right, all right,' says the engineer, 'only don't stand there with your hair down.' And he follows her and pulls her back again. Then they start saying all sorts of things, and every time the engineer lowers his voice Madame sings out, 'What did you say?' 'If only you wouldn't scream so loud,' he says, 'it would be nice and quiet here.' Then she shuts up and just smiles at him and sits still. She's quite crazy about him."

"Oh?"

"It stands out a mile. In love with a fellow like that! Then he leans over toward her and puts his hands like this—so!"

"And Madame sat still and let him?"

"Well, more or less. But then she goes to the window again and comes back again; then she goes like this with her tongue and goes right up to him and kisses him. Fancy her wanting to! Because his mouth's nothing to speak of. Then he says, 'Now we're all alone and can hear if anyone's coming.' 'Where's

Brother and his lady friend?' she asks. 'Miles and miles away, at the other end of the earth,' he says. And with that he takes hold of her and lifts her up—he's that strong, he is. 'Put me down!' she shouts.''

"And then what?" I asked breathlessly.

"Why, then you come with the letter, so I don't see any more for the time being. And when I get back to the door, they've turned the key, so it's harder to squint through than ever. But I hear Madame say, 'What are you doing? No, we mustn't.' He must have had her in his arms. In the end she says, 'Do wait a bit—put me down for a moment.' So he puts her down. 'Blow out the lamp!' she says. And then it's all dark in the room— ooh!

"But now I was almost at my wits' end what to do," Ragnhild continued. "I stood for a while with my head in a whirl—I thought of knocking on the door straightaway—"

"Of course you should have. What on earth were you waiting for?"

"Don't you see, Madame would have realized I'd been standing at the door," the girl replied. "So I nip off down the stairs. Then I turn around and go back up again, treading heavily so that Madame will hear which way I came from. The door's still fastened; then Madame hears me knocking and comes and opens it. But the engineer still has hold of her clothes, he's that crazy to get her. 'Don't go, don't go!' he keeps saying, and never once looks my way. Only, when I leave, Madame comes out with me. But merciful heavens, if I hadn't come just when I did! It was touch and go!"

A long, restless night.

When we farmhands came in for our dinner the following day, the maids began whispering about some dust-up there had been between the master and mistress. Ragnhild knew it all. The Captain had noted last night's flowing hair and extinguished lamp; now he laughed and said how nice the hair had looked. Madame kept fairly quiet until she felt sure of herself; then she said, "Well, of course I take my hair down once in a while—it's not yours, is it?" Poor Madame—answering back in a quarrel was not her forte.

Then Elizabeth had come and stuck her nose in, and she was quicker on the draw: rat-tat-tat-tat-tat! Madame managed to say, "All right, we were sitting in the house—but you two were sitting in the bushes!" To which Elizabeth answered sharply, "At least we didn't put out the light!" "What if we did put out the light?" answered Madame. "There's nothing wrong in that—we went out the moment after."

I thought, Good grief, she could have got out of it by saying they put out the light *because* they were going out!

That had been the end of the matter for the time being. But shortly afterward the Captain had hinted at how much older his wife was than Elizabeth. "You should always have your hair down," he said; "I assure you, it made you look positively girlish!" "Yes, I suppose I need to now," answered Madame. But when she saw that Elizabeth was laughing up her sleeve, she became furious and told her to get packing. And Elizabeth put her hands on her hips and said, "My carriage, please, Captain!" To which the Captain replied, "Certainly. And I shall drive you myself."

All this had been overheard by Ragnhild, who was hovering nearby.

I thought to myself, It's clear that they've both been jealous, she over his sitting there in the bushes, he over the flowing hair and extinguished lamp.

As we left the kitchen for a nap, the Captain was busying himself with Elizabeth's carriage. He called to me and said, "I oughtn't to ask you now in your dinner break, but could you go and mend the summerhouse door for me?"

"Very good."

This door had remained unrepaired ever since that evening when the engineer had burst it open; why did the Captain want it put right just now? He himself could make no use of the summerhouse while he was away with Elizabeth. Was he anxious to deny this retreat to others in his absence? If so, it was a significant move.

I took some tools and materials and went down to the grove.

This was the first time I had inspected the summerhouse from the inside. It was fairly new; it had not been there six years ago. There was plenty of room inside, with pictures on the walls, an alarm clock even (at present run-down), hassocks, tables, a fair-sized spring settee upholstered in red plush. The blinds were drawn. First I put a couple of new tiles on the roof, to replace the ones I had broken with the empty bottle. Then I removed the lock to see what the damage was; I had barely started on this when the Captain arrived. Either he had been drinking already or he had a severe hangover.

"There hasn't been any break-in," he said. "Either the door's been left open and has banged violently, or one of the gentlemen who've left stumbled against it in the dark one night. It wouldn't take much to push it open."

But the door had been subjected to considerable pressure: the lock was broken and the molding on the inside of the door frame damaged.

"Let me have a look," said the Captain. "Put in a new nail here, and compress the spring again." He sat down on a chair.

Mrs. Falkenberg came down the short flight of stone steps into the grove and called, "Is the Captain there?"

"Yes," I said.

She came up, her face trembling with emotion.

"I wanted to talk to you," she said. "Just a quick word or two."

The Captain answered, without getting up, "Go ahead. Do you want to stand or sit?" Then sharply to me, "No, you don't need to go. I haven't got all day."

This must surely mean that he wanted the door mended so that he could take the key with him on his journey.

"I may well have been . . . I mean, I oughtn't to have said what I did," she began.

The Captain remained silent.

But his remaining silent when she had come here wanting to make it up was more than she could endure, and she ended up saying, "Oh, never mind, it's all the same to me."

And with that she turned to go.

"I thought you wanted to talk to me?" said the Captain.

"Oh, forget it. I really can't be bothered."

"Very well," said the Captain, smiling. He was drunk, no doubt, and irritated about something.

But as she passed me in the doorway she turned to him and said, "You shouldn't go driving off today. There's been enough talk already."

"Well, close your ears to it," he answered.

"That doesn't help in the long run. And it's a disgrace that you don't understand that."

"Well, at least we're both involved in the disgrace," he retorted pertly, glancing around the walls.

I took the lock and went outside.

"You're not going!" the Captain yelled at me. "I've very little time."

"Oh yes, you've very little time, you're going away again," said Madame. "Only you'd better think it over. I've been thinking things over myself lately; I've given up expecting you to see."

"What do you mean?" he asked. He spoke in arrogant, unaccommodating tones. "What haven't you expected me to see? Your night-time games, when you let down your hair and go blowing out lamps, I suppose? Oh yes, of course."

"I need to go and do some riveting on the anvil," I said, and made a hasty escape.

I stayed away longer than was necessary, but when I returned Madame was still there. The voices in the summerhouse had risen, and Madame was saying, "But do you know what I've done? I've lowered myself to showing my jealousy—that's what I've done. Toward the maid, that is—I mean . . ."

"Yes, go on," said the Captain.

"No no, you don't *want* to understand anything. Have it your own way, then. Only mark my words: you'll have to take the consequences."

Those were her final words. They sounded like an arrow striking against a shield. She went out of the door and walked away.

"Are you managing all right?" the Captain asked me. But I could see that his thoughts were elsewhere and this was merely a façade. A little later he gave an artificial yawn and said, "Dear me, I've got a long drive in front of me. But there it is: Nils won't spare anyone to do it for me."

I had only to replace the lock and put a few nails in the molding and the job was done. The Captain tried the door, put the key in his pocket, thanked me for my work, and went.

Shortly afterward he drove off with Elizabeth.

"Shan't be long!" he called, first to Captain Brother and then to the engineer, waving his hand to them both. "Enjoy yourselves!" he called.

IV

Evening came. What would happen now?

A great deal happened.

We farmhands were sitting at the supper table, while the gentry were having their dinner; and already the dining room was a scene of great merriment and abandon. Ragnhild, who was waiting on them, was in and out with trays of food and bottles; and once when she came out, she giggled, and said to the other maids, "I do believe even Madame is drunk tonight."

I had neither slept the previous night nor had my afternoon

rest that day; in addition, the latest events had affected me and preyed on my peace of mind. So when I had finished my supper I wandered off into the forest, in order to sit for a while on my own. And there I stayed for a long time.

I looked down toward the manor. Now the Captain was away, the servants in bed, the beasts in the stables and barns sleeping soundly. Fat Captain Brother and his lady had doubtless found themselves a hideout the moment dinner was over; old and fat he may have been, and the lady no longer young, but he was after her like a firebrand. That left only Mrs. Falkenberg and the young engineer; and where might they be now?

Their pigeon.

I drifted back home, yawning and shivering in the cool night air, and went up to my room. Soon afterward Ragnhild came and asked me to stay awake and lend a helping hand if the need arose. It was all so unpleasant tonight, she explained; the people in the house were doing just as they pleased, walking around in their underwear from room to room, drunk. Was Madame drunk too? Yes, she was. Was she, too, walking around in her underwear? No, but Captain Brother was, and Madame was saying "Bravo!" And the engineer was. They were quite mad, all four of them. And now, drunk as they were, Ragnhild had just gone and taken them two more bottles of wine.

"Come with me and hear for yourself!" said Ragnhild. "Now they've gone up to Madame's room."

"No, I'm going to bed," I answered. "And so should you."

"But if they ring for something all of a sudden?"

"Let them ring!"

Then Ragnhild revealed that the Captain himself had asked her to stay up that night, in case Madame should need her.

This changed the whole situation at a stroke. The Captain must have had his fears and left Ragnhild to keep watch. I put on my smock again and accompanied her across to the manor.

We stopped on the upstairs landing; we could hear sounds of

great merriment coming from Madame's room. But Madame herself spoke clearly and distinctly, and was certainly not drunk. "Yes, she is," Ragnhild insisted; "she's acting ever so strange."

I would dearly have liked to see Madame for a moment.

Ragnhild and I went down to the kitchen and sat there. But my mind was ill at ease, and soon I took the lamp from the wall and told Ragnhild to follow me. We went upstairs again.

"Now ask Madame to come out here and see me," I said.

"Why, whatever for?"

"I've got a message for her."

And Ragnhild knocked and went in.

Only then did I start thinking what sort of message I might give. I could simply look Madame in the eye and say, "The Captain asked me to send you his greetings." Would that do? Or I could say, "The Captain had no choice but to drive himself, because Nils wouldn't spare anyone else."

But a moment can sometimes last an age and the brain work with the speed of lightning. I had time to reject both these plans and conceive a third before Madame came out—though I doubt if my last plan was any better than the first two.

Madame asked in tones of astonishment, "Well, what is it?"

And Ragnhild came with her and looked questioningly at me.

I held the lamp out toward Madame and said, "Excuse my coming so late, but I'm going to the post office first thing to-morrow, and thought perhaps Madame might have some letters for me to post."

"Letters? No," she replied, shaking her head.

She seemed preoccupied, but not in the least drunk. But perhaps she was merely keeping her end up.

"No, I've no letters," she repeated, and made as if to return to her room.

"Then I beg your pardon," I said.

"Is it for the Captain you're going?"

"No, for myself."

She moved away. While still in the doorway she said to her guests in an offended tone, "That was a pure fabrication!"

Ragnhild and I went down again. I had seen Madame.

But my present humiliation! Nor was I greatly soothed by something which Ragnhild now let slip—which, indeed, fairly made me shrivel up. It appeared that the good Ragnhild's story about the Captain setting her to keep watch had been sheer hocus-pocus. She maintained that I had misunderstood her, but my suspicion grew stronger and clearer: that Ragnhild was spying, tonight as at other times, entirely on her own account, purely for the love of it.

I retired to my room. Look what my unseemly officiousness had done! Pure fabrication, Madame had called it—she must have seen through me. I promised myself ruefully that from now on I would leave everything and everyone to their own devices.

I threw myself fully dressed on my bed.

After a while I heard through the open window Mrs. Falkenberg out in the courtyard, talking loudly. The engineer was with her, answering from time to time. Madame was in raptures over the fine weather, the warm evening, and how lovely it was out here—so infinitely nicer than indoors!

But now her voice seemed to be getting less clear.

I ran to the window and saw them both standing by the stone steps down to the grove. There seemed to be something the engineer had not yet managed to get off his chest. "Please listen to me for a moment," he said. There followed a short and urgent appeal, which was duly answered; indeed rewarded. She had been deaf to him so long that now he spoke as if to someone hard of hearing. They stood there by the steps, and neither gave a thought to anyone else in the whole world. Listen who dared, watch who dared—the night belonged to them, their words belonged to them, the very spring seemed to force them together. He was like a cat, all poised to throw himself upon her; every movement she made fired him afresh. And as the moment for action came nearer, there was a crude force in his desire for her. The young firebrand!

"I've pleaded with you long enough," he said breathlessly. "Yesterday you nearly said yes; today you're deaf again. Your idea is that you and Brother and Auntie and all the rest should enjoy yourselves, quite innocently of course, while I sit and watch—the ladies' tame cavalier. But by God in heaven, no! You lie before my eyes like a pleasure garden, only there's a miserable fence around the garden, with a gate—shall I tell you what I'm going to do with that gate?"

"No, what?" she asked. "No, you've drunk too much, Hugo—you're so young. We've both drunk too much."

"And then you start playing an underhanded game with me, sending a special messenger for a letter that simply can't wait— yet you can have the heart to raise my hopes, to promise me—"

"I shall never do it again."

"Never do it again? What does that mean? I've seen you go up to a man—myself, as it happens—seen you come up to me—your tongue had a life of its own—Christ, how you kissed me! So just keep quiet about never doing it again, it's done now, I can still feel it, the most fantastic sensation—thank you for giving it to me . . . You're still going around with that letter next to your breast—let me see it!"

"You're so violent, Hugo. No, it's getting late, we must break it up."

"Will you let me see that letter?"

"Why should I? Certainly not!"

He made as if to use force, but checked himself and spat out, "What? You won't? You're an absolute—I won't say bitch, but maybe something worse—"

"Hugo!"

"Precisely."

"If you *must* see the letter, here it is!" She thrust her hand inside her blouse, drew out the letter, unfolded it, waved it at him; he should see how innocent she was. "Here's the letter. It's from my mother—look, there's the signature. It's from Mama. Well?"

It was as if she had boxed his ears. All he could say was, "From Mama? But then it can't have been so important, surely?"

"There, you can see for yourself! Well, perhaps not *that* important, still . . ."

He leaned against the paling and began grappling with the problem.

"I see, from your mother. It was a letter from your mother that came and interrupted us. Do you know what I think? You've cheated me. You've fooled me from beginning to end. The light's beginning to dawn."

She tried to find a way out. "It really was an important letter; Mama's coming here on a visit, quite soon now. And I was waiting to hear."

"You cheated me, didn't you?" he resumed. "You arranged for the letter to come just at the right moment, when we'd put out the lamp. That's it. You just wanted to get me excited. You had your maid there, guarding you."

"Oh, do be reasonable! Let's go in now—it's getting so late."

"Who's being unreasonable? Well, maybe I did have a drop too much up there, and now I'm not expressing myself clearly."

He could think only of the letter, and now he came back to it again. "And besides, there was no need to make such a deadly secret of a letter from your Mama. No, I see it all now. You want to go, do you? Very well then, go, madam. Good night, madam. My filial regards."

He bowed and remained standing there, sneering.

"Filial? Yes, because I'm old," she answered; and now she was deeply agitated. "And you're so young, Hugo; yes, it's true. And that's why I kissed you. I couldn't be your mother, of course; still, I'm much, much older than you. But I'm not all *that* old; you'd see that if . . . But I'm older than Elizabeth and

the rest. What am I saying? It's not true at all. I don't know
what else the years may have done to me, but they haven't made
me old. Well? Do you think they have? What do you know
about these things in any case?"

"No no," he said evasively. "But is there any sense in going
on like this? Here you are, day after day, you're young, you've
nothing else to do except keep guard over yourself and get
others to do the same. And God knows, you promised me
something—but that means little to you; it tickles your vanity
keeping me dangling and lashing me with your great white
wings."

"Great white wings," she murmured to herself.

"Yes. Or perhaps they're great red wings. Look at you standing there now—beautiful, all right, but fit for nothing."

"Oh dear, I know I've drunk far too much. But there's plenty
of things I'm fit for." Suddenly she took his hand and drew him
down the steps. I heard her say, "Why should I care? Does he
imagine Elizabeth's so much better?"

They came up the path as far as the summerhouse. Here she
hesitated and stopped.

"No, where are we going?" she asked. "Ha-ha, we must be
mad! You wouldn't have thought I was mad, would you? I'm
not, either—well, yes, now and again. There, the door's locked;
come, let's go. What a mean trick to lock the door when we
want to go in!"

Full of bitterness and suspicion, he answered, "You're cheat-
ing again. You knew very well the door was locked."

"You really must stop thinking so rottenly of me all the
time, do you hear? But why should he lock the summerhouse so
carefully and have it all to himself? Yes, I *did* know the door
was locked, that's why I came here with you. I daren't. No,
Hugo, I won't, you must believe me. Are you crazy? Come
away!"

She took his hand again and tried to turn back. They strug-
gled for a bit; he didn't want to follow. Then he threw both

arms overpoweringly around her, and kissed her again and
again. She yielded more and more ground, punctuating the
kisses with broken words.

"I've never kissed another man before, never—I swear to
God—you must believe me—I've never kissed—"

"No, of course not," he answered impatiently, taking her
with him step by step.

At the summerhouse he released her for a moment, gave the
door a hard heave with his shoulder, and broke it open for the
second time. Then, with a single stride, he was beside her
again. Neither of them spoke.

Even in the doorway she still resisted, clinging to the frame
and not letting go.

"No, I've never been unfaithful to him, I won't, I've never,
never—"

He pulled her toward him, kissed her for a full minute, two
minutes, passionately and without pause; she bent backward
under his weight, her hand slipped on the doorframe, she let
go . . .

A white mist drifted in front of my eyes. So—now they were
there. Now he was unfolding her. Now he was taking his will
and pleasure with her . . .

A mournful lassitude descended on me; I was alone with my
pain. It was late; my heart had gone to rest.

Through the white mist I saw a leaping figure: it was Ragnhild emerging from the bushes. As she ran, her tongue was
hanging out.

The engineer came up to me, nodded a good morning, and
asked if I would mend the summerhouse door.

"Is it broken again?"

"Yes, it got broken last night."

It was early in the morning—not more than half-past four—
and we farmhands had not yet set out for the fields. The engineer's eyes looked small, and glittered as if they were smarting;

they had doubtless seen no sleep. He offered no explanation of the door's being broken.

For Captain Falkenberg's sake rather than for his, I went straight down to the summerhouse to put the door in order for the second time. There was probably no hurry—the Captain had a long way to drive, there and back; still, it would soon be twenty-four hours since he had left home.

The engineer came with me. Without at the time quite knowing why, I received a favorable impression of him: all right, he had broken the door in last night, but he was not the man to sneak out of the affair afterward—he and nobody else had got it mended. Perhaps he had merely flattered my vanity by the confidence he showed in my silence. That was it. That was why I formed a good impression.

"I'm an Inspector of Log Driving on the watercourses," said the engineer. "How long are you staying here?"

"Not long. Till the end of the season."

"If you want, you can get a job with me."

This was an occupation with which I was quite unfamiliar. Besides, it was not log drivers and proletariat that I cared to be with but men who tilled the soil or tended the forests. However, I thanked the engineer for his offer.

"It's very good of you to fix the door. The fact is, I wanted a gun and was looking everywhere for one—I wanted to do some shooting. Then I thought, Maybe the Captain keeps a gun in here."

I made no answer. I would have preferred him to say nothing.

"So I wanted to ask you before you went out in the fields," he concluded.

I mended and replaced the lock once again, and started hammering in more nails where the molding had again been splintered. While I was busy with this we heard Captain Falkenberg in the courtyard and caught a glimpse of him through the bushes, unhitching and stabling the horses.

The engineer started, fumbled for his watch, and took it out, while his eyes became large and vacant, as if they saw nothing. Suddenly he said, "No, I really must . . . I was forgetting . . ."

Then he disappeared far away down the garden.

So he was sneaking out of it after all!

The next moment the Captain came up. He was pale, covered in dust, bleary-eyed from lack of sleep, but completely sober. While still some way off he asked, "How did you get in there?"

I raised my cap and said nothing.

"Has the door been broken in again?"

"It was just—I suddenly remembered I'd been short of a couple of nails yesterday. It's done now. If the Captain would care to lock up now."

Fool that I was! If I couldn't think of a better excuse than that, he was bound to put two and two together.

He stood for a few seconds looking at the door with narrowed eyes. He must have had his suspicions; but then he put the key in the keyhole, locked the door, and went. There was nothing else he could do.

V

All the guests had departed: fat Captain Brother, the lady with the shawl, Engineer Lassen. And Captain Falkenberg was at last ready to join his regiment. I thought: He must have applied for a deferment and had a very good case, or he would have left long ago.

During the last few days we farmhands had got through an immense amount of work; it had been a strain on both man and beast. But Nils had wanted it that way, and knew what he was doing: he wished to gain time for another purpose.

One day he set me to work raking and cleaning and tidying all the way around the various buildings. This used up just about all the time gained, if not more; but somehow it improved the whole appearance of the place. And this was Nils's aim: to cheer the Captain up a little before he left home. After a while I began, on my own initiative, fastening the odd crosspiece in the garden fence that had worked loose, or straightening up an outbuilding door that had warped. Finally I started preparing two new beams for the ramp to the hayloft.

"Where are you going when you leave here?" the Captain asked me.

"I don't know. I shall wander around."

"I could do with you here for a while; there's a lot to be done."

"Is the Captain thinking of painting by any chance?"

"That too. No, I'm not sure about that. It will cost a lot of money to paint all these buildings. No, there was something else I had in mind. Do you know anything about timber? Can you select and mark trees for felling?"

So he was still pretending he hadn't recognized me from the last time I worked in his woods. But had he still got any trees left to fell?

"Oh yes, I'm used to timber. Where does the Captain mean to fell this year?"

"Everywhere. Anywhere. There must be something left."

"Very good."

Next I put the new beams in the hayloft ramp, and when I had finished that, I took down the flagpole and fixed it with a knob and a halyard. Øvrebø was already looking more shipshape, and Nils announced that he was beginning to feel like a new man. I got him to go to the Captain and put in a good word for the painting, but the Captain looked at him anxiously and said, "Yes, yes. But there's other things besides painting and painting, you know. Let's wait until the autumn and see what the harvest's like, after all the sowing we've done this year."

But when the flagpole stood there with the old paint scraped off and a new knob and halyard, even the Captain noticed, and telegraphed to order paint. Not that there was any hurry; an ordinary letter would have done.

Two days passed. The paint arrived but was put to one side: we still had a lot of seasonal work to do.

During this period we even used the Captain's two carriage horses on the harrow and the seeder; and when it came to planting potatoes, Nils had to enlist the help of all the maids. The Captain agreed to this and to everything else; then he went off to join his regiment. After that we were on our own.

But before he left there was a great matrimonial scene.

We all knew of the disharmony between the pair of them; and Ragnhild and the dairymaid went around talking openly about it. The crops were coming on nicely now, the pastures grew daily more lush, the spring was fine and favorable to growth; but Øvrebø was also a scene of strife. There were times when Madame went around with a tear-stained face, or with an exaggeratedly haughty air, as if to say she had given up crawling to anyone. Her mother came, a mild lady with spectacles on her white mouse face; but she didn't stay long—only a few days—before returning to her home in Kristiansand. She made out that the air here didn't suit her.

That matrimonial scene: it had been a final, bitter, hour-long altercation. Ragnhild gave us the full story afterward; there were no raised voices, but both the Captain and Madame had spoken in strong, measured terms; and in their bitterness they had agreed to go their separate ways.

"You don't mean it!" said the assembled company in the kitchen, clasping their hands.

Ragnhild put on an air and started impersonating the protagonists.

" 'You were involved in breaking the summerhouse door again?' says the Captain. 'Yes,' says Madame. 'And what else?' he asks. 'Everything!' says Madame. So the Captain smiles and says, 'Well, that's a plain, straightforward answer—it doesn't take long to work out what that means.' Madame says nothing. 'What merit does that young whelp possess—beyond the fact that he once helped me out of a jam?' asks the Captain. Madame gives him a look and says, 'He helped you?' 'Yes,' says the Captain, 'he countersigned a loan for me.' And Madame says, 'I never knew that.' But then the Captain says, 'Has he really never told you?' Madame shakes her head. 'But what of that?' he goes on; 'would it have made any difference if you'd known?' First she says yes, then she says no. 'Are you in love with him?' he asks. 'Are you in love with Elizabeth?' she answers back. 'Yes,' says the Captain; then he sits there, smiling. 'Good!' says Madame, sullen-like. Then they say nothing for quite a while, till the Captain starts up again and says, 'You were right when you said I ought to think things over; now I've done so. I'm not addicted to drink; it's a funny thing, but I've never really enjoyed living it up. All the same, I've done just that. But now I'm through with it!' 'How nice for you!' says Madame, sullen-like again. 'Yes,' he says, 'but it would have been nicer still if you'd shown yourself just a tiny bit pleased.' 'You'd better get Elizabeth to show herself pleased,' she says. He just says 'Elizabeth!' and keeps shaking his head. After that they sit quiet again for a while. Then the Captain asks her, 'What are you going to do now?' 'Look, don't you worry about me,' says Madame, very slow and deliberate-like; 'I can become a nurse if you want, or I can cut my hair short and become a schoolteacher if you want.' 'If *I* want!' he says—'No, you must make up your own mind.' 'I need to know first what you propose to do,' she says. 'I propose to stay where I am,' he says; 'you're the one who's thrown yourself out,' he says. And Madame nods and says, 'Very well.' "

The entire kitchen gasped. "Ye gods!" said Nils; "but surely it'll all come right again." He looked around to see what the rest of us thought.

For the first two days after the Captain's departure, Madame sat playing her piano all day long. On the third, Nils drove her to the station; she was going to her mother in Kristiansand. After that we were still more on our own. Madame had taken none of her things with her. Perhaps she felt she owned nothing; or perhaps everything had come from the Captain in the first place and she wished to have none of it. Oh, how sad it all was!

Ragnhild had been told by Madame that she needn't leave. However, it was the cook who took charge of everything and kept the keys. It was best for us all that way.

On Saturday the Captain came home on leave—something which, according to Nils, he had never done before. Despite his wife's absence he held himself erect; and he was as sober as a judge. He gave me clear, concise instructions about the trees I should mark, coming out with me and pointing here and there: battens and batten ends, a thousand dozen. He would be away three weeks this time, he told me. On Sunday afternoon he went off again. By now he was more decisive in manner, more like himself.

At last the plowing and sowing were over, and the potatoes in the ground. Now Nils and the boy could manage the day-to-day work on their own and I was able to start marking trees.

I was as happy as the days were long. We had a warm, rainy spell that made the woods all wet; I never let this keep me indoors but went out just the same. Then the hot weather set in, and during the long evenings after I got home I would take pleasure in going around and putting things to rights: here a gutter, there a window that was hanging crooked. Finally I raised the fire ladder and started to scrape the old peeling paint off the north wall of the barn. It would be a joke if, after all, I managed to paint the barn before the summer was out. The paint was there!

But now a new factor caused me to weary of the work and of the whole place. It was not the same working here now as it had been when the master and mistress were at home; I knew from experience, and was reminded again, that it is good to have someone over you in a job—unless, that is, you yourself have been placed in charge. The maids had no one now to be in awe of; Ragnhild and the dairymaid were boisterous at table, and had quarrels which the cook did not always possess the authority to quell. All this made for an unpleasant atmosphere. In addition, somebody must have gone and spoken about me to my former good comrade Lars Falkenberg, and sown suspicion of me in his heart.

Lars came to the manor one evening, took me aside, and forbade me to come to his cottage in future. His manner was comical and threatening.

I had been to his home occasionally with washing—perhaps half a dozen times in all; he himself had been out, but Emma and I had chatted about old topics and new. The last time I was there Lars had suddenly come home and at once taken Emma to task for sitting there on a stool in her petticoat. "It's too hot for a skirt," she replied. "Yes, and your hair's wandered halfway down your back," he said; "I suppose that's because of the heat, too?" He really had it in for her. Nor did he answer my "good night" when I left.

Since then I had not been there. So what had made him come here this evening? Ragnhild must have been busy again with her spy's tongue.

After forbidding me in so many words to darken his door again, Lars nodded and looked at me as if I ought to drop dead.

"What's more, I understand Emma's been down here," he went on. "She won't do that again, I rather think."

"She may have been here once or twice with washing."

"That's right, blame it on the washing. And then you come to the cottage yourself several times a week with washing—a shirt one time, a pair of underpants the next. But from now on Ragnhild can do your washing for you."

"All right, all right."

"No sirree! I know you—coming to people's homes and getting too friendly when you find they're alone! No, thank you very much!"

Nils came up; he must have realized what was going on and, like the good friend he was, wanted to help me. He heard the last few words and at once declared in my favor that he had never once seen me do anything I shouldn't, all the time I had been there.

But Lars Falkenberg at once drew himself up to his full height and measured Nils with a disdainful eye. He had, indeed, a long-standing grudge against the foreman: Able though Lars had shown himself since acquiring his own little property up in the forest, Nils had done far better work down here on the Captain's estate. And this rankled with Lars Falkenberg.

"What are you sticking your ugly mug in here for?" he asked.

"I'm only saying what happens to be true," answered Nils.

"You are, are you, jackass? You make me want to puke all over you."

At this Nils and I took ourselves off, while Lars continued to belabor us with words. Needless to say, Ragnhild stood sniffing the lilacs as we passed.

That evening I began to think I would resume my wanderings as soon as I had finished my work in the forest. The Captain came after three weeks, as he had said, and praised me for scraping the paint off the north wall of the barn. "I can see it's going to end with your repainting it too," he said. I told him how much timber I had marked, and reported that there was not much left to do. "Carry on marking!" was his answer. Then he rejoined his regiment for another three weeks.

But I had no desire to spend another three weeks at Øvrebø now. I marked enough trees to make a few score dozen more, and reckoned it all up on my work sheet: it would have to do. But it was still too early to live in the woods and hills: there were flowers but no berries; mating birds with their chirrup and song, butterflies, flies and midges, but no cloudberries, no angelica.

Here I was, in a town.*

I had called on Engineer Lassen, Inspector of Log Driving, and he had kept his promise and given me work, even though the season was far advanced. To begin with, I had to do a tour of the river, marking on a map the points where the worst log-jams had occurred. The engineer was a straightforward enough fellow; merely very young still. He plied me with superfluous good advice on matters about which he thought I was ignorant; this made him feel more grown-up.

So this man had helped Captain Falkenberg out of a jam! Now, probably, the Captain regretted this and wanted to free himself; hence the felling of his timber down to the last batten. And I, too, wished him free; I even began reproaching myself for not having marked down another few days' timber, for stinting the help I had given. Supposing, now, it proved just a fraction too little!

Engineer Lassen was clearly a man of means, living as he did in a hotel, where he had two rooms. I only saw his office, but even this was expensively appointed—books and magazines, a silver writing set, a gilt theodolite, and so on; his silk-lined summer topcoat hung on the wall. Beyond doubt, he was one of the town's richer and more important citizens; there was even a large picture of him in the local photographer's display case.

---

* From the description, the town would appear to be Drammen, at the head of Drammenfjord, southwest of Oslo.—Trans.

Of an afternoon, moreover, I would see him taking the air with the young ladies of the town. As supreme head of log-driving operations, he liked best of all to stroll out onto the 475-foot bridge over the rapids, where he would stop to peer upstream and downstream. Just here—around the piers of the bridge and on the flat rocks downstream—was where the logs were most inclined to jam, and for this reason alone the engineer kept a team of log drivers almost constantly on call. When he stood on the bridge surveying the men out on the logjam, he was like a ship's captain, young, strong, and able to command. His fair companions would wait patiently on the bridge, however strong the current below. And to hear each other speak above the roar of the torrent they had often to lean their heads together.

But it was precisely when the engineer took up his station on the bridge, and stood there turning fore and aft, that he lost in stature and elegance: his athlete's build and tight-fitting jacket that pinched at the back conspired to make his bottom quite absurdly large.

The very first evening, when he had already briefed me for my journey upriver in the morning, I met him promenading with two ladies. At the sight of me he stopped, halted his retinue, and gave me the same instructions all over again. "Lucky I met you," he said. "Because tomorrow you must be up early. Take a pike pole with you and free as much timber as you can. If any logjam is more than you can manage, mark it on the map—got the map, have you? And carry on until you meet my other man working his way down. But remember to mark in red, not blue. And make sure you do the work properly." Then to the ladies: "This is a man I've appointed to work under me; I really can't be bothered traipsing everywhere myself."

How busily engaged he was! He even took out a notebook and made a note. He was so young, and had such a charming retinue to show off to.

Next morning I started out early; by the time it was light, at four o'clock, I was already a fair distance up the river. I had food with me, and my pike pole—which is the same as a boat hook.

Here was no young, luxuriant growth as at Øvrebø; the forest floor was barren and stony, heather and pine needles covered the ground for mile after mile. The felling had been ruthless, the pulp mills too greedy in their demands, a load of scantling was all that remained; and the virtual absence of young trees made this a dreary landscape that I wandered through.

By midday I had cleared several small jams and marked in one large one. I ate some food, drank from the river, and after a short rest continued on my way. Toward evening I came to a biggish logjam where a man was at work. This was the man I was scheduled to meet. I didn't at once come forward but amused myself for a while watching him furtively. He guarded his life with the utmost care, and was even afraid of getting his feet wet. The first hint of danger, of being carried out into the stream on a loosened log—and he was away. Then I went right up close and looked at him—and yes, it was my good friend Grindhusen.

Grindhusen, my companion at Skreia in the days of my youth; Grindhusen, my well-digging partner of six years ago.

And now here he was again.

We exchanged greetings, we sat on the logjam and talked, we questioned and answered for the space of an hour. By then it was too late to do more work that day, so we got up and walked a short distance up along the river to where Grindhusen had his little wooden hut. We crept in, lit a fire, made coffee, and had a meal. Then we went out again, lit our pipes, and lay full length in the heather.

Grindhusen had become old; he was in just the same plight as I, and he didn't at all care to remember the gay nights we had danced through in our youth. He it was who had been after the girls like a red-haired wolf; now he was well chastened by age and toil, and he had even ceased to smile. If I had had some brandy with me, he might have livened up, but I had none.

In his younger days Grindhusen had been as stubborn and awkward as they come; now he was mild and stupid. "Maybe, maybe" was his answer to everything; "you're right, you know, dead right," he would say—not because he meant it but because life had made him evasive and vacillating. It was unpleasant meeting him again; evasive and vacillating—that is what life makes us all, year by year.

One day followed another, he said, but where he was concerned things weren't what they used to be; he'd suffered lately from rheumatism, also from heartburn—cardialgia, they called it. Still, as long as he could keep this job with Engineer Lassen, he'd just about manage; he knew the river all the way up, and spent the whole spring and early summer here in his hut. As for clothes, he wore nothing but trousers and smocks, summer and winter. Oh, and last year he'd been lucky, he suddenly told me: he'd found a sheep that didn't belong to anyone. Sheep in the forest? "Up there!" he answered, pointing. He'd had mutton on Sundays from that sheep till far into the winter. Mind you, he had people in America now, that wasn't the problem, children who'd married and settled nicely. They'd sent him a little help the first year or so—but then they'd stopped, and now it was close on two years since they'd even written. Yes, that was the way it was for him and his wife in their old age.

Grindhusen grew pensive.

There came a faint soughing from the forest and from the river, as of millions of nothings flowing ceaselessly away. No birds dwelt here, no animals frisked around; but when I rolled a stone aside I would find some crawling insect underneath. "Can you understand what these tiny creatures live on?" I asked. "What tiny creatures?" said Grindhusen; "they're only ants and the like." "It's some kind of beetle," I said; "put him on the grass and roll a stone over him and he'll live." Grindhusen answered, "Maybe, maybe." But he hadn't paid my words the slightest heed. So I pursued the line of thought for myself: slip an ant under the same stone, however, and soon there will be no more beetle.

And the forest and the river went on soughing—one eternity agreeing with another eternity about something. In tempest and thunder, however, there is war between them.

"Yes, that's the way it is," said Grindhusen at long last; "it'll be two years come the fourteenth of August since I got the last letter. There was a nice photograph inside, from Olea—she lives in Dakota, as they call it. A swell photograph, that was, but could I sell it? Ah well, with God's help something will turn up," said Grindhusen with a yawn. "What was I going to say— how much are you getting per day?"

"I don't know."

But Grindhusen gave me a suspicious look, thinking I was reluctant to tell him.

"Well, it's all the same to me," he said. "I was only asking."

So I guessed a figure, just to satisfy him. "I suppose I'll get a couple of kroner, two or three kroner?"

"Yes, I dare say you will," he said enviously. "I only get two kroner, mind, and I'm an old hand at this game."

But now he must have become nervous lest I noise his discontent abroad, for he started boasting about Engineer Lassen, how he was a damned fine fellow in every respect—"He'd never do me an injustice. A likely idea, indeed! Why, he's been like a father to me, that I will say for him."

The engineer a father to Grindhusen! It sounded ineffably droll, coming from that almost toothless mouth. I could doubtless have learned a thing or two about the engineer from this source, but I asked no questions.

"He didn't say anything about me coming down into town?" asked Grindhusen.

"No."

"There's times he sends for me, all in aid of nothing in particular—just wants to chat with me a bit. A mighty good sort, he is."

Dusk gathered. Grindhusen yawned again, crept into the hut, and bedded down.

Next morning we cleared the logjam. "Come with me up my way for a bit," said Grindhusen. So off we went. After walking for an hour we saw buildings and fields: a hill farm up in the woods. Some association of ideas made me think of Grindhusen's sheep.

"Was it somewhere about here you found that sheep?" I asked.

Grindhusen gave me a look.

"Here? Lord no. That was miles from here—over Trovatn way."

"Isn't Trovatn in the next parish?"

"That's right. So it's miles and miles from here."

But now Grindhusen wished me to come no farther with him; he stopped and thanked me for my company. Surely I could come as far as the farm, I objected; but Grindhusen wasn't even calling at the farm—a place he never set foot in. I was left alone with the day, and the long walk into town.

So I turned and went back the way I had come.

VI

This was not my idea of work at all: walking and walking along the riverbank, upstream and downstream, clearing the smaller jams, then on again. And at the end of each trip, fetching up back at my boardinghouse in town. During this period I had only one man to talk to: the underporter at the engineer's hotel, a giant of a man with childlike eyes, and hands that could span eleven inches. He had fallen and hit his head when he was small, he told me, and had never got further in life than heaving and carrying heavy loads. With him I exchanged a few words from time to time, and with no one else.

That little town!

When the river was high, it raged and roared through the middle of the town, dividing it in two. North and south of the roar, people lived in their wooden houses, apparently scraping a livelihood from day to day. Of the many children who crossed the bridge or ran errands to the shops, none went naked, few probably suffered any want, all were good-looking. Most amusing of all were the older girls, tall and thin and bony, cheerfully absorbed in each other and their own little world. Sometimes they would stop on the bridge to watch the men down on the logjam, and help them as they hauled at the timber by singing "Yo-o heave ho!" Then they would giggle and dig each other in the ribs.

But no birds sang.

Strange, this absence of birds. On quiet evenings, at sundown, the great enclosed log pond lay there, deep, its surface immobile; midges and butterflies swarmed over it; the trees on the bank were mirrored in it; but no birds perched in the trees. Perhaps the deafening roar of the torrent was to blame: no birds could thrive where they could not hear each other sing. And that was why the only winged creatures here were midges and flies—though God alone knows why even the crows and the magpies shunned our town.

Every small town has its daily event that people turn out for; so, for that matter, does every big town that boasts a promenade. On the west coast it is the mail boat; how hard it is to live there and keep away from the quay when the boat comes in! Here, in this inland town a full twenty miles from the sea, and only hills and mountains all around, we had the river. Had the water risen or fallen during the night? Would they be clearing

logs from the booms today? How absorbing we found it! To be
sure, we also had a narrow-gauge railroad, but this was nothing
to write home about: the line ended here, it went as far as it
could, then stopped, like a cork in a bottle. And the tiny little
cars were enchanting, but people were bashful about objects so
ridiculously old and stunted—why, one could hardly sit upright
in them with a hat on.

And then of course there were the markets and churches and
schools and post offices; and sawmills and pulp mills all along
the river. As for grocery stores, their number was beyond belief.

We had this, we had that. I was a stranger here—as everywhere—yet I could count a multitude of things we had in addition to the river. Had the town once been a big one? No, it has
remained small for two hundred and fifty years. Once, however,
there was a greater man over all the lesser men—a grandee who
rode with a servant behind and lorded it over many an acre.
Now we were all equal—except, perhaps, for Engineer Lassen,
this twenty-something-year-old Inspector of Log Driving who
could afford two rooms at his hotel.

Having nothing to do, I caught myself meditating as follows:
Here stands a great house, about two hundred years old, once
the home of the wealthy Ole Olsen Ture; a huge two-story
house the length of a block, now used as a depot. At the time
when this house was built, there was plenty of massive timber
in these parts; three beams together made the height of a man;
they were filled with ore, with iron, and would blunt any ax.
And inside there were halls and cells, as in a castle. Here the
great Ture reigned like a monarch.

Times changed. It was no longer enough for a house to be big
and to afford shelter from cold and rain; it had also to give
pleasure to the eye. On the opposite side of the river stands an
old archaic building with a nicely balanced Empire-style ve-
randa, complete with pillars and a pediment. It is not beyond
criticism, but it is beautiful in its way, and stands out like a
white temple against the green hills behind. And there is yet

another house which I have stopped to look at, near the market-place. Its double door onto the street has ancient handles and cut-glass rococo mirrors; but the frame around these mirrors is fluted in the style of Louis XVI. The cartouche over the door bears the date 1795 in arabic figures—the transitional period has arrived! Even in this little town there were people in those days who kept abreast of the times, without the aid of the telegraph or of steam.

But later generations built against snow and rain, and for no other purpose. The houses were neither large nor beautiful. They were intended, Swiss-fashion, to provide a dwelling place for wife and children; and that was all. From this wretched little people up in the Alps, which throughout its history has never been anything or done anything, we learned to set no store by how a human dwelling looked to the eye, as long as it went down well with globe-trotting tourists. Why get excited because the white building on the hillside has something of a temple's peace and beauty? Why preserve the great big house from Ole Olsen Ture's days, when it could make way for twenty little homes?

Things have gone downhill until they have reached rock bottom. Now cobblers are filled with glee, not because we have all grown equally great, but because we have all grown equally small. Our pigeon!

The long bridge is excellent for walking on, being paved with planks and as even as a floor; any young lady can walk gracefully here. It is airy, too, and open at the sides—the perfect vantage point for inquisitive people like me.

Shouts rise to us from the men down there on the logjam, as they struggle to free the timber that has caught on rocks and boulders in the river. Log after log comes drifting down, to join the logs already stuck there; the jam grows and grows, until there may be a couple of hundred dozen balks at a single spot on the river. If all goes well, the men can free them again in a reasonably short time; if things go badly, some unfortunate driver may even be carried down the rapids to his death.

Out on the logjam are ten men with boat hooks, all of them more or less wet from falling in. The foreman points to the log which needs freeing next; but at times we spectators recognize signs of dissent among the gang of drivers. The din prevents our hearing anything; but there are clearly those who favor freeing some quite different log first, and one old hand has started voicing his discontent. Knowing his language, I seem to hear him say, stubbornly and deliberately, "Happen we'd do better to take *him* first!" Now ten pairs of eyes are cast on the new log, working out a fairway for it through the magpie's nest of other logs; if all agree, ten boat hooks descend on it. For a moment these boat hooks extend from the log like the strings of a harp. Then there is a cry of "Heave!" they all pull, and the log moves forward a little. Fresh grips, another cry, and again it moves forward a little. It is like watching ten ants at work on a twig. Finally the log sails down over the rapids.

But certain logs are almost immovable, and often it is just such a log, and no other, which has to be freed first of all. Then the drivers fan out and surround it, digging their boat hooks in wherever it is visible in its magpie's nest, some pulling, others pushing; if it is dry they splash water over it by way of lubrication. And the boat hooks no longer extend from the log in regular formation, like strings on a harp, but radiate from it crisscross in all directions, like a spider's web.

At times the ten-man chorus on the river can be heard all day long, except during meals; at times, indeed, we hear them for days on end. Then suddenly a new sound falls on the ear: the stroke of an ax. Some swine of a log has settled so awkwardly that it cannot be dragged clear. And yet it is holding the entire mass together; therefore, it has to be cut. Not many blows are needed; the immense pressure brought to bear soon causes it to crack, and the huge magpie's nest caves in and starts turning around. At once the men break off and stand at the ready; if the section they are on breaks loose, they must move with catlike agility to a safer place. Every day, every hour of their work is fraught with fearful tension; their lives depend entirely on themselves.

But this is a dead-alive little town.

It is a sad spectacle, a dead town trying to pretend it is alive. It is the same with Bruges, that great city of former years; likewise with many cities in Holland, southern Germany, northern France, the Orient. Standing in the marketplace of such a town, you say to yourself, This town was alive once—and look, I can still see people walking about in its streets!

It is very strange: our town is tucked away, shut in by mountains; yet it seems to possess its share of female beauty and male ambition, just like any other town. Only it's a queer, mysterious life, the life lived here, with short crooked fingers, mouse eyes, and ears filled day and night with the everlasting roar from the torrent. A beetle walks in the heather, occasional blades of yellowing grass loom up—great trees they seem to the beetle! Two local merchants are walking across the bridge, doubtless on their way to the post office. Today they have clubbed together to buy a whole sheet of postage stamps at one go, for the sake of the discount!

Oh, these local merchants!

Every day they hang out their ready-made clothes and display their fabrics and goods in the windows; but seldom is anyone seen entering their doors. I guessed at the outset there must be the odd peasant-farmer from up the valley, coming to town on business; and I guessed correctly. Today I saw that farmer—and what splendid entertainment he provided!

He was dressed like the peasants in our folktales, in a short knitted jacket with silver buttons, and gray trousers patched with black leather behind. He was driving a tiny little hay wagon with a tiny little horse; in the wagon stood a little red-

flanked cow, doubtless en route for the butcher. All three—
man, horse, and cow—were so diminutive and paleolithic as to
resemble subterranean gnomes on a brief visit to the haunts of
men; I was expecting to see them vanish before my eyes. Suddenly the cow let out a bellow from its Lilliputian carriage; and
even this preposterous sound came as if from another world.

Some two hours later I saw the man again, without his horse
or cow, wandering around the stores on his errands. I followed
him into the emporium of one Vogt: Saddler, Glazier, and (for
good measure) Leather Merchant. This versatile man of com-
merce wanted to serve me first; but I said I needed to look at
a saddle and some glass and a sample of leather first; no hurry
where I was concerned. The merchant then turned to the
gnome.

The two were acquainted.

"Well, if it isn't himself back in town!"

"Ay, that's about long and short on't."

The whole gamut: the weather, the wind, the state of the
roads; the wife, the kids (much the same as usual); the crops;
the river (fallen by a quarter this last week); the price of meat;
the hard times we're living in. Then they started in on the
leather: feeling it, turning it, bending it, talking it over. And
when at last a strip had been cut and weighed, the gnome
thought it must be bewitched and all to weigh so much. Best
reckon in round sums—no sense in fiddle-faddling with all
them bits and pieces of weight. On this issue they racked their
brains for a while, as form and custom prescribe. When finally
the moment for paying arrived, a leather purse was conjured up
as if from a fairy tale, one by one the prehistoric coins were
solemnly and gingerly fished out, both parties counted them
again and again, and the gnome closed the purse with an anxious movement: that was all he had!

"But you've paper money too, as well as change? Didn't I see
a bank note?"

"Bank note? Nay, I'm not breaking into *him*."

More racking of brains, prolonged discussion, a little give-and-take on both sides—and the deal was done.

"That was a cruelly dear piece of leather," said the purchaser.

And the seller replied, "No, you got it dirt cheap. Now don't forget to look me up any time you're in town."

Late in the afternoon I saw the gnome driving home again after his visit to the haunts of men. The cow had stayed behind with the butcher. The little man's parcels and sacks were in the wagon, but he himself was plodding along behind, the leather on his backside standing out in a triangle at each step. Whether his wits were naturally weak, or whether they had been over-taxed by a visit to the liquor store, he was wearing a roll of shoe leather around one arm like a bracelet.

And so, once more, money had poured into town: a peasant farmer had been in and sold his cow, and bought himself out of small change again. The event was immediately noted every-where: even the three lawyers took note, even the three little local newspapers took note—the circulation of money was on the increase. Unproductive activity; and the town lived on it.

Every week, however, town houses were offered for sale in the local papers; every week, the authorities published a numbered list of properties on the tax rolls which were to be sold in liqui-dation of unpaid tax. Well, what of it? Ah, but the sheer number of houses for sale in this way! The barren mountain valley with its great river could not feed this moribund town; a cow now and again was not enough. Hence the enforced surren-der of town houses and Swiss chalets and dwellings of every kind. On the west coast, if once in a while a small town house is up for sale, it's a major event; the natives gather on the mack-erel quay, putting their heads together and whispering. Here in our little town, which had lost all hope, it occasioned no remark when a property slipped from an exhausted hand. My turn today, my neighbor's turn tomorrow! And no one to shed a tear.

Engineer Lassen came to my lodgings and said, "Put your cap on and come with me to the station to fetch a trunk."

"No," I answered. "I'm not doing that."

"Not doing that?"

"No. There's a man at the hotel for that. I don't grudge him his earnings."

I had made my point. The engineer was so young, he could only stare at me in silence. And when, being persistent by nature, he returned to the attack, his tone had changed.

"I'd sooner have you than anyone on this occasion," he said; "and I'm sure you wouldn't mind."

"That's another matter; in that case I'll do it."

I put on my cap and was ready. He led the way to the station; I followed behind. We waited ten minutes, then the train arrived: three little boxlike cars, out of which crawled a handful of passengers. From the last car there crawled a lady; the engineer strode off to assist her.

I took no special notice of what went on. The lady, who was gloved and veiled, handed the engineer a yellow summer coat. She seemed shy and spoke only a few quiet words; but when, by contrast, the engineer talked loudly and freely and begged her to take off her veil, she grew bolder and did as he said. "Do you recognize me now?" she asked. And at once I pricked up my ears—it was Mrs. Falkenberg's voice. I turned and looked her in the face.

How hard it is to be old and superannuated! The moment I realized whom I was standing before, I was concerned only with my own aged person, with my dignity of bearing, with the depth of my bow. I was now the possessor of a tunic and trousers of brown corduroy such as workmen wear in the south—a handsome outfit, and brand new; but alas, I wasn't wearing it that day. How irritated, how downcast this made me! And while they stood there talking, I started to wonder why the engineer had so particularly wanted me to accompany him to the station. To save the tip to the porter, perhaps? To strut around with his own personal servant? Or did he wish to cheer Madame with the sight of a familiar face? If so, the idea was sadly misconceived; the moment she saw me, Madame went rigid with displeasure at finding me here, where she might have fancied herself well hidden. I heard the engineer say, "See this fellow here? He'll take your trunk. Got the ticket?" But I gave no sign of greeting and turned away.

Afterward I stood gloating over him in my miserable soul, and thinking: Ah, now she will take against him for his tactlessness! He has presented for her inspection a man who has been in her employment when she had a home; but that same man had a sense of delicacy, he turned away without recognizing her! (And God alone knew why the ladies ran after this kid, with his concave back and enormous bottom.)

There were fewer and fewer people on the platform; the train's crew uncoupled the three little boxes and began forming them into another train; in the end we were the only people left. The engineer and Madame still stood there talking. Why had she come? Search me! The young firebrand must have missed her and wanted to have her again. Or perhaps she had come of her own free will, to explain the lie of the land and seek his advice. Sooner or later, no doubt, it would end in their getting engaged and then married. Mr. Hugo Lassen was a knight-at-arms, of course, and she his beloved here on earth. It only remained to be seen if her path would be strewn with happiness and flowers ever after.

"No, that won't do at all!" exclaimed the engineer, laughing. "If you won't be my aunt, then you'll have to be my cousin."

"Sh!" she answered. "Can't that man go away?"

Whereupon the engineer came up to me with the luggage ticket in his hand and said, in the lordly manner of an Inspector of Log Driving addressing his team, "Bring the trunk up to the hotel."

"Very good," I answered, touching my cap.

As I carried the trunk I thought: So now he's asking her to be his aunt, his elderly aunt! Again, he could have been more tactful—as I would have. I would have said to all and sundry, "There is come a fair angel unto King Hugo. Behold how young she is and how comely. Her gray eyes tell of a heavy heart; yea, her glance is grave. But a myriad lights shimmer in her hair, and I do love her. Behold her also when she speaks, her mouth is altogether good and delicate; sometimes it cannot choose but yield a smile. I am King Hugo this day, and she is my beloved!"

The trunk was no heavier than many another burden, but it was fitted with bronzed iron bands, one of which tore a hole in the back of my smock. Then I thanked my lucky stars that it wasn't my corduroy tunic which had been ruined.

VII

Several days passed. I was bored with my futile occupation, which consisted of doing precisely nothing, of idling in fact; and I applied to the log drivers' foreman for a place in his team. But he turned me down.

These lords of the proletariat are tremendous swells; they look down on the farm worker and don't want him anywhere near them. They roam from watercourse to watercourse, live a free and easy life, get cash in their hands once a week, and as likely as not drink most of it away. They are also in good favor with the girls. It's the same with road workers, railroad workers, and factory workers of every kind: they regard even the craftsman as a lower form of being, while as for the farm worker, he is a serf!

By now I felt certain that I could join the gang whenever I chose, by telling the Inspector of Log Driving that I wished to do so. But, in the first place, I had no desire to place myself further in the man's debt; and, in the second place, I would have to be prepared for my worthy colleagues giving me hell—right up until the moment when, with great difficulty, I had earned their respect. And that might take longer than I was prepared to spend.

In any case, the engineer came to me one day with instructions which I was to observe with all possible care. Speaking courteously and reasonably, he said, "There's been no rain for a long time now; the river's falling and the jams are growing. I want you to tell the man higher up and the man lower down to take every possible care at present; I need hardly say that goes for you too."

"There's bound to be rain very soon now," I said, for the sake of saying something.

"Be that as it may," he replied with all the seriousness of youth, "I have to act as if it were never going to rain any more. Now remember every syllable I've said. I can't be everywhere myself, especially now that I've got a visitor."

At this I took him as seriously as he took himself and swore to do my level best.

But this meant I couldn't yet give up my idle life; instead, I continued wandering upstream and downstream with my boat hook and my provisions. For my own satisfaction I took to clearing bigger and bigger jams unaided, singing to myself as if I was an entire team of log drivers, and working as hard as a dozen men. I also conveyed the engineer's instructions to Grindhusen and put the fear of God in him.

But then came the rain.

And now the logs fairly danced down the waterfalls and rapids, like great tawny snakes that darted on and on, with sometimes the heads and sometimes the tails in the air.

Carefree days for the engineer, I presumed.

As for myself, I disliked both the town and my boardinghouse; I had my own little room, but took no pleasure in it, since it let in every sound in the place. Besides, my nose was put well and truly out of joint by all the young log men who lodged there. At this period I paced the riverbank assiduously, even though there was little or nothing for me to do. At times, however, I would steal away to a hiding place under a cliff, where I would sit feeling old and forsaken, and wallowing in the sensation. And in the evenings I would write letter after letter to my acquaintances as a way of talking to them; but I never posted the letters. In short, these were cheerless days. The greatest pleasure I had was to crisscross my way through the town, observing trivial things and reflecting a little on each.

But was the engineer still so carefree? I began to have my doubts.

Why was he no longer out in the streets early and late with the visiting cousin? He was even capable of stopping another young lady on the bridge and asking about her health—something he had not done these last two weeks. Once or twice I had seen him with Mrs. Falkenberg; she looked young and chic and happy, even a trifle wild—she laughed aloud. That's what it means, I thought, to be a newly compromised woman; but tomorrow or the day after it may be different. The next time I saw her I was irked by the frivolity that I found both in her clothes and in her nature; she had lost some of her former appeal, her sweetness. What had become of the tenderness in her gaze? Now there was only boldness. I said to myself in a fury: That's what her eyes are like—the two flickering lights at the entrance to a cabaret show.

But then it seemed as if they had started to weary of each other's company, since the engineer increasingly went about on his own, leaving Mrs. Falkenberg to sit at her window in the hotel, gazing out. This, perhaps, was why fat Captain Brother now reappeared on the scene; his high spirits and capacity for enjoyment were to infect others than himself. And the monstrously misshapen companion of mirth certainly did his best. One whole night through the little town rang with his roguish laughter; then his leave ran out and he had to rejoin his regiment. The engineer and Mrs. Falkenberg were left on their own once more.

One day, while standing in a shop, I heard that Engineer Lassen had had some slight disagreement with his cousin. Or so a traveling salesman reported to the storekeeper. But such was the respect in which the wealthy engineer was held in our town that

the storekeeper would scarcely believe his ears. With an incred-
ulous air he said to the tattletale, "It must have been a joke between them. Did you hear them yourself? When was it?"

And now the salesman did not dare to make too much of his
tale.

"My room's right next to the engineer's," he said, "so I
couldn't help hearing what went on last night. No doubt about
it: they were arguing. Mind you, I'm not saying it was anything
very much; quite the opposite, the merest bagatelle. All she
said was that he was different from before, he'd changed, and he
answered by saying he didn't dare do as he'd like, not in this
town. Then she asked him to dismiss some man she'd taken
against, one of the log drivers, I guess. And he said he would."

"Well, that's nothing at all," said the storekeeper.

But the traveling salesman looked as if he had certainly heard
more than he chose to come out with now.

And had I not noticed myself how the engineer had changed?
The man who had spoken so loudly and happily that first day at
the station was now given to stubborn silences on the rare oc-
casions when he walked with Madame on the bridge; I saw
them both, just standing there, staring in different directions.
God in heaven, love is a volatile substance!

At first all was well. Doubtless she said something like,
"How lovely it is to be here; the river is so big, and the torrent
so swift, and its roar so strange; and here is a little town with
streets and people, and here are you!" And he answered, "Yes,
and here are you!" And each was peerless in the other's eyes.
But soon they were sated with pleasure, they drove it too hard,
they fashioned love to an article measured by the ell, such fools
they were. The conviction grew on him that things had taken a
wrong turning; the town was so small, his cousin a stranger
there; he could not go on being her constant cavalier, they must
tear themselves away from each other a little, must perhaps occasionally—just once in a while, you understand!—eat at different times at the hotel's board. Otherwise those traveling

salesmen would start putting two and two together about this pair of cousins. For remember, it's a small town! And she—how incapable she was of understanding this! Surely the town was no smaller now than at first? No, my darling, it is you who have changed!

We now had abundant rain, and the work went at a rattling pace. Yet the engineer had started taking little trips up and down the river. It seemed as if he wanted, above all, to get away from home. His face, too, was deeply careworn these days.

One day he asked me to go up to Grindhusen and fetch him down to the office. Was it Grindhusen, perhaps, who was about to be dismissed? But Madame had never even set eyes on Grindhusen since she arrived; what could he have done to her?

I fetched Grindhusen to the town, where he reported at once to the engineer. The latter put on his hat and coat, and off they went together; they set out up the river and were soon out of sight.

Later that day Grindhusen came to my boardinghouse, clearly eager to talk; but I asked him no questions. In the evening he got some brandy from the log drivers and began to open up. What kind of cousin was this that the Inspector of Log Driving had got hold of? Wasn't she due to be on her way again shortly? No one knew the answer to that—why should she be on her way again? "It's nothing but everlasting monkey business and ruination with these cousins," Grindhusen declared. "He'd do much better to find himself a girl he could marry—and what's more, I told him so." "Go on, you didn't!" someone else said. "I did, you know," said Grindhusen, pleased as Punch with himself; "there I was, sitting talking to the inspector just like he was one of you. Why do you suppose he sent for me? You'll never guess, not if you sit there till the cows come home. He sent for me, let me tell you, so he could conversate with me. Just so as he could conversate with me. Not but what he hasn't done so before, only it's this time I'm referring to." "What did he talk to you about?" someone asked. Grindhusen puffed and preened. "Now, look here, I'm not so dumb that I don't know how to talk to a man. And I'm not what you'd call a contradictious type either, as far as I'm aware. 'Grindhusen,' the inspector says to me; 'you know a thing or two, you do,' he says; 'here's two kroner for you.' Those were his very words. And if you don't believe me, you can see the two-krone piece. There it is!" "Yes, but what did you *talk* about?" shouted several voices at once. "I don't think he ought to tell us," I said.

It occurred to me that the inspector must have been in a state of torture and despair when he sent me to fetch Grindhusen. He was so little versed in the world that the moment anything went wrong he felt the need of someone to confide in. At present he was going around day after day feeling sorry for himself, with a long face as if to let the world know of the sorrow that God had laid on him in interrupting his fun and games. This sportsman with the protruding bottom was a mere travesty of young manhood, a sniveling Spartan. What sort of upbringing had he had?

Ah, but had the engineer been old, I would have found excuses for him in plenty; maybe I only hated him for being young. Who could say? All the same, he struck me as a travesty.

When I had said my little say, Grindhusen stared at me, and all the others stared at me.

"Well, perhaps I shouldn't really tell you," said Grindhusen, vacillating.

But the log drivers protested, "Why shouldn't he tell us? We'd never dream of spreading it any further."

"Certainly not," said another. "But maybe *you're* one of those who go in for mailing poison-pen letters to the inspector."

Whereupon Grindhusen too plucked up courage and said, "I'll say what I like, don't you worry! I'll tell you just as much as I choose. Yes. Because I'm not saying anything but what's the honest truth. And if you really want to know, the inspector will be coming any day now and giving *you* a small item of news. That's what he'll be doing, according to my information. So you don't need to bother yourself. And with regard to anything I choose to tell you about this, that, or the other, I'm telling you no more than what's the honest truth. So put that in your pipe. Yes. And if you knew what I know, you'd know that she's nothing but an aggravation and a scandal to the inspector, and he can't go out in the town because of her. Cousin indeed!"

"All right, all right," said the log drivers, trying to calm him.

"Why do you suppose he sent for me? Yes, there sits the guy who brought the message! But he'll be getting a message himself one of these days, if I understand the inspector correctly. I say no more. And with regard to anything I choose to tell you, why, he's been like a father to me, and I'd need to have a heart of stone to say any different. He says to me, 'I'm so depressed and miserable all day—do you know a cure for that, Grindhusen?' 'No,' I says, 'but the inspector himself knows one,' I says. Those were my very words. 'I don't know about that,' he says, 'but it's these wretched females,' he says. 'Ah,' I says, 'if it's females, they're a regular pain in the neck.' 'You're dead right there,' he says. 'But,' I says, 'it strikes me the inspector can take them and do his bit with them, and then give them a couple of good hard raps over the tailbone,' I says. 'By God, I believe you're right there too, Grindhusen,' says the inspector, cheering up no end. I've never seen anyone cheer up so quickly and get right back on top again, just for a word or two. It was quite something to see, I can tell you. Stone me if it isn't gospel truth, every syllable I've told you. I sat there just like I'm sitting here now, see, and the inspector, he sat like it might be *there* . . ."

Grindhusen maundered on and on.

Next morning, before it was properly light, I was stopped in the street by Engineer Lassen. It was only half past three.

I stood there with my boat hook and rations, fully armed for a march upriver. Grindhusen had embarked on a drinking bout in town, and my plan was to cover his district as well, then continue right to the watershed. For this reason I had double rations in my knapsack.

The engineer, it was obvious, had come from a party: he was laughing and talking loudly with two other men—all of them the worse for drink.

"Go on ahead!" he told the others. Then he turned to me and asked, "Where are you off to?"

I explained my plans to him.

"Hm, I'm not so sure about that," he said. "No, it's not worth it—surely Grindhusen can manage. Besides, I'm about to make a tour of inspection myself. What do you mean by planning a trip like this without saying a word to me about it?"

He was right enough; and I apologized. Indeed, I ought to have had more sense—knowing how much he liked being the boss and ordering us about.

But my apology had merely given him the taste of blood. His righteous anger boiled over, and he said, "I won't have this kind of thing. My workers are here to do as I tell them, period. I took you on because I wanted to help you, not because I needed you—and anyway, I don't need you any longer."

I just stood there, staring at him.

"You can come to my office later today and collect your wages," he added, turning as if to go.

So I was the one to be dismissed! Now I understood Grindhusen's veiled allusions. Mrs. Falkenberg must have found she couldn't stand the sight of me here, reminding her of home, and had arranged for me to be sent packing. But surely I, and I alone, had shown a sense of delicacy toward her at the station, turning away instead of recognizing her. And had I ever once paid her any mark of attention on meeting her in the street? Didn't one display of delicacy deserve another?

And now here was this young engineer dismissing me with exaggerated anger. How well I fancied I understood him! For

days he had been shrinking from this task; finally he had managed it, after a whole night spent in drinking his way to
courage. Was I doing him an injustice? Perhaps; and I fought
against my own reasoning. I reminded myself again that he was
young, while I was old and probably eaten up with envy on that
account. So I refrained from sarcasm and simply said in reply,
"Ah well, in that case I'd better empty my knapsack again."

But the engineer evidently wanted to strike again while the
iron was still hot, and reminded me about the incident of the
trunk.

"And when I get a flat no after giving an order," he said, "I
don't find it funny at all. I'm not used to that. And since I can't
be certain it won't happen again, it's best if you go."

"Yes, all right," I said.

At the window of the hotel I glimpsed a figure in white, and
guessed it was Mrs. Falkenberg who stood there watching us. So
I made no more ado.

But then the engineer seemed suddenly to remember that he
couldn't quite get rid of me here and now: he still had to pay
me, we were bound to meet once more. So he changed his tone
and said, "Well—come sometime during the day and collect
your wages. Have you thought about what you should have?"

"No. That's for the engineer to decide."

"Well, well," he said, mollified. "All in all, you've been a
good man to have around, I can't deny it. But various circum-
stances—besides, it's not just my idea, you know how these
females—I mean ladies . . ."

Yes, indeed—he was young all right. And denied himself
nothing.

"Well—good day!"—and with an abrupt nod he was gone.

But the day proved too short for me: I wandered into the forest,
and stayed there so long on my own that I never got to the office for my wages. Not that there was any hurry; I had plenty of
time.

What should I do now?

I had no great affection for our little town; but I had begun to find it more interesting and could have wished to remain there yet awhile. Certain complications were arising between two people whose fortunes I had followed closely for some weeks; at any moment now some further development might occur—who could tell? To avoid leaving town, I toyed with the idea of becoming a blacksmith's apprentice; but for one thing the work would have tied me to the smithy all day and generally restricted my movements, while, for another, the apprenticeship would have taken too many years of my life. And years were the very article I was now so short of.

So I let the days go by, one after another; they were warm and sunny days once more. I lived in the same lodgings, mended my clothes, and had some new ones made at a store. One of the servants at the boardinghouse came one evening and offered to do my mending; but I was in a joking mood, and showed her instead how well I could fend for myself: look at this patch, and look at that one! After a while a man came up the stairs and began rattling my door and saying, "Open up there!" "It's Henrik, one of the log men," said the girl. "Is he your sweetheart?" I asked. "Lord, no!" she answered; "I'd sooner go without than have someone like him." "Open up, I tell you!" shouted the man in the corridor. But the girl said boldly, "Let him go on standing there!" So we did—though at times my door buckled visibly under his more furious assaults.

When we had run out of jokes about my patches and her sweethearts, I had to reconnoiter the corridor before the girl would venture out. But the man had gone.

It was now late in the evening. I went down to the parlor, where Grindhusen was drinking with some of the log drivers. "That's him!" called out one of them—Henrik, no doubt—as I entered. He at once started egging on his mates; and even Grindhusen ganged up with the others in trying to bait me.

Poor Grindhusen! He went around nowadays with a permanent hangover, which he couldn't shake off. He had had yet
another conference with Engineer Lassen; they had wandered
away upstream as before and sat talking for an hour; on his return Grindhusen produced another two-krone piece he'd been
given. And again he had got drunk and blustered away about
being the engineer's confidant. Tonight, too, he was as high
and mighty as a polar explorer who has wintered in the Arctic;
he wouldn't crawl, not even to the king.

"Come and sit down," he said to me.

I sat down.

But one or two of the log drivers objected to my company,
and as soon as Grindhusen became aware of this, he swung right
around and set about teasing me and committing further in-
discretions about the engineer and his cousin.

"Well, have you been fired?" he asked, with a wink at the
others as if to command their attention.

"Yes," I said.

"Really? Well, I knew that weeks ago, but I never said a
word. I don't mind saying that I knew before anyone in the
whole world of us here, but did I utter a single squeak? The
inspector, he says, 'I want your advice, Grindhusen,' he says;
'it's about whether you'd fancy being down here in the town for
a while instead of the other man who I'm going to fire,' he says.
'As far as that's concerned,' I says, 'it all depends on what the
inspector commands.' Those were my very words, down to the
last syllable. But did I utter a single squeak?"

"*Have* you been fired?" one of the log drivers asked.

"Yes," I said.

"As for that cousin," Grindhusen continued, "the inspector
asked me about her, too. Wants my advice about every blessed
thing, he does. And this last time we were upriver together, he
sort of slapped his knee at the thought of her. Yes. Well, you
can go on guessing till the cows come home. Posh food and

drink she has to have, and posh everything—it's costing a fortune every week; and still she doesn't go. Shit! That's what I
say—I don't believe in mincing words."

But now my dismissal seemed to be working in my favor;
some of the men may have felt sorry for me, while others, no
doubt, were glad I'd been sent packing. One offered me some of
his brandy, and called to the maid for a glass—and mind it's
properly clean! Even Henrik forgot his grudge and clinked
glasses with me. And we sat for a long while idling away the
time.

"Only don't forget to go for your money," Grindhusen advised me. "Because the inspector's got no intention of bringing
it to you, according to my information. 'There's some money for
him sitting in my office,' says the inspector; 'but perhaps he ex-
pects me to come and hand it to him on a platter,' he says."

VIII

In the event, the engineer was not so far from handing me
the money on a platter. However, it was an unsought victory
and a meaningless one.

The engineer called on me at my lodgings and said, "Would
you come with me, please, and collect your money? There's a
letter for you, too; it came in the post."

We went up to the engineer's office—and there was Mrs.
Falkenberg. I was greatly surprised, but bowed and remained
standing near the door.

"Do sit down, please," said the engineer. He went to his
desk and found my letter. "Here you are. No, do please sit and
read it here; I'll just be working out your pay in the meanwhile."

And even Mrs. Falkenberg motioned me to a chair.

Why did they both look so tense? Why all this sudden politeness and "please" every other word? The explanation was not long in coming: the letter was from Captain Falkenberg.

"Do you want to borrow this?" asked Madame, handing me a paper knife.

A short, friendly letter, and nothing more; the opening even mildly jocular:

I had left Øvrebø before he knew I was going; what was more, I had left without my pay. If I had got the impression that he was in difficulties and unable to pay me until harvest time and that was the reason for my sudden departure, then he hoped I would realize I had been mistaken. And now he wished very much that I would come back as soon as possible unless I was committed elsewhere. He wanted to have all the various buildings painted, then there would be the harvest, and finally he would value my help in felling timber. "It all looks lovely here now—crops growing tall and grass growing fat! Please let me have an answer to this letter as soon as possible. Kind regards, Captain Falkenberg."

The engineer finished his calculations, turned sideways in his chair, and gazed at the wall; then, as if he had hit on something, he turned quickly back to the desk again. Pure nervousness. Madame stood looking at her rings; but I sensed that she had been observing me on the sly throughout. How frightened they both were!

Then the engineer said, "Oh, by the way, I see your letter's from Captain Falkenberg. How are things with him? I know his handwriting, of course."

"Would you like to read it?" I said at once, offering it to him. What harm could there be?

"No. No, thank you, I didn't mean that. It was just . . ."

All the same, he took the letter. And Madame went up to him and looked over his shoulder as he read.

"Uh-huh," said the engineer, nodding. "Yes, everything seems to be all right. Thanks." And he held out the letter to give it back.

But Madame chose to interpret his movement another way; she seized the letter and began perusing it for herself. The paper shook slightly in her hand.

"Now, how about settling up?" said the engineer. "Here you are—your money. I don't know whether you feel that's enough?"

"Yes, thank you," I answered.

The engineer seemed relieved to find that Captain Falkenberg's letter concerned me and no one else. He made another attempt to play down my dismissal, saying, "Well, well. If you ever come this way again, you know where you can find me. The log driving's finished for this year in any case—the weather's been so dry lately."

Madame stood there, reading. Then she was reading no longer—her eyes never moved—but merely staring at the letter, lost in thought. What was she thinking about?

The engineer glanced at her impatiently and said with a half smile, "My dear, you surely don't need to learn that letter by heart! Can't you see the man's waiting for it?"

"I'm sorry," said Madame; and she handed me the letter with a quick, embarrassed movement. "I was forgetting myself."

"Evidently," said the engineer.

I bowed and left.

On summer evenings the bridge was thick with promenaders: teachers and merchants, teenage girls and children. I would wait until the evening was far advanced and the bridge deserted; then I too would stroll out there and station myself in the midst of the roar for an hour or so. Why do anything but listen? However, my brain was so well rested, with all my idleness and good sound sleep, that it found innumerable things to busy itself with. The evening before, I had decided in all seriousness to go to Mrs. Falkenberg and say, "Take the first train, Madame, and go!" Today I had laughed at myself over this idiotic idea and exchanged it for another: Take the first train yourself, my dear sir, and go! Are you her peer and counselor? No, indeed; and what one does must not be hopelessly at odds with what one is!

That evening I continued to treat myself according to my deserts. I started to hum, but could scarcely hear my own humming; it was roared to death by the torrent. "You should always stand over a torrent when you want to hum," I told myself in cutting tones; then I laughed at myself. Such were the childish fancies with which I frittered away the time.

An inland torrent does to the ear what ocean breakers do. But a breaker surges forward, now strongly, now feebly, whereas the roar of a torrent is like an audible fog, absurd in its monotonousness, totally lacking in reason, a miracle of idiocy. What's the time? No, not at all! Is it day or night? Yes! Like laying a stone across twelve keys of an organ, then going away.

Such were the childish fancies with which I frittered away the time.

"Good evening!" said Mrs. Falkenberg at my elbow.

I wasn't greatly surprised; I suppose I had been expecting her. After her performance with her husband's letter, she might well proceed further.

There seemed to be two ways of viewing Madame's appearance: either she had turned sweet and sentimental at being so directly reminded of her home, or she wanted to make the engineer jealous; he might at that very moment be watching us from his window—and I had been summoned back to Øvrebø. For that matter, it was on the books that yesterday too she had been practicing her wiles, trying to make the engineer jealous by studying the Captain's letter so intently.

But neither of my flashes of insight, it seemed, was going to be confirmed. It was on my account that she had come—merely to apologize, after a fashion, for getting me dismissed. A bagatelle like that should have left her completely indifferent! Was she so utterly frivolous as not to appreciate the dismal nature of her own present position? Why the hell should she concern herself over mine?

I thought of saying a few terse words and pointing toward the train; instead, I found myself being gentle with her, as with someone not fully responsible, a child.

"So now I suppose you're off to Øvrebø?" she said. "If so, I'd like to . . . Hm. It's a bad business for you, I dare say, having to leave—yes? No? No, no. But there's something you don't know: it was I who got you dismissed."

"It doesn't matter."

"No, no. But just to let you know. And now that you're going back to Øvrebø, I suppose, I wanted to tell you. You can understand it was a bit embarrassing for me to . . ."

She broke off.

"To have me around. Yes, it would be embarrassing."

"To keep seeing you. I mean, just a bit embarrassing. Because, of course, you knew where I came from. So I asked the engineer if he couldn't fire you. Not that he wanted to, of course—but in the end he did. I'm glad you're going to Øvrebø."

I said, "Really? But when Madame comes home again, won't it be just as embarrassing to see me there?"

"Home?" she said. "I'm not going there."

Pause. She had knitted her brows as she spoke. But then she nodded, even smiled a little, and started to go.

"Well, you'll forgive me, then," she said.

"Do you mind at all my going back to the Captain?" I asked.

She stopped and looked me full in the face. How to read her mind correctly? Three times she had mentioned Øvrebø; was she figuring that I might let slip a good word for her when I got there? Or was she afraid of being indebted to me for the favor of my *not* going?

"No, no, *I* don't mind," she answered. "Go, by all means." Then she walked away.

She had been neither sentimental nor calculating, as far as I could see. Or again, she might well have been both. And what had I to show for my attempt to gain her confidence? I ought to have known better than to try. Whether she was here or elsewhere was no business of mine. Her pigeon!

I said to myself: You're all agog, aren't you? You kid yourself that she's merely literature to you—yet that wizened soul of yours puts out fresh shoots the moment she is friendly toward you and starts looking at you with those eyes of hers. You fill me with shame and grief, and tomorrow you're going!

Only I didn't go.

But it was true that I was all agog, all ears, for news of Mrs. Falkenberg; and equally true that many a night I took myself to task on this account, and tortured myself with self-contempt. From early morn till night I thought of her: Is she up? Has she slept well? Is she going back home today? And at the same time my head was full of schemes: I might get work for a while at the hotel where she was staying. Or I could write home for some clothes, turn gentleman myself, and stay at that same hotel. This last idea would at once have cut the ground from under my feet, and left me further removed from her than ever; yet it was one that I particularly favored—I had no more sense than that. I had been cultivating the friendship of the under-porter at the hotel, purely and simply because he lived nearer to her than I did. He was a big, strong fellow who used to meet the trains; and once every two weeks he would collect a salesman coming to display his wares in the hotel room dedicated to this purpose. He never had any news for me; I neither questioned him directly nor tried to manipulate him into saying something of his own accord; besides, he was not strong in the head. But he lived under the same roof as Madame—ah, that he did! And one day this acquaintanceship of ours led to my learning a great and good piece of news about Mrs. Falkenberg—and from her own lips.

So not all days in that little town were equally unpleasant.

One day I accompanied the underporter back from the station, where he had met the morning train and collected a salesman of some substance—the horse and cart were needed for his heavy gray trunks.

I had helped him with some lifting at the station; now, back at the hotel, he looked at me and said, "You could do me a favor helping get these trunks in—and I'll buy you a beer this evening."

So we carried the trunks in together; they were needed at once in the display room on the second floor, where the salesman was waiting for them. It was no problem for two big, strong fellows like us.

When there was only one trunk left in the cart, the underporter was detained for a moment in the display room by the traveler's giving him some errand or other to run. Meanwhile, I stood waiting for him in the corridor; I was a stranger here and didn't care to slink off down the stairs on my own.

At that moment Engineer Lassen's office door opened, and he and Mrs. Falkenberg came out. They looked as if they had only just got up; they were bareheaded, and doubtless on their way to the breakfast table. Whether they failed to see me standing there, or whether perhaps they took me for the underporter, they continued their conversation. He was saying, "Quite so. And it's not going to change. I simply don't understand why you should feel so lonely."

"You understand very well," she retorted.

"I do not. And I think you should make an effort to be more cheerful."

"You think nothing of the kind. You prefer me to stay like this—heartbroken because you don't want me any more."

"Are you crazy?" he asked, stopping at the head of the stairs.

"Yes, I think I must be," she answered.

Which was a fairly feeble thing to say; but then she always got the worst of a quarrel. Why could she not exert herself to find some wounding, deadly reply?

He ran his hand along the banister and said, "So you think I enjoy this state of affairs? I can't tell you the torture it is. And it's been torture to me for a long time."

"And for me too. But now I'm going to put an end to it."

"Really. You've said that before—you said it last week, in fact."

"Yes, but this time I'm leaving."

He looked up. "You're leaving?"

"Yes, very soon."

But then he must have wanted to gloss over the eagerness, the positive joy, with which he had jumped at her words. He said, "Nonsense, you're going to be a nice, cheerful cousin, and then you won't have to leave."

"No, this time I'm leaving," she said, passing him and going down the stairs.

He followed.

Then the underporter came out and we went down together. The last trunk was smaller than the others, and I asked him to carry it up on his own, pretending I had hurt my hand. I helped him lift the trunk onto his back and went home. Now I could leave in the morning.

Late that afternoon Grindhusen, too, was dismissed. The engineer had sent for him and given him a dressing down for doing no work, but loafing around the town, getting drunk; now he didn't need him any longer.

I reflected on the astonishing speed with which the engineer had gained new courage. He was so young, he had needed this man to comfort him and say yea to his every word; but now that a certain tiresome cousin would soon be on her way, he no longer needed comfort. Or was my aged soul doing him an injustice?

Grindhusen was deeply dejected. He had counted on remaining in this town the whole summer, as the inspector's odd-job man; now that hope had collapsed in ruins. No, the Inspector of Log Driving was no longer like a father to him; and Grindhusen took his disappointment very hard. In paying him off the inspector had wanted to deduct the two-krone pieces which he had given Grindhusen at different times, maintaining that they had only been meant as an advance. Grindhusen sat in the parlor telling us all about this, and adding that the inspector paid meanly enough in any case. At this someone laughed and said, "But did he do like he'd threatened? He didn't, did he?"

"No," answered Grindhusen, "he didn't dare knock off more than the one."

There was general laughter at this, and some wag asked, "Was it the first or the second two-kroner he knocked off? Ha-ha-ha-ha, that's the funniest thing I've ever heard!"

But Grindhusen didn't laugh; he only fretted more and more. What should he do now? All the seasonal jobs had gone by this time, and here he was. He asked me where I was going and, when I told him, begged me to put in a word for him with Captain Falkenberg about his working there for the summer. Meanwhile, he would stay on in the town and wait till he heard from me.

But what would become of Grindhusen's money if he stayed on in the town? It seemed best to take him along with me; and this I did. Among other things, he had once been a demon for painting, had my mate Grindhusen; had I not watched him paint old Gunhild's cottage on the island? Now he could give me a hand. And later, no doubt, a solution would be found; there must be all kinds of seasonal work on the Captain's estate to keep him going throughout the summer.

The sixteenth of July saw me at Øvrebø once more. I remember dates better and better, partly because I am older, so that the interest which the senile take in dates has been sharpened, partly because as a worker I have to keep track of my working days. But while the old man remembers his dates, he cheerfully forgets more important things. Until now I have forgotten to mention that my letter from Captain Falkenberg had been addressed to me care of Engineer Lassen. Well, it had. And this had immediately struck me as significant: it meant that the Captain was aware of whom I was working for. And I thought to myself at the time, Perhaps the Captain knows who else has been care of Engineer Lassen this summer!

The Captain was still away with his regiment and was not expected home for another week; but Grindhusen got a good reception nonetheless. Nils was delighted that I had brought my mate with me; but, instead of handing him over to me to help with the painting, he sent him on his own responsibility to work in the potato and turnip fields, where there was any amount of weeding and thinning out to be done. Nils himself was well on with the haying.

He was the same blissfully dedicated farmer as ever. At the first break, while the horses were feeding, he took me out and showed me the cornfields and the meadows. Everything was fine; but spring had been late that year, so the timothy was only just beginning to form spikes and the clover to flower. During the recent rain, part of the first year's crop had been flattened too badly to rise again, so Nils had set to work on it with the reaper.

We returned home through billowing grass and corn; there was a rustling in the winter rye and the fat six-rowed barley, reminding Nils of a lovely line of Bjørnson's he had learned at school: *Begynder som en susen i kornet sommerdag*—"Beginning like a whisper in the corn one summer day."

"No—it's time I was taking the horses out again," said Nils, lengthening his stride. Then, with a final sweeping gesture toward the fields, he added, "What a harvest we shall have if only we can get it safely in!"

So Grindhusen went to work in the fields, while I started on the painting. I began with the barn, and everything that was to be red; then I primed the flagpole and the summerhouse with oil. The house itself I wanted to save till the end. It was built in good, traditional manor-house style, with massive, richly ornamented eaves and a carved Grecian border over the main entrance. At present the house was yellow, and a fresh supply of yellow paint had arrived; but I took it upon myself to send this paint back and get it exchanged. In my view the house should be stone-gray, with doors and windows and gableboards picked out in white. But the Captain would have to decide.

Though everyone in the place was as nice as could be, the cook mild in her authority and Ragnhild as bright-eyed as ever, we all missed the master and mistress. Only the worthy Grindhusen missed no one and nothing. With regular work and good food he grew fat and contented within a matter of days. His only worry was that the Captain would dismiss him when he arrived.

But no: Grindhusen was allowed to stay.

IX

The Captain arrived.

I was giving the barn its second coat of paint; on hearing his voice I descended the ladder. He bade me welcome back.

"Leaving without your money, you!" he said. And I thought he had a suspicious look in his eye as he asked, "Why?"

I answered, briefly and coldly, that I had had no intention of doing the Captain a kindness. My money could wait for me here.

At this he brightened and said, "But of course. Well, I'm very glad you've come. So you think the flagpole should be white?"

Not daring to reveal at once the full extent of what I proposed should be white, I answered only, "Yes. And I've laid in some white paint."

"Have you? Good. You have a companion with you, I hear."

"Yes. But that's for the Captain to decide."

"He can stay. In fact, Nils has already set him to work in the fields. You all do just as you like with me, in any case," he added as a joke. "You've been on the log driving since I saw you last?"

"Yes."

"Hardly the thing for you, was it?" But then, as if afraid of appearing to cross-examine me about my work with the engineer, he changed the subject completely and said, "When are you starting on the house itself?"

"This afternoon, I thought. I need to do some scraping here and there first."

"Fine. While you're at it, put in a nail any place where the board siding's loose. Have you been out in the fie.ds?"

"Yes."

"They look good. You chaps did a fine job in the spring. Now we could do with some rain for the upper fields."

"Grindhusen and I came past lots of places in worse need of rain than the Captain's land. Here we're on clay, even high up on the hills."

"True enough. How did you know that, by the way?"

"I looked around a bit when I was here in the spring," I answered. "And I did a bit of digging here and there. I was thinking that sooner or later the Captain would want to have a water pipe down to the house, so I was looking for water."

"A water pipe? Why, yes, I thought of it at one time, but . . . Yes, in fact I looked into it a few years ago. But I wasn't able to do it all at one go, and then something or other got in the way. And the money I get from this harvest is needed for other purposes."

A wrinkle appeared for a moment between his eyes; he stood looking down, thinking.

"Still, with the thousand dozen battens I should manage and to spare," he said suddenly. "Water pipe? It would need to go to the house *and* the outbuildings—a regular network, eh?"

"But you'll have no rock to blast your way through."

"Really? Well, we'll have to see. By the way, did you like it in the town? It's not much of a town, but there's more people there, of course. And the odd visitor arriving by train."

Aha, I thought; he certainly knows who's been visiting Engineer Lassen this summer. I answered, truthfully, that I hadn't much cared for the town.

"No? I see."

And as if this had given him food for thought, he gazed into the distance, whistling softly to himself. Then he walked away.

He was in good spirits, and more communicative than I had known him; he nodded to me as he went off. I recognized him from of old: brisk and decided, full of interest in his affairs once more, and sober as a judge. The sight of him put new heart in me as well. Here was no defeated man: for a time he had kept open house for foolishness and debauch, but his own resolution would put an end to that. An oar in the water appears to be broken; but it is whole.

Then the rain set in, and I had to abandon my painting. Nils had been lucky enough to get in all the hay he had cut. Now we were all employed, men and women alike, in weeding the potatoes.

Meanwhile, the Captain stayed indoors, striking an occasional note on Madame's piano, from loneliness and boredom. Now and again he came out to us in the fields, with no umbrella either, letting himself get soaked. "Splendid weather for the soil, eh?" he would say; or, "Looks like being a bumper year." But when he went back home, it was back to himself and his loneliness. As Nils said, "We're better off than he is."

So we weeded the potatoes, and when we had finished with them too, the rain started easing off. Ideal weather, bumper year! Both Nils and I were as proud and contented as if we owned Øvrebø.

And now the haying began in earnest, with the girls out following the machine and spreading the cut hay, and Grindhusen scything wherever the ground was too rough for the machine to go. Meanwhile, I coated the house with stone-gray paint.

The Captain came and asked, "What kind of paint's that you're using?"

How should I answer? My solution was rather cowardly, but what I feared most was the Captain's forbidding me outright to paint the house gray. I said, "Oh, it's just some paint—I don't know—it's all the same what color we use for the under-coat . . ."

At least I gained a reprieve: the Captain said no more.

When I had coated the house gray, and the doors and gable-boards white, I went down to the summerhouse and painted that the same way. But the resulting color was hideous—the yellow paint showed through and made all the buildings look sallow. The flagpole I took down and painted white all over. Then I spent a few more days with Nils, helping him harvest the hay. We were now in August.

By the time I set to work on the house again, I had conceived the idea of starting so early one morning that I would be far advanced with the painting before the Captain was up—irrevocably far, so to speak. I started at three in the morning; there had been a fall of dew, and I had to rub the walls down with a sack. I worked until four, had some coffee, then on again till eight, which I knew was the Captain's hour for rising; then I went off and helped Nils for an hour. I had reached my target with the painting, and my idea was to give the Captain time to recover from my stone-gray paint, in case he should have got out of bed on the wrong side.

After breakfast I climbed the ladder again and continued painting, all industry and innocence. Up came the Captain.

"Are you putting on a second coat of gray?" he called up to me.

"Good morning! Ye-es. But I don't know—"

"Look, what the hell is going on? Come down off that ladder!"

I came down. But I had completely lost my timidity: I had thought of a sentence which might perhaps do the trick when the moment came. Or had my instinct led me wildly astray?

I began by trying to maintain that it made virtually no difference what color we used for this second coat either; but the Captain cut me short, "Nonsense! Put yellow on top of that gray of yours and the whole thing will be one filthy mess—can't you see that?"

"Then perhaps we could finish off with two coats of yellow?"

"Four coats? No! And look at all that zinc white you're squandering! It's far more expensive than the ocher."

He was right there, and this was an objection I had feared all along. The moment had come to speak out.

"You should let me paint the house gray, Captain."

"What!" he exclaimed.

"The house deserves it. And the background too, with the green of the woods behind. Oh, I don't know, but the house has a style—"

"The gray style, perhaps?"

He took a few impatient strides away, then back again.

At this I became more innocent than ever: a thought came to me—it could only have come from above—and I said, *"Now* I remember! I must have seen the house manor-house gray in my mind's eye ever since—it was your wife I got it from."

I was observing him, and saw a spasm run through him. He gazed at me for a second with wide-open eyes; then he took out his handkerchief and wiped one eye as if to remove a speck of dirt.

"Really?" he said. "She said that?"

"Yes, I seem to remember it quite clearly. It was a long time ago, but—"

"It's a load of nonsense," he said, and strode away. I heard him once, over in the yard, clearing his throat noisily.

I lounged about for a while, feeling good for very little. Not daring to continue painting and thereby increase the Captain's displeasure, I spent an hour or so chopping and sawing in the woodshed. Finally I ventured back to my ladder. As I did so, the Captain stuck his head out of an upstairs window and called down, "You may just as well carry on, now that you've got so far. But I've never seen anything like it."

Then he slammed the window shut, although it had been open before.

And I painted.

A week went by; I alternated between painting and helping with the hay. Grindhusen was good enough at ridging potatoes and raking over the meadows; but his forkloads of hay were distinctly on the feeble side. As for Nils, he was a glutton for work.

One afternoon, as I was going over the house for the third time, and the elegant gray with white details was transforming the house into a residence of real style, the Captain came walking up from the road. He looked at me for a while, then took out his handkerchief as if the heat was bothering him and said, "Yes, having got so far you'd better continue. I must say, her taste wasn't bad when she said that. All the same, it's a load of nonsense. Hm!"

I made no answer.

The Captain continued, using his handkerchief the while:

"It's been hot today—pooh! What was I going to say? No, come to that, it's not bad, not bad at all. Looks as if she was right there—I mean, that's the right color you've got there. I was out in the fields just now, and I thought it looked really good. In any case, you've gone too far now."

"I agree with the Captain," I said. "It suits the house."

"Yes, it seems to suit the house. Did she say that about the woods too? My wife, I mean. Did she say that about the background?"

"It's so long ago, but I'm fairly certain—"

"Well, never mind. I must say, I'd never imagined it could be so—be just so. But aren't you going to run out of white paint?"

"Hm. No. I traded the yellow in."

At which the Captain smiled, shook his head, and walked away.

No, my instinct had not led me astray.

After that the hay took up all my time until it was finished; but in exchange Nils helped me in the evenings and spent an hour or so painting the summerhouse. Even Grindhusen joined in and wielded a brush. He was not *exactly* a painter, he said; but he figured he could be trusted to coat a wall. Grindhusen had altogether ceased being a dead weight.

And now at last the buildings all shone in their new glory, changed beyond recognition; when, for good measure, we had set to and tidied up a little in the lilac grove and the little park, Øvrebø was a different place. The Captain came and thanked each of us individually.

As we started harvesting the rye, the autumn rain started too; but we pushed ahead, cutting the rye and hanging it on stakes; and at intervals the sun came out again. There were acres of thick, fat rye, not to mention acres of barley and oats which were not yet ripe—a rich landscape to work in. The clover was starting to seed, but the turnips still had some way to go. They could do with a thorough good soaking, said Nils.

Several times the Captain employed me in fetching and carrying mail; and one day I carried a letter addressed to his wife. He handed me a bunch of letters, with the one to his wife in the middle, addressed care of her mother at Kristiansand. The first thing the Captain said when I brought back the mail that evening was, "You posted the letters all right?" I said I had.

Time passed. Then the Captain told me that, on wet days when we couldn't do much out of doors, he wanted me to do various bits of painting in the house. He showed me some enamel paints he had laid in and said, "Right: first of all, the staircase here. I want it painted white, and I've written off for a dark-red runner. Then there are various doors and windows. Only there's a certain amount of urgency over this work—I've neglected it far too long."

Beyond doubt, this was an excellent idea of the Captain's. For years he had been living it up, without a thought for how his home appeared. Now his eyes had been opened again; it was like an awakening. He showed me around, upstairs and downstairs, pointing out what needed to be done. In the course of this tour I saw pictures and busts, in the living room a big marble lion, and paintings by Askevold and Johan Christian Dahl. Heirlooms, they must have been. Madame's room upstairs still looked lived-in, with all manner of trifles laid out neatly in their places and clothes hanging on the hooks. The whole house was old and elegant, with molded ceilings, and costly wallpaper on some of the walls; but all the paintwork was yellowed or peeling. The staircase was broad and easy, with landings and a mahogany handrail.

While I was busy painting one day, the Captain came and said, "I know it's harvest time; but we need to push on with this painting too—my wife will soon be here. I'm not sure what we'd better do. It would be nice to have it all spick-and-span."

So that letter must have been summoning Madame back! But then I reflected that it was several days since he wrote, and that since then I had been going for the post, but there had been no answer from Madame, whose writing I remembered from six years ago. The Captain doubtless imagined that he only had to say come and she would come. Well, perhaps he was right; perhaps she was just getting ready. How was I to know?

Such was the urgency over the painting that the Captain went up to the cottage in person and asked Lars to take my place and lend a hand in the fields. Not that Nils was particularly pleased by this exchange: the worthy Lars Falkenberg had little appetite for obeying orders in the place where he had once been foreman.

But the urgency over the painting proved exaggerated. The

Captain sent the lad to the post a couple of times, but I watched his comings and goings, and he brought no letter from Madame. Perhaps she had not the slightest wish to come; perhaps things had reached that pass. Or she felt herself cheapened, and was too stiff and proud to answer yes when her husband called. Perhaps that was it.

But the paint was put on and had time to dry, and the red runner was fastened with brass stair rods, and the staircase looked singularly handsome, and likewise the windows and doors in the upstairs rooms looked singularly handsome; but Madame did not come. No.

We harvested the rye, and set to work in good time cutting the barley; but Madame did not come. The Captain would stand gazing down the road, whistling; he looked thin. Time and again, when he came out to us in the fields, he would accompany us for a long time, watching us without saying a word. But if Nils asked him a question, he never needed to call back his thoughts, as it were, from a great distance, but answered at once and to the point. He was not depressed, and if he looked thin it may have been because he had got Nils to cut his hair.

But now I was sent for the post once more, and this time there was a letter from Madame. It had a Kristiansand postmark. I hurried home with the letter, put it in among the rest of the mail, and gave the bundle to the Captain, out in the courtyard. "Thanks," he said, with no apparent interest; he had grown used to being disappointed. "Everyone got their grain in? What are the roads like?" he asked, as he glanced at letter after letter. While I was answering about the state of the roads and his neighbors' grain, he reached the letter from Madame; whereupon he snapped the bundle together and started questioning me even more closely about the state of the roads and his neighbors' grain. He had schooled himself, no doubt, not to display emotion. As he went in, he thanked me again and nodded.

Next day the Captain himself set to, washing and greasing

the landau. Another two days passed, however, before he needed to use it. One evening we were sitting over our supper when the Captain came into the kitchen and said he needed someone to drive him to the station in the morning. He could have driven himself, but he was fetching his wife, who had returned from a journey abroad, so he needed to take the landau in case it rained. Nils decided then and there that Grindhusen could best be spared as coachman to the Captain.

The rest of us went on with our work in the fields. There was plenty to do: apart from the rye and barley not yet under cover, there were potatoes waiting to be ridged and turnips to be weeded. At intervals, however, Ragnhild and the dairymaid gave stalwart help, setting to work like two young hurricanes.

It might have been fun to be working once again with my former mate Lars Falkenberg; but he and Nils hit it off so badly that the atmosphere in the fields was one of somber silence rather than cheerful good humor. Lars seemed to have got over some of his earlier resentment against me, but for the foreman's benefit he was short and surly with us all.

Finally Nils decided that Lars should take the pair of chestnuts and start on the autumn plowing. Lars took offense at this and flatly refused. It was the first time he had heard of anyone plowing in a field that hadn't yet been harvested! "Ah," said Nils, "but we'll find you at least a hundred acres that are harvested already."

More bickering. Everything had become so dreary and dismal at Øvrebø, Lars reckoned. In the old days he did his job and then sang songs to the master and mistress and their guests; now there was damn-all rhyme or reason in anything. "Autumn plowing, did you say? No, thank you very much!" "You don't understand these things," said Nils; "you don't realize that nowadays people plow in between the hay-drying racks or the corn poles, as the case may be." "No, I should just think I don't," said Lars, turning up the whites of his eyes; "understanding stuff like that's more in your line—you jackass, you!"

But it ended with Lars not quite daring to disobey the foreman, and agreeing to plow until the Captain returned.

It came back to me that when I went away I had left some washing with Emma. However, it seemed best to refrain from going up to the cottage to collect it, as long as Lars remained so bloody-minded.

X

The Captain and Madame came next day. Nils and I had debated whether to hoist the flag. I couldn't quite muster the courage; but Nils had fewer qualms and went ahead. It flapped proudly and handsomely from its white mast.

I was close at hand when the master and mistress descended from the landau. Madame walked some distance into the yard, gazed at the buildings, and clapped her hands. I heard her, also, uttering loud exclamations of wonder from inside the entrance—doubtless at the sight of the staircase, with its red runner.

Grindhusen had hardly stabled the horses before coming to me all agape and taking me aside for a few words. "There must be something wrong somewhere," he began; "that can't be Mrs. Falkenberg. Is it her the Captain's married to?"

"That's correct, Grindhusen, it's his wife the Captain's married to. Why do you ask?"

"But it's the cousin! Stone me if it isn't the very same person—the Inspector of Log Driving's cousin."

"Nonsense, Grindhusen! Her sister, perhaps."

"You can stone me. I saw her any number of times with the inspector."

"Well, all right, she could be his cousin, for that matter. What business is it of ours?"

"I saw it the moment she got off the train. And she looked at me too, and gave quite a start. She kept kind of gasping for a long while. Don't come and tell me—but what I can't make out—is she from here?"

"Did she seem happy or unhappy?"

"Can't say really—yes, I suppose so." Grindhusen shook his head, unable to grasp that this was the Captain's wife. "Surely you saw her yourself with the inspector—do you mean to say you don't recognize her?"

"Did you say she was happy?"

"Happy? Oh, I guess so. Can't say really. They talked a load of queer stuff in the carriage—no, they started talking queer at the station. There was a whole lot I couldn't make out at all. 'I'm not sure if I'm finding the right words,' she says, 'but I beg and implore you to forgive me for everything,' she says. 'And I ask the same of you,' he says. Would you believe it? And in the carriage I'll swear they were crying, both of them. 'I've had the whole place painted and done up a bit,' says the Captain. 'No, have you really?' she says. Then he talked about all her things, how they were still there and hadn't been touched; I don't know what he meant by 'things,' but that's what he said: 'I think I can safely say that they're all where you left them.' Would you believe it? 'Your things,' he said. And then he went on about someone called Elizabeth and said she was not in his thoughts and never had been—that's what it sounded like. Then the lady cried and cried and said she was sorry and carried on like she was beside herself. But she never said nothing about being abroad, like the Captain said. No, she's come from the inspector all right."

I began to fear I had been ill advised to bring Grindhusen to Øvrebø. It was done now; but I regretted my action. And I stood Grindhusen against a wall and told him so in no uncertain terms. "The mistress here has always been kindness itself to everyone, and the Captain likewise, just remember that. But you'll be out on your ass before the day's over if you go around spreading tittle-tattle. I suggest you think it over—you've got a good place here, with good wages and good food. Just remember that and keep your trap shut!"

"You're right, you know, dead right," said Grindhusen, vacillating. "I'm not denying that; I'm only saying she's the dead spit and image of that cousin. Have I ever said more than that? I don't know what's eating you. For that matter, her hair's probably a bit fairer than the cousin's was, I won't swear it's the same hair. And I never said it was. But if you want to know what I really thought from the word go, I don't mind telling you straight out that I thought she was too good to be that cousin. Those were my very thoughts. Because it was a crying shame for her to be the cousin of a fellow like that, and it beats me that anyone would want to. It's not the money I'm thinking of, mind, you know as well as I do that people like you and me don't worry about sending a two-krone piece down the drain, only it was mean giving it right into my hand and then knocking it off from my pay. Yes. I say no more. But I don't know what's been eating you lately, flying out at a man the moment he opens his mouth. What have I said, anyway? He was that tight-fisted, he only gave me two kroner a day—no board, mind—and he haggled over every blessed thing. Yes. I won't talk to you any more, but these were my very thoughts, if you really want to know . . ."

But for all his prattle Grindhusen was unable to gloss over the fact that he had recognized Madame and was still convinced that she was the person he thought.

And now everything was in order, the master and mistress home again, fair days and a fat harvest. What more could we ask for?

Madame greeted me kindly and said, "Do you know, I can hardly recognize Øvrebø since you painted it so beautifully all over. The Captain's delighted with it."

She seemed calmer than when I last saw her, on the hotel stairs in the town. She didn't kind of gasp on seeing me as she had on seeing Grindhusen—and that must mean she doesn't mind seeing me again, I thought joyfully. But why had she not yet given up that new habit of flickering her eyes? If I were the Captain, I would speak to her about it. In addition, a number of curious little pimples had appeared about her temples, though these made no difference to her looks.

"But I'm sorry to say it wasn't my idea, this beautiful gray for the walls," she continued. "Your memory's at fault there."

"Well, I can't make it out. But it makes no difference in any case—it was the Captain himself who decided on it."

"The staircase is quite exquisite; so are the rooms upstairs. They're twice as cheerful now . . ."

It was Madame herself who wished to be twice as cheerful and twice as good—that much was clear to me. For some reason or other, she felt she owed me these courtesies, and I thought: Good—but now that is enough, let it rest there!

Autumn was setting in: the scent from the jasmine in the grove was strong and importunate, while up on the wooded slopes the leaves had long since turned yellow and red. There was not a soul in the place but rejoiced at Madame's return. The flag, too, helped make it seem like a Sunday, with the girls in newly ironed aprons.

In the evening I went down the stone steps into the grove and sat there. After the heat of the day, waves of scent from the jasmine were wafted toward me. Then Nils came down, looking for me. He said, "No more guests here now—and no more racketing around either, that I've heard. Have you heard any racketing around at night since the Captain came back from maneuvers?"

"No."

"And that was a good ten weeks ago. What do you say to my cutting this off right now?" Nils asked, indicating his temperance badge. "The Captain's left off drinking, Madame's home again, and there's no need for me to go around being mean to either of them."

Whereupon he handed me his knife and I cut the badge away.

We talked for a while about the fields—he had fields on the brain. "Yes," he said, "by tomorrow evening, thank God, we'll have most of the grain in. After that we'll sow the winter rye. Isn't it strange, here's Lars been using the machine to sow with, year after year, and thinking that was good enough. No, no; we're going to sow by hand."

"But why?"

"On land like ours! You take a look at the next property over that way: he sowed by machine three weeks ago—some of it's come up, some of it hasn't. The machine loosens the soil too much."

"Mmm—just smell the jasmine this evening!"

"Yes. The barley and oats have come on a lot these last few days. Well, I guess it's time to go to bed."

Nils got up, but I remained seated. Nils surveyed the sky and prophesied a fine morning; then he talked a little about cutting some of the excellent second crop of hay which the meadow here had produced.

"Are you going on sitting there?" he asked suddenly.

"Yes, why? No, perhaps I'd better be going too."

Nils took a few steps, then returned and said, "You shouldn't sit here any longer. You ought to come with me."

"Should I?" I said, and rose at once; I realized that Nils had come here on purpose to fetch me, for some reason of his own. Could he have seen through me? But what was there to see through? Did even I know what I had gone to the grove for? I remember lying there on my stomach, chewing a straw. There was a light in a certain upstairs room in the main building; and this I was looking at. That was all.

"I don't want to be inquisitive, but what's up?" I asked.

"Nothing," Nils answered. "The girls said you were lying here, and so I came down. Why should anything be up?"

So the girls must have seen through me, I thought dejectedly. That'll be Ragnhild, the confounded girl—and she's so sharp, she's certainly said much more than Nils here wants to come out with. And what if Madame herself has seen me from her window?

I resolved to be indifferent and cold as ice for the rest of my days.

Ragnhild was in her element: the thick stair carpet muffled her footsteps—she could go up whenever she wanted and down again in a flash without a sound, if the need arose.

"I can't make Madame out," said Ragnhild. "Now she's come back, she ought to be happy and nice, but all she does is whine and cry. The Captain said to her today, 'Do be a bit reasonable, Louise,' he said. 'I'm sorry, I won't do it any more,' she said, and cried because she'd been unreasonable. But that bit about not doing it any more—she's said that every day now since she came home, and still she goes on doing it. Poor thing, she had such a bad toothache today, she was howling—"

"Look, go and lift some more potatoes, Ragnhild!" Nils broke in. "We haven't time to stand around talking today."

And so back to the fields again for one and all. Oh, how much there was to do! Nils was afraid of the corn spoiling on the poles, and preferred getting it in on the damp side. Fair enough. But that meant threshing the worst of it at once, and spreading the grain over every outbuilding floor in the place; even the floor of the great servants' hall had a layer of corn lying there to dry. Any more irons in the fire? Yes, any number more, and all white hot. The weather had turned nasty and might get worse, and none of the work would brook delay. After threshing we had the fresh straw to cut up and salt down in bins, or it might spoil. That the lot? Far from it, many irons still glowing. Grindhusen and the girls were taking up potatoes. Nils was using the precious time after a couple of dry days to sow some three acres of rye, while the lad did a good job harrowing in his wake; and Lars Falkenberg was still plowing. The good

Lars had knuckled under and become a mighty plowman since the Captain's return with Madame; when the cornfields were too wet, he plowed the meadows; then, after a few days' sun and wind, he plowed in the cornfields again.

All went smoothly and well. One afternoon the Captain himself came out in the field and lent a hand. We were bringing in the last of the corn.

Captain Falkenberg was no mean worker: big and strong, with a capable pair of hands. He was loading up oats from the drying frames, and was on his second load.

At this point Madame came walking along the road; then she cut across to the drying frames, where we were working. Her eyes were bright, and she seemed to enjoy the sight of her husband loading up corn.

"Bless the work!" she said.

"Thank you," said her husband.

"We used to say that up north," she continued.

"What?"

"We used to say that up north."

"I see."

The Captain went on working, and the crackling of the stubble meant that he did not always hear what she said and had to ask her to repeat herself. This irritated them both.

"Are the oats ripe?" she asked.

"Yes, thank God."

"But they're not dry, are they?"

"I can't hear you!"

"Oh, nothing."

A long, sullen silence. From time to time the Captain tried to put in a cheerful word, but met with no response.

"So you're making a tour of inspection, eh?" he said, attempting humor. "Have you been over to the potato field?"

"No. But I'll gladly go there if you can't bear the sight of me here."

It was so unpleasant that I may well have expressed distaste with my eyebrows. Moreover, I suddenly remembered that I had a particular reason for being as cold as ice, and this made me wrinkle my brows still more.

Madame looked straight at me and said, "Why are you pulling a face?"

"What—pulling faces, are you?" said the Captain, with a forced laugh.

Madame rounded on him. "You heard *that* all right!"

"Come, come, Louise," said the Captain.

The tears welled up into her eyes. For a moment she stood there; then, leaning forward from the waist, she ran behind the drying frames and burst into sobs.

The Captain followed her.

"What is it, Louise, can you tell me?"

"Oh, it's nothing. Do go away!"

I could hear her vomiting now behind the frames, and wailing, "Oh, God help me!"

"My wife isn't at all well at present," the Captain remarked to me. "We're all puzzled by what it is."

"There's supposed to be a bug going around," I said, by way of saying something. "A kind of autumn flu; I heard it at the post office."

"Really? Do you hear that, Louise?" he called. "There's a bug going around—it must be that you've got."

Madame didn't answer.

We continued loading up from the frames, while Madame moved farther and farther along as we approached her. Finally she lost her last shred of cover and stood there as if caught in some act. She was very pale after her nausea.

"Shall I see you home?" asked the Captain.

"No, thanks. Quite unnecessary," she answered, starting to go.

And the Captain stayed with us until evening, loading up the corn.

But now everything was in chaos again. How difficult life was for the Captain and his wife!

And, of course, it was not a thing that could be put right with a little goodwill on each side, as sensible people say; it was something insurmountable, a disharmony at the deepest level of their beings. It had culminated with one of the marriage partners in a state of mutiny: Madame now locked her door at night. Ragnhild had heard the Captain speaking in injured tones through the wall.

But that evening the Captain had demanded and obtained an audience with his wife in her room, before she went to bed, and there had been a new fracas. Each, no doubt, desperately wanted to put things right. But this was beyond their powers; they had left it till too late. Nils and I sat in the kitchen listening to Ragnhild; I had never seen Nils so despondent.

"If things go wrong again now," he said, "it's the end. I kept wondering, in the summer, if perhaps what she needed was a good thrashing; now I can see that would have been madness. Did she say she was leaving him again?"

"She hinted as much," said Ragnhild, and proceeded to tell her story, somewhat as follows: "It started with the Captain asking if she didn't think it was this stomach bug she'd got. But she said it was hardly a stomach bug, her taking such a dislike to him. 'Have you really taken such a dislike to me?' 'Yes, I could scream. That awful habit you have of eating vast quantities of food.' 'Do I?' says the Captain. 'I don't know if that's an awful habit exactly, it's the way I'm made—there are no fixed rules about the size of meals.' 'Yes, but watching you all the time makes me throw up—that's the reason I keep throwing up.' 'Well,' he says, 'at least I don't drink too much any more—so surely things are a bit better than they were.' 'On the contrary, they're much worse.' Then the Captain says, 'To be quite frank, I think you might try and be a bit patient with me after I've—after what you did in the summer.' 'Yes, you're right,' says Madame, and then she starts crying. 'It gnaws and gnaws at me night and day,' he says, 'but I've never once mentioned it.' 'No, I know,' she says, and cries more than ever.

'And what's more,' he says, 'it was I who asked you to come back.' But then she must have thought he was totting up the score too much, because she stops crying and tosses her head and says, 'Yes, and you'd have done far better not to have written to me if this was all you were bringing me back to.' 'And what may that be?' he asks; 'you do just as you please, and always have; only you take no interest in anything—you don't even touch your piano; all you do is go around being touchy and difficult and thinking nothing's good enough for you. And then you shut your door on me at night. That's fine by me, just carry on shutting it!' And she answers, 'You're the one who's touchy and difficult, if you ask me. I never go to bed at night or get up in the morning without being in terror of my life in case you should be reminded of that business in the summer. Never once mentioned it, did you say? Oh no, indeed. Oh *yes*, my friend, you never go five minutes without rubbing my nose in it. There was one day when I made a slip of the tongue and said Hugo— and what did you do? You could easily have patted my hand gently and helped me over it, but all you did was sneer and say, "I'm not Hugo, you know." Well, of course I knew you weren't Hugo, and I was really and truly sorry about what I'd said.'

" 'That's precisely the point,' says the Captain; 'are you really and truly sorry about that Hugo business?' 'Yes,' says Madame, 'I'm really and truly sorry about it.' 'I don't believe you are— seems to me you're as standoffish as ever.' 'And what about you then? Haven't you by any chance got something to be sorry about?' 'Haven't you got photographs of Hugo standing on your piano to this very day? And have you ever shown any sign of removing them, even though I've made it clear, not once but fifty times, how much I wanted it—positively begged you to do so?' 'How you do harp on those photographs!' she says. 'Look, don't get me wrong: if you go and remove them now, it no longer means a thing to me, after I've coaxed you about it fifty times or more. Only it would have been a little less shameless if of your own free will you'd burned those pictures the day you came home. Instead of which, you've still got books with his name in floating about in your room. And there's a handkerchief with his initials on, I see.' 'Sheer jealousy on your part,' says Madame; 'why should a thing like that matter? I can't kill him, much as you'd like it, and Mama and Papa say the same. After all, I've lived with him and been married to him.' 'Married to him?' 'That's what I said. It's not everyone who looks at Hugo and me as you do.' After that the Captain sat there for a long time shaking his head. 'And in any case, it's all your own fault,' says Madame after a while; 'driving off with Elizabeth that time, even after I'd come and begged you to stay at home. That was when it happened. And we'd had a lot to drink that evening, my head was going round and round.' The Captain still sits there saying nothing; then he says, 'Yes, it was wrong of me to go away that time.' 'Yes, it was,' says Madame, and starts crying again. 'You wouldn't listen to anything. And you're always rubbing my nose in it over Hugo, and forgetting what you yourself have done.' 'There's only one small difference,' says the Captain; 'namely, that I've never lived with the lady you have in mind, never been married to her, as you call it.' Madame just cocks an eyebrow at that. 'Never!' says the Captain, and hits the table with his fist. Madame jumps a foot, then sits there staring at him. 'Then perhaps,' she says, 'you can explain why you were always running after her and sitting in the summerhouse with her and lurking in all the dark corners?' 'It was you who sat in the summerhouse,' he says. Then she says, 'That's right, it's always me, never you!' 'No,' says the Captain, 'the reason why I ran after Elizabeth was simply to get you back. You'd drifted away from me and I wanted you back again.' Madame sits and thinks about that for a moment; then she jumps up and throws her arms around him and says, 'Then you loved me after all! And I thought it was all over. Because you'd been drifting away from me too, for years—you remember? What a mess it all was! I never thought—I never knew—and to think it was me you loved all the time! But goodness me, then everything's all right again!'

" 'Sit down,' he says. 'There's only this to remember, of course—that something has happened since then.' 'Happened? What?' 'You see, you've forgotten already. May I ask now if you're at all sorry about what's happened?' Then Madame gets all wound up again and says, 'Oh, you mean Hugo. That's over and done with now.' 'You haven't answered my question.' 'Whether I'm really and truly sorry about it? And you—are you so utterly blameless?' Then the Captain gets up and starts pacing up and down. 'Our trouble is not having any children,' says Madame. 'I've no daughter I can bring up to be better than I am.' 'I've thought about that,' says the Captain, 'and perhaps you're right.' And then he turns and looks straight at her and says, 'It's as if a vicious landslide has swept over us, Louise. But we've survived—shouldn't we set to work now and clear away all the stones and tree trunks and gravel that have been burying us for years and start breathing again? You could still have a daughter!' Then Madame gets up and wants to say something, only she can't get it out. All she can say is 'Yes' and then 'Yes' again. 'You're tired now and your nerves are on edge, but think about it later. Good night, Louise.' And 'Good night,' says Madame."

XI

The Captain told Nils that he had it in mind to put all his logging out on contract, or alternatively, to sell the standing timber. Nils took this to mean that he wished to avoid taking on more new people. "It looks as if he and his wife are back to square one."

Once we had lifted the potatoes, the immediate pressure was removed. But we still had plenty to do: the autumn plowing was behind schedule, and Lars Falkenberg and I were both kept busy on this now—fields and meadows alike.

That singular creature, Nils, now found Øvrebø so depressing again that he would gladly have given notice and gone, but the shame of abandoning his service was more than he could endure. He had strong, clear views about honor, views handed down through many generations: a boy from a large farm did not behave like a boy from a small holding. Besides, he had not been there long enough yet: before he came, Øvrebø had been shamefully neglected, and it would take many years to get the place back on its feet. This year, with the extra help he had had, was the first in which he had managed to gain some ground. But from now onward he could start seeing the fruits of his toil—look at the harvest this year, look at that fine heavy grain! And the Captain had had occasion, for the first time in many years, to look at this rich harvest with wonder and gratitude. He could sell by the bushel.

But in that case it made no sense for Nils to leave Øvrebø. He needed, however, to pay a flying visit to his home, a bit to the north; and to this end he took two days' leave when all the potatoes were harvested. We speculated on his purpose, which must surely be a valid one—perhaps to see his girl. He returned the same straightforward, active fellow as ever and resumed his work.

As we sat in the kitchen one lunchtime, we saw Madame come rushing out of the house and away down the drive in the greatest agitation. The Captain followed, calling, "Louise—no, *Louise*—where are you going?" But Madame's only answer was "Leave me alone!"

We all looked at each other, and Ragnhild left the table to follow Madame.

"That's right," said Nils, calmly as always. "Only first go in the living room and see if she's removed those photographs."

"They're still there," answered Ragnhild as she left the room.

Out in the yard, we heard the Captain say, "Go and look for the mistress, Ragnhild."

No one thought of leaving Madame to her fate; everyone felt concerned about her.

On our way back to the fields, Nils said to me, "She ought to remove those photographs. It's not right of her to leave them there. She's a changed person."

I thought: What do you know about it? I, of course, was full of wisdom about people, after all I had learned on my wanderings. Perhaps our foreman was merely taking up a stance. I decided to test him a little.

"I find it strange," I said, "that the Captain hasn't taken those pictures and burned them long ago."

"I don't," Nils answered. "I wouldn't have done so either."

"Really?"

"It would be for her to do it, not for me."

We walked on a little. Then Nils said something that showed the soundness and depth of his instinct. "Poor Madame! I don't think she's ever got over that false step of hers in the summer; it's done her an injury. That's how I see it: there are some who pick themselves up after a fall and continue on their way through life, with their blue and yellow bruises. And there are others who never rise again."

"Well," I said, still testing him, "she certainly has the appearance of taking it lightly enough."

"One can't tell," he answered; "but to my mind she's been a changed person ever since. She has to live, of course; but perhaps her harmony is gone. I'm no judge in these matters, but it's harmony I mean. No, of course she can eat and laugh and sleep, but . . . I've just seen someone like that into the grave."

At this I stopped being wise and unbending, and was foolish and ashamed. I could only say, "You have? She died?"

"Yes. That's what she wanted most." Suddenly he said, "Right, carry on plowing, you and Lars. We haven't got all that much left."

And with that he went his way and I went mine.

I thought perhaps it was a sister of his that had got into trouble, that he'd just been seeing into her grave. Dear God, there are indeed some who never get over it; it shakes them to their foundations, like a revolution. It all depends on how

coarse-fibered they are! Blue and yellow bruises, Nils said . . .
A thought struck me and I stopped dead: perhaps it was not his
sister but his girl!

Some association of ideas made me think of my washing. I
decided to send the lad up to the cottage for it.

Evening.

Ragnhild came to my room and begged me to stay awake
again—everything was at sixes and sevens with the master and
mistress. She was greatly agitated, and now in the dusk the only
place she dared to sit was on my knee. It was always the same:
under the stress of emotion she grew timid and tender, timid
and tender.

"Can you leave the kitchen like this?" I asked. "Is anyone
taking your place?"

"Yes, the cook's listening for the bell. Do you know," she
announced, "I'm on the Captain's side—I've been on his side all
along."

"That's only because he's a man."

"No, it's not."

"And you ought to be on the mistress's side."

"You only say that because she's a woman," Ragnhild retorted. "But you don't know all that I know. Madame's so unreasonable. Saying we don't care about her, saying we just let her
go to rack and ruin. Did you ever hear the like—when I'd run
after her and all? And the dreadful way she's behaved!"

"I don't want to hear about it," I said.

"But I haven't been listening—are you crazy? I was there in
the same room and heard them."

"I see. In that case, we'll stay here till you've calmed down a
little; then we'll go down and join Nils."

And so timid and tender was Ragnhild that she threw her
arms around me for being kind. She really was an extraordinary
girl.

And so we went down and joined Nils. I said, "Ragnhild
thinks one of us ought to stay awake a bit longer."

"It's so sad down there, you see," said Ragnhild; "worse than it's ever been. God knows what the Captain's going to do—maybe he won't even go to bed. Oh, she loves the Captain all right, and the Captain loves her too; only everything's gone wrong. When she ran off today, the Captain was in the yard and said to me, 'Go and find the mistress, Ragnhild!' So I went and found her—there she was, standing behind a tree by the side of the road, just standing there crying and smiling at me. I wanted her to come in again, but she said we didn't care about her—it made no difference where she went. 'The Captain's sent me to find Madame,' I said. 'Has he?' she asked. 'Now? Has he sent you just now?' 'Yes,' I said. 'Wait a bit then!' she said. She stood there for quite a while; then she said, 'Will you take those detestable books lying in my room and burn them? No, I'll do it myself,' she said, 'but I'll ring for you after supper, and then you must come up straightaway.' 'Very good,' I said. And then I got her to come with me.

"And to think she's with child," said Ragnhild suddenly.

We looked at each other. The foreman's face became indistinct and blurred; he shriveled up, his eyes seemed to go to sleep. Why did he take it so much to heart?

To break the silence, I said, "Madame was going to ring, did she say?"

"Yes, and she rang. There was something she wanted to say to the Captain, but she was scared and wanted to have me with her. 'Light a candle,' she says to me, 'and then pick up all these hundred and one buttons that I've dropped.' Then she calls to the Captain in his room. So I light a candle and start picking up buttons, dozens and dozens of them, all sorts and sizes. The Captain comes, and Madame immediately says to him, 'I only wanted to say how kind you were, sending Ragnhild to look for me today. God bless you for it!' 'Well, well,' he says, smiling, 'you *were* a bundle of nerves, my dear.' 'It's true,' she says, 'my nerves are bad, but I hope it'll get better. The trouble is my not having a daughter that I could bring up to be a really nice girl. There's nothing left for me to do.' The Captain sits down on a chair. 'Surely there is,' he says. 'Surely there is, did you say? Oh, I know it says in that book over there—ugh, those wretched books—take them away and burn them, Ragnhild!' she says; then she says, 'No, I'm going to tear them to shreds myself and throw them in that stove.' And she starts pulling the books to pieces, taking a handful of pages at a time and throwing them in the stove. 'Don't let your nerves run away with you so, Louise!' says the Captain. '*The Monastery*,' she says—that's the book in her hand. 'But I can't go into a monastery, or even a convent. So there's nothing left for me to do. When I laugh, you think I'm laughing,' she says to the Captain; 'but really I'm taking it seriously and not laughing at all.' 'Is your toothache better?' he asks. 'You know very well my toothache won't be better for a long time yet.' 'I know nothing of the kind.' 'Don't you?' 'No.' 'Good God, can't you *see* what's the matter with me?' she says. The Captain just looks at her and doesn't say anything. 'Why, I'm—oh, you said today I could still have a daughter, don't you remember?' I happened to look up at the Captain . . .''

Ragnhild smiled and shook her head. Then she continued, ''God forgive me for laughing, but the Captain's face was so funny—he looked like a half-wit. 'Haven't you realized that before now?' says Madame. The Captain looks my way and says, 'What's that you're doing all this time?' 'I asked her to pick up all my buttons for me,' says Madame. 'I've finished now,' I said. 'Have you?' says Madame, getting up; 'let me see.' And she takes the box and drops the buttons all over the floor again—rolled everywhere, they did, under the table and the bed and the stove—everywhere. 'Did you ever see such a mess?' says Madame. But then off she goes again on her own tack. 'Well, fancy your not realizing that I—what was wrong with me.' 'Can't those buttons stay there till the morning?' says the Captain. 'Yes, I suppose so,' says Madame, 'except that I'll be treading all over them. I'm not good at—I'm hardly capable of picking up—but never mind, let them lie there,' she says, and starts stroking his hand. 'Darling, darling!' she says. But then he takes his hand away. 'Ah, now you're angry with me,' she says; 'but then why did you write to me?' 'My dear Louise, we're not alone,' he says. 'Surely you must know why you wrote to me?' 'I suppose I hoped things would turn out all right.' 'But they didn't?' 'Well, no.' 'But what was in your mind when you sat down and wrote to me? Me? You wanted me again? I can't make out what was in your mind.' 'Ah, Ragnhild's finished, I see,' says the Captain. 'Good night, Ragnhild!' "

"So off you went?"

"Yes, but I didn't dare go very far from Madame. You can imagine the pickle she was in when I went—I had to be somewhere handy. And if the Captain had come and said anything, I'd have told him straight that I had no intention of going any farther off, with Madame in the state she was. Not that he came, as it happened; they only started talking again in there. 'I know what you're going to say,' says Madame; 'it could be that it's not you who—it could be that you're not the father. Yes, I think perhaps you may be, after all. Only I wish to God I could find words to make you forgive me,' she says, sobbing. 'Say you do, dearest, say you do!' she sobs; and then she goes down on her knees on the floor. 'You've seen me now getting rid of the books, and that handkerchief with the initials on I've burned already, and look, there are the books—' 'Yes, and there's another handkerchief with the same initials,' says the Captain; 'good ness, how considerate you are toward me, Louise!' Madame gets all upset. 'I'm sorry you should have seen that,' she says; 'it must have come back with me in the summer, and I keep forgetting to go through my things. But does it really matter so very much? Well?' 'Of course not,' he says. 'And if you'd only listen to me for a moment,' she says, 'it's very likely you who—I mean, that it's your child. Why shouldn't it be? It's just that I don't know how to put it.' 'Do get up off your knees,' says the Captain. But Madame must have misunderstood him, because she stands up and says, 'There you are—you won't listen to me. But in that case I'm jolly well going to ask you why you wrote to me at all, instead of leaving me alone.' The Captain says something about a man who's grown up in a prison yard—that was what he called it. Take him out of his prison yard, he said, and he'll long for it again—something like that. 'Yes,' she says, 'but I stayed with Papa and Mama, and they weren't as hard as you are—they said I'd been married to him, and they weren't at all unreasonable with me. Not everyone looks at it as you do.' 'Why don't you blow out that candle that Ragnhild was using?' says the Captain. 'It looks silly standing next to the lamp—almost as if it was ashamed.' 'Ashamed of me, I suppose,' she says; 'yes, that's what you meant. But you've been greatly to blame as well.' 'Don't misunderstand me,' he says quickly; 'I know I've been greatly to blame—but nothing for you to make a song and dance about.' 'That's what *you* think. Well, of all the—so you're blameless, are you?' 'I didn't say that. For many years I've been to blame—does that satisfy you? But not in the way you mean. And I certainly don't come home to you carrying the fruits of my blameworthiness under my heart.' 'No,' says Madame, 'but you were really the one who never wanted me to get—never wanted us to have children; and if I didn't either, it was up to you to know better. That's what they said at home, too. Because if I'd had a daughter—' 'You can spare us that magazine story,' says the Captain. 'But it's true,' says Madame; 'how can you possibly deny it?' 'I'm not denying anything. Do sit still and listen to me, Louise. These children and this daughter you keep plugging away at are something you've picked up quite recently. And the moment you came across the idea you made it your hope and salvation. But you never made children an issue before that I ever heard.' 'Yes, but you ought to have known better.' 'That's something else you've picked up recently. Still, this is beside the point—it may well be that we'd have done better to have had children. I've come to realize that for myself—too late, unfortunately. And look at the state of you now!' 'Oh God, yes! But perhaps

you *are*—I don't know—no, I suppose not . . .' 'Me?' says the
Captain, and shakes his head. 'Oh, it *ought* to be the mother
who knows, of course; but in this instance it seems she doesn't.
In this marriage of mine the mother doesn't know. Or do you?'
Madame says nothing to that. 'Do you know? I'm asking you.'
Still she says nothing—just collapses on the floor and cries.
Honestly, I don't know—perhaps I'm on Madame's side after
all—it was *dreadful* for her. In the end I was going to knock and
go in, but then the Captain started off again. 'You don't say
anything,' he says. 'But that too is an answer. It's as clear as if
you'd shouted it from the rooftops.' 'I can't say more,' says
Madame, and cries and cries. 'There're many things I love you
for, Louise,' says the Captain, 'and one of them's your truthful-
ness.' 'Thank you,' she says. 'They haven't yet taught you to lie.
Get up, now.' And he helps her up and settles her on her chair
again—it was pitiful to see how she cried. 'Be quiet, now,' he
says. 'I want to ask you something: shall we wait and see what
it looks like, what sort of eyes it has, and so on?' 'Yes, God
bless you—let's do that! Oh darling, darling, God bless you!'
'And I shall simply try to bear it. It gnaws and gnaws at me,
but . . . And I too am to blame.' 'God bless you! God bless
you!' she says again. 'And you too!' he says. 'Good night now—
see you in the morning.' Then Madame flops forward over the
table and cries as if her heart's going to break. 'What are you
crying about now?' he asks. 'Because you're going,' she says;
'earlier on, I was afraid of you—now I'm crying because you're
going. Couldn't you stay a little?' 'Here? With you, now?' he
asks. 'No, I didn't mean—it wasn't that,' she says; 'but I'm so
lonely. Oh no, I didn't mean what you think.' 'Ah well, I'm
going now,' says the Captain; 'you must surely understand that
I don't particularly feel like staying here any longer. Ring for
the maid.'

"So off I ran," Ragnhild concluded.

After a while Nils asked, "Have they gone to bed now?"

Ragnhild didn't know. Yes, perhaps; but in any case the cook was keeping an eye on things. "But good heavens, what a mess Madame's got herself into—I can't imagine her being able to sleep."

"You'd better pop over and see how she is."

"Yes," said Ragnhild, getting up. "No, honestly, I'm more on the Captain's side, whatever you may say. Yes, really and truly."

"It's not so easy to know what's right."

"Just imagine being got with child by *him!* How could she do such a thing? And she's been staying with him in that town since then, or so I hear—what sense is there in that? And all those handkerchiefs of his I've seen, and any number of hers missing—they must have been using each other's. Lived with him, she said! When she had a husband and all!"

XII

The Captain had done what he'd said and had put the logging out on contract: there came a cracking and a crashing from the forest. It was a mild autumn, too, with no frost as yet— good plowing weather. Nils piled up the hours like a miser, to lighten the burden of work in the spring.

The question arose whether Grindhusen and I should join in the logging. I remembered that really I ought now to be on my way to the region where the berries grow, to the mountains thick with cloudberries—what about that journey? As for Grindhusen, he was hardly much use to the Captain as a logger nowadays: all he was fit for was to hang around and hold one end of a saw from time to time.

No, Grindhusen had grown sluggish—devil only knows how to explain it. He still had all his hair, and that hair was still red. But he had picked up nicely at Øvrebø, thank you, and maintained the appetite and digestion of an ox. How he flour-

ished! All that summer and autumn he had sent regular sums of
money home to his family; and he poured out his panegyrics
about the Captain and his wife, who paid so reasonably and
were such a model master and mistress. Not like the inspector,
who haggled and dickered over every little øre and ended up, so
help me God, knocking off two kroner, which he'd fairly and
squarely—ah shit! He, Grindhusen, would cheerfully send a
two-krone piece down the drain if it served any earthly use or
purpose; but bloody hell! Catch the Captain doing a thing like
that!

But Grindhusen was so evasive and vacillating nowadays; he
couldn't even get properly angry with anyone. He might yet go
back to the Inspector of Log Driving for two kroner a day, and
say a faithful yea to his every word. Age and time had caught
up with him.

As they catch up with us all.

The Captain said, "That water pipe you mentioned once—is
it too late in the year to do anything about it now?"

"Yes," I said.

The Captain nodded and walked away.

I did another day's plowing; then the Captain came to me
again. He was here, there, and everywhere these days, working
hard himself and keeping an eye on everything. He barely finished his food before he was out again: in barn and stable, in the
fields, in the forest with the loggers.

"You may as well get cracking on that water pipe," he said.
"It could be quite a while yet before the first frost. Who do you
want helping you?"

"Grindhusen can help me," I answered. "But—"

"Right, and Lars. What were you going to say?"

"We *could* start getting frosts any day now."

"Or we could get snow, in which case there'd be no hard
frosts. We don't get hard frosts every winter here, not by any
means. You'd better take several men with you, and have some
of them digging, others doing masonry work. I take it you've
done this kind of work before?"

"Yes."

"I've warned Nils, so you don't need to be afraid of any un-pleasantness," he said with a smile. "Now take the horses in."

He was so impatient that I too caught the itch to plunge right in, and ran rather than walked the horses home. The Captain had set his heart on this water supply after seeing the beauty of the newly painted house and the richness of the harvest. And now he was cutting his thousand dozen battens, and paying off his debt, with something to spare!

So I set off uphill and rediscovered the site that I had long since earmarked for the reservoir; then I took a bearing on the house below me, paced out the distance, measured and calculated. There was a stream with its source far up the hill; its channel was so deep, and its fall such, that it never froze in winter. At the chosen spot I intended to build a small reservoir, with built-in overflow outlets for the spring and autumn flood waters. Yes, Øvrebø would get its water supply all right. Our building materials we would quarry *in situ*—there was layer upon layer of granite.

By noon next day the work was in full swing: Lars Falkenberg was digging the trench for the pipeline, Grindhusen and I quarrying—work we both knew well from our road-building days at Skreia.

Good.

We worked for four days; then it was Sunday. I remember that Sunday: high, clear sky, the trees stripped of their leaves, the hills green and peaceful on every side, smoke from the cottage chimney rising into the air. In the afternoon Lars Falkenberg had borrowed a horse and cart from the Captain to drive his newly slaughtered pig to the station en route for the town. On his way home Lars was to collect the Captain's mail.

It occurred to me that this was a suitable evening for sending the lad to fetch my washing from the cottage: Lars was away, and no one need be offended by that washing any more.

Oh yes, I said to myself, your motives are impeccable, sending the lad for the washing. Only it's not a case of having worthy motives, or any motives at all; mark my words, it's merely old age.

I chewed on this for an hour or so. Yes: most probably I'd been deluding myself with a lot of nonsense. Besides, it was a singularly mild evening, Sunday at that, nothing to do, the servants' hall deserted. Decrepitude of old age? Hills getting too much for me?

So I made the journey.

Early next morning Lars Falkenberg was down at the manor again. He took me aside, as once before, and for the self-same purpose. I had been up at the cottage yesterday; it was for the last time—just remember that!

"It was also the last piece of washing," I pointed out.

"Washing, washing, washing! Couldn't I have brought you that miserable shirt of yours a hundred times this autumn?"

"I didn't want to remind you of that washing again."

What witchcraft was this, that he had already heard about my little walk yesterday evening? The insufferable Ragnhild must have been out telling tales; there was no one else it could have been.

As fate would have it, Nils, our foreman, was close at hand on this occasion too. He came innocently across the yard from the kitchen—and at once replaced me as the main target for Lars's rancor.

"Ah, here comes the other caricature too," said Lars. "And he looks even more of an insult to his Creator."

"What's that you're saying?" asked Nils.

"What's that you're saying?" retorted Lars. "Go and rinse your mouth out with some patent mouthwash or other, and speak intelligibly."

Nils stopped to see what it was all about, and said, "I don't understand a word of all this."

"You don't, huh? Understand, huh? No, indeed! Plowing in uncut corn, that's what you understand. When it comes to understanding that, there's no one to touch you."

Nils's cheeks turned pale with unaccustomed anger, and he

said, "You really are an incorrigible fool, Lars! Can't you shut your trap and stop talking baloney for once?"

"Fool, eh? Just listen to that jackass," said Lars, turning to me. "Doesn't he talk posh? 'Incorrigible,' he says—and turns pale with the effort . . . I've spent more years than you at Øvrebø, *and* I've sung to the master and mistress more than once of an evening, let me tell you. Whereas nowadays it's nothing but maundering and megalomania. You remember"—turning to me again—"what it was like here in the old days? It was Lars here and Lars there, and I never heard of the work not getting done. And after me came Albert—he was in charge for eighteen months. And after Albert came *you*, Nils. And now it's all pushing people around and plowing and carting manure day and night, so to speak, till a man goes as thin as a frostbitten fingertip with it all."

At this point Nils and I were unable to keep a straight face. Far from being offended, Lars felt he had made a hit as a humorist; he was instantly appeased and joined in the laughter himself.

"Yes, I'm telling you straight," he said. "And if it wasn't for the fact that at times you're quite a nice lad—nice? No, I won't go as far as that, but helpful and pleasant in a way—if it wasn't for that, then—"

"Yes, what would happen then?"

Lars had become more and more good-humored; he laughed and answered, "Well, I suppose I could always pick you up and stuff you into your own boots."

"Want to feel my arm?" said Nils.

"What's going on?" asked the Captain, walking toward us. It was only six o'clock, but he was already up and about.

"Nothing," said Lars; and "Nothing," said Nils.

"How's the reservoir going?" the Captain asked me. But without waiting for an answer, he turned to Nils and said, "I need the boy now to drive me to the station. I'm off to Christiania."

Grindhusen and I resumed our work on the reservoir, and Lars his digging. But a cloud had come over our spirits.

"Pity about the Captain going away," even Grindhusen acknowledged.

I felt the same. But of course the Captain had business to transact—timber and crops to sell. Only why was he leaving so early in the day? He couldn't, in any case, catch the morning train. Had there been conflict again? Did he wish to be gone before his wife was up?

And indeed there was often conflict.

It had now reached the point where the Captain and Madame no longer made any perceptible movement of the lips when they spoke to each other; if obliged to exchange a few words, they did so in tones of complete indifference, their eyes well and truly averted. From time to time the Captain might look his wife in the face and urge her to go out and enjoy the fine weather; once he even called to her to come in from the courtyard and play a little on her piano. But this, I suspect, was done for the sake of appearances, and for no other reason.

How sad it all was!

Madame was quiet and pretty; sometimes she would stand outside on the steps, with her soft features and reddish-yellow hair, gazing up at the hills. Already she looked like a good young mother. But the place was utterly desolate for her now—no visitors any more, no games or music, no joy; only sorrow and shame.

The Captain had, of course, promised to bear his burden for the present; and doubtless he bore what he could. More he could not do. A calamity had struck the house; and a calamity is harder to bear than seven burdens. If Madame in a hasty moment forgot to show gratitude, the Captain would look down at the floor and shortly afterward take his hat and go out. The maids could all quote instances of this, and I myself witnessed it once or twice. Naturally, he could never forget her faux pas—no, never. Still, he could keep quiet about it. But how was he to keep quiet about it when she forgot herself and said, "You *know* I'm not well, you *know* I can't walk as much as usual"? He would frown and answer, "Hush, Louise!" And the conflict would be in full swing: "Do you have to keep reminding me of it?" "On the contrary, it's you yourself who keeps reminding us both of it; you've lost your modesty since your fall, you've become brazen and shameless." "Oh, why did I come back here? I was far better off at home." "Yes, or with the whelp." "I thought you said he helped you once? Yes, dear God, I often wish I was back with Hugo—he's worth any number of you."

Her words were completely irresponsible; possibly they went further than she herself intended. But she had become unrecognizable to us all—and corrupt. Mrs. Falkenberg corrupt? Perhaps not—God alone knows. Be that as it may, she had the nerve to come out into the kitchen of an evening and address flattering words to Nils about his youth and strength. I suppose I was a little jealous again, and envied the foreman his youth, for I thought: Has everyone gone mad? Surely we older men are much to be preferred! Was it Nils's innocence that had caught her eye? Or was she merely keeping her end up, trying to be younger than she was? But then one day she came up to the reservoir and sat for a while watching Grindhusen and me. For half an hour the work was child's play, the granite amenable and obedient to our wills, and we ourselves a Herculean pair of stonemasons. Yes, but she was being irresponsible again, playing around with her eyes. Why did she not cure herself of this new habit? Her eyes were too grave for such a game; it didn't suit her. I thought: Either she's using Grindhusen and me to cancel out her foolishness with Nils, or she's playing a new game, for new stakes. But which? I couldn't make up my mind. As for Grindhusen, he understood nothing—all he said when Madame went away was "I reckon she's a mighty fine sort, that lady; she's almost like a mother. Why, she even went to feel if the water was cold for us!"

One day, as I stood by the kitchen steps, she said to me, "Do you remember this place in the old days? The first time you were here?"

She had never alluded to that time before, and all I could think of saying in reply was yes—indeed I remembered it.

"You drove me to the parsonage on one occasion," she said.

I began to entertain fancies that she was by no means averse to talking with me a little by way of amusement. And I wanted to help her, to make it easier for her to get going; I was also, I guess, rather touched. I answered, "Yes, I remember. It was a glorious drive; only the last part was rather cold for Madame."

"No, it was you who were cold," she replied; "you'd lent me your own blanket from the box. Poor you!"

I was still more touched by this; but then, of course, I had to start giving myself airs—so she hadn't entirely forgotten me! The handful of years since then couldn't have told on me all that severely!

"I think Madame's memory must be mistaken about the blanket," I said; "but we ate in a cottage, and an old woman made coffee for us, and you gave me food."

I put my arms around a post and leaned against the handrail.

This may have offended her, by suggesting I was all set for a prolonged gossip with her; furthermore, I had said, "*We* ate in a cottage." I had gone too far, of course; but I had grown unused to watching my step, after all those months of wandering.

As soon as I sensed her displeasure, I straightened up, but by then it was too late. That is to say, she was still kindly enough, but the bad days she had fallen on must have made her hypersensitive and suspicious, so that she found discourtesy even in clumsiness.

"Ah yes," she said. "Well, I hope you like it as much at Øvrebø now as you did then."

And with that she nodded and walked away.

Several days passed. The Captain was still away, but Madame had received a friendly postcard from him: he hoped to be home again next week. Also, he was sending pipes, faucets, and cement for the water installation.

"Look!" said Madame, coming to me with the card. "The Captain's sending these things for you and asking you to have them fetched from the station."

We stood there, the two of us, at noon in the middle of the courtyard, reading the card. I can't explain it, but standing there right beside her, with my head inclined toward hers, made me feel good in my inmost being. When she had finished reading she looked up at me. She was playing no game this time; yet, aware as she must have been of a new expression on my face, she continued to look at me. Did she feel my presence as I felt hers? Those two heavy eyes, raised toward mine and held there, were loaded to the brim with love. She could not be held to account: that gaze welled up from pathological depths, blending on its way with the life she carried under her heart. She began breathing heavily, her face flushed dark all over; then she turned on her heel and walked slowly away.

I stood with the card in my hand. Had she given it to me? Had I taken it?

"Your card," I said. "Here, I'm coming . . ."

She held out her hand behind her without turning around, and walked slowly on.

This incident haunted me for several days. Should I have followed her when she walked away? I could have tried, I could have had a shot; her door was not far away. Pathological? But why had she brought me that card in the first place? She could simply have told me its drift. And now I recalled how six years ago we had stood in just the same way, reading a telegram that the Captain had sent her. Did she seek these situations? And did they do her good?

The next time I saw her I detected no trace of embarrassment; she was friendly and reserved. Better drop the whole business. What did I want with her in any case? Really!

Some callers came one day: a neighbor and her daughter.

They had doubtless heard that the Captain was away and wanted to give his wife some diversion; perhaps, too, they had come from curiosity. Mrs. Falkenberg received them hospitably, was her old amiable self with them, and ended by playing for them on her piano. When they left, she accompanied them down to the road, making sensible conversation, although she must have had other things in her head than domestic economy and slaughtering. How nice and interested she was! "Come again soon—you, Sophie, at the very least." "Thank you, I'd love to. But aren't you ever coming over to Nedrebø again?" "Me? If it hadn't been so late I'd have come with you now." "Well, there's always tomorrow." "Yes, I might well come over tomorrow. Oh, are *you* there?"—this to Ragnhild, who had followed her down with a shawl. "You really make me laugh, thinking I'm cold."

All in all, there was a better atmosphere about the place; that sense of malaise no longer weighed on us all. Grindhusen and I worked away at our famous reservoir, and Lars Falkenberg came farther and farther uphill with his trench. Seeing the Captain was away so long, I was keen to push ahead in the hope of getting most of the work completed by the time he returned; what a lark it would be if we got the whole thing done! He could do with a nice little surprise, because—well, yes, there had indeed been conflict the night before he left. Something may have reminded him of the calamity afflicting his home; perhaps an unburned book still lying around in his wife's room. His last words had been, "Well, now I'm felling timber to pay that debt; and the harvest will bring in a lot of money, too. So I hope the Lord will forgive me—as I forgive him. Good night, Louise!"

When we had laid the last stone of the reservoir and cemented the whole thing, Grindhusen and I joined forces with Lars for the last of the digging. It went with a will. Here and there a boulder needed blasting, here and there a tree had to come down; but the trench crept up and up, until finally there was a long black line all the way from the reservoir to the manor. Then we worked our way back, digging down to the right depth. Naturally the trench was not intended as a work of art; rather as an underground resting place for some water pipes that needed burying without delay. It was merely a question of getting below the deep-frost level, and of getting there before the frost set in. It was already coating the fields at night. Nils dropped all his other work in order to help us.

Building or digging, however, I was using only my hands; and my mind in its idleness toyed with all manner of notions. Each time I remembered the postcard incident, it sent a glow all through me. Yes, but why give it another thought? Really! Besides, I hadn't followed her to the door, had I?

But there was she, and there were you. Her breath was on you, you tasted flesh. She came from some darkness—she was certainly not of this earth. Remember the eyes?

And each time the glow was followed by a wave of nausea. Into my mind would pour a meaningless succession of wild and tender names of places she might have come from: Uganda, Antananarivo, Honolulu, Venezuela, Atacama. Was it verse? Were they colors? I could make nothing of them.

XIII

Madame ordered the carriage; she needed to go to the station.

She seemed in no great hurry: she told the cook to prepare some food for the journey, and when Nils asked if she wanted the calash or the landau, she thought for a moment before choosing the landau and pair.

Then off she went, driven by Nils himself.

That same evening they were home again, having turned back when halfway there.

Had Madame forgotten something? Now she demanded fresh horses and another hamper of food; she intended to leave again at once. Nils objected that night was coming on, that they would be driving in the dark; but Madame repeated her order. While she waited she sat in the living room with her things on, doing nothing—she had not forgotten anything—just sitting there, staring. Ragnhild went in and asked if she could help with anything. No, thank you. Madame sat leaning forward, as if bowed down with some mortal sorrow.

The carriage was ready; Madame came out.

On seeing Nils all set to drive again, she took pity on him and said that Grindhusen should drive her. While waiting for Grindhusen, she sat on the steps.

Then off they drove. It was a fine evening, pleasantly cool for the horses.

"I can't make it out," said Nils; "she's a changed person. I had no idea of anything until she knocked on the glass and told me to turn back; we were about halfway. But she never said a word about wanting to go straight out again."

"Surely she must have forgotten something."

"Ragnhild says no. She was in the living room, and I wondered about those photographs, whether she was going to take them and burn them; but no, they're still there. All the time she was back she never did a single thing."

I crossed the yard with Nils, who continued, "No, there's something very wrong with Madame; she's got no harmony left for anything. Where do you suppose she's off to now? Heaven knows—she hardly seemed to know her own mind. We stopped to rest the horses and she said, 'I'm so busy, Nils, there's so many places I ought to be at the same time, and I shouldn't be away from home either.' 'Madame shouldn't be so busy,' I said; 'Madame should just take things easy.' But you know how she is these days—you can't say anything to her. She just looked at her watch and said we must be off again."

"Was this on the way to the station?"

"No, on the way home just now. She seemed almost more edgy then."

"Perhaps the Captain's written for her to join him?"

Nils shook his head.

"No. Or rather, heaven knows. By the way, tomorrow's Sunday, isn't it?"

"Yes?"

"Oh, nothing really. It's just that I want to use the day working out a route for fetching firewood in the winter. I've had it in mind for some time. It's easier now than when the snow's on the ground."

Nils had the running of the place constantly in mind. It was a matter of honor; and now, in addition, he was anxious to show himself grateful for the handsome increase the Captain had given him since the harvest.

Sunday.

I took a stroll up the hill, and inspected the reservoir and trench. A few more good days and we would have the pipe laid. I was all keyed up and could hardly wait for Sunday to be over before returning to the attack. The Captain, moreover, had never meddled in my project by as much as a single word, but had left me completely in charge, so to me it was by no means a matter of indifference if the frost came and spoiled things for us.

When I got back, there was the landau standing in the court-yard; but the horses had been unhitched. It was more or less the time when Grindhusen was due back; but why had he pulled up by the front steps? I went into the kitchen.

The maids came running to me: Madame was sitting in the landau; she had come home a second time. She had been all the way to the station; now she wanted to go there again. What did I make of it all?

"Must be her nerves," I said. "Where's Nils?"

"Up in the forest. He said he'd be out for quite a while. There's only us here, and we can't say more to her than what we've said already."

"And where's Grindhusen?"

"Gone to change the horses again. And Madame just sits in the carriage and won't get out. Do go and talk to her."

"Well, it's not all that serious if she goes for a drive or two. So take it easy."

I went out to Madame, my heart beating fast. How completely she had gone to pieces, how hopeless everything must seem to her! I opened the carriage door, bowed, and said, "Will Madame allow me to drive her this time?"

She looked at me calmly and said, "No, why?"

"Grindhusen may be a bit tired—I don't know—"

"He promised to drive me," she said. "No, he's not tired. Is he coming soon?"

"I don't see him," I answered.

"Shut this door again, and go and tell him to come," she commanded, wrapping herself more closely as she spoke.

I went across to the stables, where Grindhusen was harnessing the fresh horses.

"What's up?" I asked. "Are you off again somewhere?"

"Yes? Aren't I?" said Grindhusen, breaking off for a moment.

"It all looks very odd to me. Where's Madame going—do you know?"

"No. She wanted to come straight back from the station last night, but I said neither of us could stand it. So she slept at the hotel. But this morning she still wanted to go home, or so she said. And now she wants to go to the station again, she says. I don't know."

He continued harnessing.

"Madame told me to hurry you up," I said.

"All right, I'm coming now. But these bellybands are the devil's own work."

"Aren't you too tired to make that journey again?"

"No, I dare say I'll manage it. And she's given me quite a bit extra."

"Has she, indeed?"

"Sure. Oh yes, she's a mighty nice creature."

Then I said to Grindhusen, "I don't think you ought to start off again now."

He broke off abruptly. "You think not? No, perhaps you're right."

At this point Madame called, from just outside the stable door, "What, aren't you ready yet? How much longer am I to sit there waiting for you?"

"I'm coming this minute!" Grindhusen answered, and set to work more busily than ever. "It was only these bellybands."

Madame ran back to the landau. The thick fur coat she had on was too heavy for her, and she flailed with her arms to keep her balance. There was something pathetic in the sight—like a hen trying to escape across a barnyard and flapping its wings to help.

I went over to Madame again; I was polite, indeed humble; I took off my cap and begged her to give up this new journey.

"You're not driving me," she answered.

"No. But if Madame would make up her mind to stay at home . . ."

But now she took offense. She measured me, inspected me, and said, "Excuse me, but you're not to meddle in this. Even if I did get you dismissed once—"

"No no, it's not that!" I said despairingly, and was lost for words. When she took that line she reduced me to pulp.

For one moment a paroxysm of rage seized me: I had only to reach into the carriage and lift out this child, this pitiful hen! My arms must have twitched, for she gave a frightened start and shifted her position. Then suddenly reaction set in; I turned soft and foolish, and embarked on another attempt.

"It's so cheerless when you're away—we all feel it. Can't we find something here to amuse you with instead—I can read a little, read aloud a little, and of course Lars sings beautifully.

And perhaps I can tell stories—one thing or another. Grindhusen's coming now—shall I send him away again?"

She seemed mollified, and thought for a moment. Then she said, "I think you must have got it all wrong. I'm going to meet the Captain. He didn't come the day before yesterday, and he didn't come yesterday, but sooner or later he's bound to come. I want to go and meet·him."

"Oh!"

"So be off with you. Is Grindhusen there?"

I felt as if I had been struck across the mouth. She was right, it sounded so plausible—and oh, I had made a fool of myself again!

"Yes, Grindhusen's here," I managed to get out.

And I put my cap on again and even helped Grindhusen hitch the horses. I was so bewildered and shamefaced that I didn't even offer an apology, but could only flutter this way and that, checking the harness all over.

"So it's you who's driving me, Grindhusen?" called Madame.

"What, me? Why, sure!" he answered.

Then she slammed the door to, and the landau rolled out of the yard.

"Has she gone?" asked the maids, clasping their hands.

"Certainly she's gone. She's going to meet her husband."

I went back up to the reservoir. With Grindhusen away, the team was a man short; could the rest of us manage the extra work?

But it had already dawned on me that Mrs. Falkenberg had caught me off guard with that trumped-up story about going to meet her husband. Not that it mattered: the horses were thoroughly rested, having done no work while Nils was helping us with the trench. All the same, I had behaved stupidly. Why couldn't I have got up on the box myself, without asking permission? Yes, and then? Well, in that case any subsequent follies would to some extent have been channeled through me, and I might have been able to stop them. Ha-ha—you infatuated old man! Madame must have known what she intended: to get her own back on the Captain and be away when he returned. She vacillated endlessly, kept wanting to and not wanting to, wanting to and not wanting to; but the intention was there. And bless my soul, I had not set out on my wanderings for the sole purpose of looking after the bourgeois interests of married couples involved in love affairs. Their pigeon! But how corrupt Mrs. Falkenberg had become! She had indeed received an injury, an injury tantamount to her destruction: she no longer cared what she did to herself. And she had taken to lying. After the cabaret eyes, the pack of lies: the white lie today, the compulsive lie tomorrow, one leading to the other. But where would it end? Life could afford to waste her, to fritter her away.

We worked on the trench for another three days, till we had only a few yards left. There were now up to five or six degrees of frost at night, but this did not prevent us from pressing steadily forward. Grindhusen had returned and been set to work digging a tunnel for the pipe under the kitchen; I myself dug under the barn and stables as being the most important. Meanwhile, Nils and Lars Falkenberg were putting the finishing touches to the trench.

On the third day I at last questioned Grindhusen about Madame. "So she didn't come home with you again that last time?"

"No, she took the train."

"It was her husband she was going to join, was it?"

But Grindhusen had become extremely wary of me; for two days he had never opened his mouth, and now he only said, "That's about what it comes to, I should say. Well, yes, I suppose so—her own husband, you understand . . ."

"I thought perhaps she might have been going to her parents in Kristiansand."

"Yes, maybe, maybe," said Grindhusen, finding this an improvement. "Gee, it's as clear as day she's gone there for a while. Well, I dare say she'll be home again soon."

"Did she say she would?"

"Sounded like that, yes. Though the Captain hasn't come home yet either, for that matter. Yes, she's a mighty fine woman. She says to me, 'Here's something for food and drink for you and the horses—and here's something extra,' she says. Ah, you won't find another such mistress."

But Grindhusen felt safer with the maids; and to them he had said it was a toss-up whether Madame would be coming home again. She had quizzed him about Engineer Lassen all the way, and had certainly gone to stay with him. Ah, that was a man she wouldn't go disappearing from—not with his wealth and splendor!

Then came another postcard from the Captain to his wife, just to ask if she would please get Nils to meet him at the station on Friday, and to bring his fur coat without fail. The card had been delayed; Friday meant tomorrow. Incidentally, it was fortunate on this occasion that Ragnhild had happened to take a squint at the message side of the card.

We sat in Nils's room talking about the Captain, wondering what his reaction would be when he got home, what we should say, whether indeed we should say anything. All three maids were present at this conclave. There was comfortable time for Madame to have reached Christiania by the time the Captain wrote her that card; since she had evidently not done so, she must have been going elsewhere. The whole thing was sad beyond words.

Nils asked, "Didn't she leave any letter?"

But no such letter was lying about. As against that, Ragnhild had, on her own initiative, done something which perhaps she oughtn't: she had taken those photographs off the piano and thrown them in the stove. Was that wrong?

"No, Ragnhild, indeed not."

She also told us she had gone through Madame's things and

sorted out all the handkerchiefs that weren't hers. Oh, and she had found various things in her room—a purse with Hugo Lassen's initials embroidered on it, a book with his name in full, some sweets in an envelope with his address on—and had burned the lot.

Ragnhild really was an extraordinary girl. What an instinct! A case of the devil turned monk? After making such heavy use of the red stair carpet and all those keyholes.

For myself and my work, it fitted like a glove that the Captain had not demanded transport until this moment. The trench was now complete over its entire length; and for laying pipes I could dispense with Nils. On the other hand, when it came to covering them up, I would need every man jack. The weather, by the way, had turned mild and rainy, with the temperature well above freezing.

It was doubtless an excellent thing for me at this period that I had the water installation to hold my interest: it saved me, probably, from many a mad caprice. From time to time I would clench my fists in pain, and when I found myself alone at the reservoir, I was liable to stand and scream at the forest; but there was no chance of my getting away. Besides, where would I go?

The Captain was back.

Without even taking off his fur coat or snow boots, he went all around the house: in the living room, in the kitchen, in all the upstairs rooms, then down again.

"Where's the mistress?" he asked.

"The mistress went to meet the Captain," answered Ragnhild. "We expected her by now."

The Captain's head began to droop. Feeling his way, he said, "You mean, she drove down with Nils to the station? But how maddening that I didn't look for her more carefully!"

Ragnhild said, "No, Madame left on Sunday."

The Captain took a fresh grip on himself and said, "Sunday. So she must have been going to meet me in Christiania. Hm.

We've missed each other: as it happens, I made a little side trip yesterday, to Drammen—I mean Fredrikstad. Have you got any food for me, Ragnhild?"

"It's on the table, sir, if you please."

"Come to think of it, it was the day before yesterday I made that side trip. Well, at least she'll have had a little outing! Everything all right here? Men busy digging that trench?"

"They've finished it, I believe."

The Captain went in.

And Ragnhild came running to us at once and repeating every word, to give us something to go by, and to save us from making bad worse.

Later on the Captain came out to see us, greeting us officer-style with "How's it going, boys?" He was amazed to find the pipes all laid; indeed, we had already started covering them over.

"Splendid fellows!" he exclaimed. "You don't take as long over a job as I do!"

With that he left us and went up to the reservoir. When he came back he was less keen-eyed, more withdrawn; perhaps he had been sitting there in solitude, thinking various thoughts. Now he stood watching us, one hand on his chin. After a moment or two he said to Nils, "Well, I've sold the timber."

"Dare say the Captain got a good price for it too?"

"Yes, I did. A good price. But I've taken all this time over it. You've been quicker here."

"Ah, but there've been several of us on this job," I said. "Sometimes as many as four."

He tried to make a joke. "Oh yes, I know you're an extravagant man to have around."

But there was no mirth in his face, and his smile hardly deserved the name. He was flagging now, with a vengeance. After a while he sat down on a stone we'd removed from the trench—it was covered with fresh clay; and from this position he followed us with his eyes.

Feeling sorry for his poor clothes, I went up to him, spade in hand, and said, "Shall I scrape some of the clay off that stone?"

"No, it doesn't matter."

All the same, he got up and allowed me to clean it a little.

At that moment Ragnhild came running along the trench toward us. She had something white in her hand, a piece of paper. And she ran and ran. The Captain sat watching her.

"It's only a telegram," she said breathlessly. "It came express."

The Captain got up and took a few quick steps toward this telegram. Then he tore it open and read it.

We could see at once it must be something serious: the Captain gave a great gasp. Then he made for the house, at a walk, at a run; a short way off he turned and shouted to Nils, "The carriage, at once! I'm going to the station."

Then he ran on again.

And the Captain set out once more. He had only been home a matter of hours.

Ragnhild told us how jittery the poor man had been: trying to get into the carriage without his fur coat, forgetting the hamper of food prepared for him, leaving the telegram wide open on the stairs.

ACCIDENT, it said . . . YOUR WIFE . . . CHIEF OF POLICE. "What's it all about?"

"I thought as much when it came express," Ragnhild said in an unfamiliar voice; then she turned away. "I've a strong feeling it's a terrible accident."

"No, surely," I said, reading and rereading. "Look, it's not so serious—listen to this: REQUEST YOUR IMMEDIATE PRESENCE, ACCIDENT INVOLVING YOUR WIFE. CHIEF OF POLICE."

It was an express telegram from the little town, the dead town. Yes, that was it. A town with a roar right through it—a long bridge—rapids. All screams died on the screamer's lips; no one heard them. And no birds sang . . .

But all the maids were coming and talking to me in unfamiliar voices; misery reigned supreme among us. So I had to be grave and confident. "Madame must have fallen and hurt herself; she hasn't been too steady on her feet of late. But I dare say she picked herself up again and walked off hardly the worse for it—just a little bleeding. They're too hasty sending telegrams, these police chiefs."

"No, that's not true," said Ragnhild. "You know very well that if the Chief of Police sends a telegram, it probably means that Madame's been found dead somewhere. Oh, I can't—I just can't—bear it . . ."

They were evil days that followed. I worked harder than ever before, but like a sleepwalker, without interest and without pleasure. Was the Captain never coming?

Three days later he came, silent and alone. The body had been sent to Kristiansand; he had only come home to change his clothes before following it there, to the funeral.

This time he was home for at most an hour; then off again, to catch the morning train. I never even saw him, being out in the grounds.

Ragnhild asked if he had seen his wife alive.

He looked at her and frowned.

But the girl refused to give up—she begged him, please, in God's name, to say. And the two other girls stood behind her, equally despairing.

Then the Captain answered—in a voice so low that he seemed to be speaking only to himself—"She had been dead for several days when I got there. It was an accident—she tried to cross the river and the ice was too thin. No, there was no ice; it was the stones that were slippery. Or rather, there was ice as well."

And now the girls set up a wailing; but this was too much for the Captain. He got up from his chair, cleared his throat hard, and said, "There, there—all right, girls, you must go now. Wait, Ragnhild!" And what he had to say to her in private was this: "By the way, is it you who's taken down some photographs from the piano? I can't make out where they've got to."

Then Ragnhild recovered her wits and answered gloriously—God bless her for the lie—"Me? No, it was Madame took them down one day."

"So. Well, well. It's just that I was puzzled by their having gone."

It helped—helped the Captain, this enlightenment.

As he left, he told Ragnhild to say I was not to leave Øvrebø, before he returned.

XIV

No, I did not go away.

I worked, trudged through the dreariest days of my life to their end, and got the water installation completed. It made a bit of a change the first time we were able to turn on the water, and we all felt better for having something new to talk about for a while.

Lars Falkenberg had left us now. All differences between him and me were finally resolved; it was just as in the old days when we wandered around the countryside together.

He was better off than many another man: his heart was light, his head empty, and his health immutably sound. To be sure, his singing days down at the manor were gone forever; but he himself had evidently come in later years to mistrust his voice a little, and now he merely larded his speech with tales of how at one time—in his day—he used to sing at dances and before the gentry. No, for Lars Falkenberg things were not too bad—he had his little patch of earth with two cows and a pig, not to mention his wife and children.

But what were Grindhusen and I to do? I could wander off anywhere, but the good Grindhusen was incapable of wandering. He was only fit for staying put in one place after another and working until he was fired. And each time the harsh announcement came, he had grown so flabby that he took it very hard and thought it was mighty tough on him. After a while, however, he regained his confidence and his childhood faith— not in himself but in destiny, in providence, saying in his shiftless way, "Ah well, with God's help something will turn up."

But he too was well enough off. He had a unique gift for making the best of every place he came to, and could happily stay there till he died if the choice rested with him. Home was a place he never needed to go: his children were grown up, his wife managed nicely without him. No, this old, red-haired firebrand of yesteryear needed nothing now but a place to lay his head and use his hands.

"Where are you going from here?" he asked me.

"Far away up in the mountains, to Trovatn, to a forest."

And for all his total disbelief he said, quietly and evasively, "Maybe, maybe."

After we had finished the plumbing, Grindhusen and I were set to work on the firewood until the Captain returned. We cut up and stacked the top ends the loggers had left—nice, steady work.

"I'll bet you we're both laid off when the Captain gets back," said Grindhusen.

"You could get work here for the winter," I suggested. "Out of these thousand dozen battens there'll be a mass of cordwood left, which you could saw up for a reasonable wage."

"Yes—speak to the Captain about it, will you?"

And now the hope of a long spell of work for the winter made this man a contented soul again. Grindhusen was good at enduring his own company. Grindhusen, therefore, was by no means badly off.

That left me. And alas, I found my own company was scarcely to be endured a moment longer.

That Sunday I loitered here and loitered there: I was waiting for the Captain, who was expected home that day. Then, just in case, I went for a long walk up along the stream that fed our reservoir; I wanted to see once again the two little pools of water up on the hillside, the sources of the Nile.

On my way down through the woods, I met Lars Falkenberg on his way up, going home. The full moon was just rising, red and enormous, and lighting up the whole landscape. There had also been a little snow and frost; the air was easy to breathe. Lars was as friendly as could be; he had been drinking brandy somewhere, and now talked fifteen to the dozen. But I would not have chosen to meet him.

I had stood for a long time up on the hillside, listening to the sough from heaven and earth; there was nothing else to be heard. Then there might come a rustling sound, which would prove to be a shriveled, curled-up leaf fluttering down through the frozen branches; it was like listening to a tiny fountain. Then heaven and earth would sough again. A mildness enveloped me, as though all my strings were muted.

Lars Falkenberg wanted to know where I had been and where I was going. Stream? Reservoir? A load of monkey business the whole caboodle—as if people couldn't carry water for themselves. The Captain had gone in for so many newfangled inventions and plowing among the crops and suchlike paraphernalia, he'd come a cropper one fine day. A rich harvest it was supposed to be. Fair enough. But they never stopped to consider the cost, with a machine for every blessed thing, and several men to each machine. Imagine what Grindhusen and I must have cost this summer! What he himself must have cost this autumn, for that matter! In the old days there had been music and plenty at Øvrebø, and a certain person had been in the living room and sung— "I don't care to talk about it," said Lars. "And soon there won't be a decent stick of timber in the forest."

"And in a few years it'll be as thick as ever."

"A few years? Years and years, if you ask me. No sirree, it's not just a matter of being a Captain and shouting *Hut-two-three*—and hey presto, Bob's your uncle. And he's not even spokesman for the district any longer, and you never see a soul coming to ask his advice on everything under the sun—"

"Did you see the Captain down at Øvrebø? Is he back yet?" I interrupted.

"Just back, and looking like a skeleton. What was I going to say . . . When are you leaving?"

"Tomorrow."

"Tomorrow already!" Lars was full of goodwill and all-the-best toward me; he had never dreamed I'd be off so soon.

"Well, in that case it's a toss-up if I'll see you again this time," he said. "But there's one thing I don't mind telling you: it's time you stopped frittering away your life and never settling down anywhere. I'm saying this for the last time now—so don't you forget, mind. It's not that I'm all that well off; but how many of the likes of us have done better, I'd like to know—certainly not you. I do at least have a roof over my head, and that's a fact. Wife and kids, two cows—one to calve in the spring, the other in autumn—and a pig, and that's as much as I possess in the world. Nothing to boast about—but it all adds up to a farm, such as it is."

"It's all right for a chap like you who's come out on top," I said.

Lars grew still more friendly at this acknowledgment; he positively overflowed with goodwill toward me.

"I don't know anyone who could be more on top than you, for that matter," he continued. "You're good at all sorts of work, and writing and doing sums into the bargain. But it's your own stupid fault. You could have done as I told you six or seven years ago and taken one of the girls here like I took Emma and settled down for good. Then you wouldn't be traipsing around now from parish to parish. And that's what I'd still advise you to do."

"It's too late now," I answered.

"Yes, you've gone hideously gray, so I don't know who'd have you now from around these parts. How old are you?"

"Really, what a question to ask!"

"Well, you'd hardly be a chicken exactly, still. There was something I meant to say—come up my way for a stretch, maybe it'll come back to me."

I went with him, talking all the way. He offered to put in a good word for me with the Captain, so that I too could get a clearing in the forest.

"Well, that really is funny," he said, "my forgetting so completely what I had in mind. Come on home with me now, and it's bound to come back."

He was goodwill incarnate. But I had one or two things to sort out and didn't feel like accompanying him any farther.

"You won't see the Captain tonight in any case."

No, but it was getting late; Emma must have gone to bed; I would only be disturbing her.

"Not a bit of it!" said Lars. "If she's gone to bed, well then, she's gone to bed. I wouldn't be surprised, either, if there isn't a shirt of yours still lying around at our place. Come and take it with you, and save Emma going all that way with it."

"No, I'd better not—but remember me to Emma," I ventured to say now.

"Shall do. And if you really haven't got time to come up to my little place, such as it is—are you leaving early in the morning?"

Forgetting that I wouldn't be able to see the Captain that evening, I said yes, I'd be leaving first thing.

"In that case I'll send Emma down with that shirt of yours this instant," said Lars. "And goodbye for now! Don't forget what I've told you!"

And so we parted.

When I had gone a little way, I slackened off speed: there was really no great hurry about my packing and other preparations. I turned and set off uphill again, whistling in the moonlight. It was a lovely evening, no hint of cold, only a soft, compliant peace enveloping the woods. After half an hour or so I was surprised to find Emma on her way with my shirt.

Next morning neither Grindhusen nor I went out in the woods. Grindhusen was uneasy and asked, "Have you spoken to the Captain about me?"

"No, I haven't spoken to him at all."

"No, you mark my words, he's going to lay me off. If there was any go in him, he'd let me chop up that cordwood; but not him! It's about as much as he can do to keep a man at all."

"What's all this, Grindhusen? Surely you liked Captain Falkenberg well enough before?"

"Yes, you know that. Well, yes, that's to say, the man may be all right. Hm . . . I can't help wondering if the Inspector of Log Driving mightn't find some job or other for me to do now. He's a very effluent man, you know, that inspector . . ."

At eight o'clock I managed to see the Captain, and talked with him for a while; then a couple of neighbors called, doubtless to offer their condolences. The Captain looked strained but by no means crushed, his bearing was steadfast and straightforward. He questioned me a little about a plan of his for a big drying house for hay and grain.

And now, it seemed, there was no more disorder at Øvrebø, no agitation of the mind, no derailed soul! I thought of this almost with melancholy. No one placed impertinent photographs on the piano, but no one played the piano either. It stood there, dumb, since the last note died away. No, Mrs. Falkenberg was no longer here to injure herself or others. Of the old days nothing was left. It only remained to be seen whether Øvrebø would be strewn with happiness and flowers forever after.

"As long as he doesn't take to drink again," I said to Nils.

"No, surely," he replied. "And I don't think he ever really took to drink. He was just a bit foolish, I'd say, living it up the way he did for a time. To change the subject—are you coming back in the spring?"

"No, I shall never come back again now."

So Nils and I said our farewells. I wanted to fix in my memory the man's equanimity and honorable way of thinking, and stood watching as he walked away across the yard. Then he turned and said, "Were you in the woods yesterday? Is there enough snow for me to use the sleigh getting firewood today?"

"Yes," I said.

His mind set at ease, he went to the stables to harness up.

Then Grindhusen in turn passed me on his way to the stables. He stopped for a moment to tell me that the Captain had, of his own free will, offered him work cutting firewood. " 'Saw up as much of that cordwood as you can,' he says; 'just carry on for the time being—I'm sure we'll agree all right about wages.' 'My thanks and respects, Captain,' says I. 'Go and report to Nils,' says he. Ah, what a fine fellow! You won't find many like him."

Shortly afterward I was sent for by the Captain, and went up to his office. He thanked me for my work, both indoors and out, and paid me my wages. That just about finished our business; but he asked me one or two questions about the proposed drying house, and we talked it over for a while. It would all have to wait till after Christmas, in any case, he said; but when the time came he would be glad to have me back. As he said this he looked at me; then he added, "But I suppose you're never coming back now?"

I was taken by surprise. But I met his gaze and answered, "That's correct."

On my way down I turned his words over in my mind. Had he seen through me? At all events, he had trusted me in a way that I valued highly. He was a real gentleman.

Trusted me? But what had it cost him? I belonged to the ranks of the superannuated. He had allowed me to go and do and pretend as I pleased, all on the strength of my eminent harmlessness. That must be it. In any case, there was nothing to see through.

I went all around the house, upstairs and downstairs, taking my leave of one and all, of Ragnhild and the girls. Then, as I crossed the courtyard with my knapsack on my shoulder, Captain Falkenberg called from the steps, "It's just occurred to me—if you're going to the station, the lad can drive you."

Ever the gentleman! But I thanked him and declined the offer. I didn't feel so superannuated but that I could manage that stretch on foot.

And now I was back in my little town again. I had come here on my way to Trovatn and the mountains.

Here everything was as before, except that a thin layer of ice now covered the river above and below the rapids, and the ice was coated with snow.

I kept a weather eye open and bought some clothes and equipment, and after picking up a good pair of new shoes, I took the old pair to the cobbler to get them half-soled. The cobbler chatted a while, then begged me to be so good as to be seated. "And where's himself from, now?" he asked. And at once I was soaked in the spirit of the place.

I sauntered up to the churchyard. Here, too, they were keeping a weather eye open and preparing for winter. Bundles of straw had been lashed around plants and bushes, many a delicate tombstone was crowned with a high wooden hat; while the hats themselves had been protected with paint. It was as if people had said to themselves: Look, I own this tombstone now—with care and foresight it can serve as a tombstone for me and my kith and kin for many generations.

There was a Christmas fair on, too, and here in turn I sauntered. There were toboggans and skis, wooden butter dishes from the nether regions and subterranean chairs carved from logs, rose-colored mittens, clothes mangles, fox skins. And then there were horse dealers and cattle dealers mingling with drunken folk from up the valley; yes, and Jews who had come to palm off an ornamented pocket watch or two, in this town that had no money. And the watches came from that country up in the Alps where Böcklin was at pains *not* to come from, where nobody and nothing ever came from.*

---

* Arnold Böcklin (1827–1901), at one time an immensely popular painter who peopled his romantic landscapes with classical nymphs and satyrs, was born and died in Switzerland but lived most of his life abroad.—Trans.

Oh, this Christmas market of ours!

But the evenings offered noble entertainment for all: dancing in two large halls, virtuoso performances on the Hardanger fiddle, and eh but it's grand—that's about long and short on't. The Hardanger fiddle has iron strings, it produces no melodious phrases, it is music with a sting in it. It affects different people in different ways: some of us soak it up with national mawkishness, others of us bare our teeth and howl with melancholy. Never was such a powerful effect produced by stinging music.

And the dance went on.

> Poor aged mother, toiling hard,
> Spending your sweat like blood,

sang the local schoolmaster during an interval. But some of the wilder lads wanted dancing and nothing but. What was all this? Stand about with your arm around a girl, *singing?* No sense in that! The singer broke off. "What, no sense in Vinje?" Dancing versus the poet Vinje. Argument for and against, yelling and screaming, uproar. Never was such a powerful effect produced by poetry and singing.

And the dance went on.

The lasses from up the valley were five pink petticoats thick; but this counted for nothing with such experienced bearers as these. And the dance went on, and the thunder went on, and the brandy was potent, and a steam arose from the witches' caldron. At three in the morning the local police force appeared and banged on the floor with its baton. Period. The dancers went out in the moonlight and spread out over the town and its environs. And nine months later the lasses from up the valley produced conclusive evidence that they had still been one pink petticoat short. Never was such a powerful effect produced by the want of one pink petticoat.

The river had grown quieter now—not much of a river to

look at; winter had mantled it over. It still drove the pulp mills
and sawmills along its banks, because it was and remained a
great river—but a river with no life in it, a river that had shut
the lid on itself.

As for the rapids, they too were in poor shape. Once I had
gazed down at them and listened to them and thought: If I
lived down there in the world of that roar forever, what in the
end would become of my brain? Now the rapids were shrunk
and murmured meekly; it would have been a mockery to speak
of a roar. Dear God, the rapids were in utter ruin! They had
sunk into poverty; great boulders stuck out all along the bank,
logs had wedged themselves at all kinds of angles; one could
jump dry-shod from bank to bank, by way of stone and timber.

And now I stood with my knapsack on, having finished my
business in the town. It was Sunday; the weather was fine and
clear.

I went to the hotel and announced myself to the underporter.
The great, good-natured creature wanted to come with me up
along the river for part of the way, and also to carry my knapsack—as if I couldn't carry it myself.

We followed the right-hand bank, although the road proper
was on the left; ours was only a summer path trodden by log
drivers, and showing now a few fresh tracks in the snow. My
guide couldn't quite make out why we didn't follow the road;
he was not strong in the head. But I had already been up this
way twice in the last few days, and wanted to do so once again.
It was my own tracks we could see the whole way.

I asked, "The lady you mentioned once—the one who got
drowned—was it about here?"

"The one who fell in, eh? Ay, we're just about there. It was
terrible; in the end there must have been twenty of us searching
for her—police and all."

"Did you drag the river?"

"Ay, we dragged it. Laid planks and ladders down—stood on

'em—crack! Broke up nearly all the ice that way. Here, you can see where we went," he added, stopping.

I made out the dark stretch of ice where the boats had rowed around, crushing the ice and dragging; now it had frozen over again.

The underporter went on with his story. "We found her in the end. I must say, it was a blessing the river was so low. She'd gone straight to the bottom between two rocks and stuck there. There was no current to speak of; if it had been in the spring, she'd have gone for miles."

"So she thought she'd cross the river?"

"Ay, they all want to go out on the ice the moment it freezes over; it's asking for trouble. Someone had been across already— two days earlier, it was. She came walking along, just here, this side we're on now, and the engineer he came down the road on the other side—he'd been out on his bicycle. Then they saw one another and signaled to each other—just saying hello or something of the kind, because they were related together, both of them. But then the lady mistook one of the signals, so the engineer says, and thought he was beckoning to her, because she started to cross. And the engineer he yelled, but she didn't hear, and he had his bicycle, which he couldn't leave—and, in any case, somebody had been across already. The engineer told the police about how it all happened and they wrote down every word. Well, then when she was halfway across, down she went. She must have happened to tread on a really rotten part of the ice. And the engineer he came flashing through the town on his bicycle, back to the hotel, and started ringing. I've never heard such ringing in all my days. 'Someone's fallen in the river!' he shouted. 'My cousin!' he shouted. We all turned out, the engineer too. We had ropes and boat hooks with us, but it was no use; then the police came, and the fire brigade came, and they got hold of a boat somewhere up there—carried it between them till they reached us, then they got it out and started dragging. But we didn't find her, not the first day we didn't. But then the second day we found her. Ay, it was a nasty accident, that."

"Did you say her husband came—the Captain?"

"Ay, the Captain came. And you can imagine the state he was in—though to tell you the truth we all were, for that matter—the whole town. As for the engineer, he was quite beside himself for a long time, they said at the hotel, and when the Captain came, the engineer went off inspecting up the river; he just couldn't bear to talk about the accident any more."

"So the Captain never saw him?"

"No. Hm. Well, I don't rightly know." He looked around him. "No, I don't really know at all."

His answer was so shifty that I realized he *did* know something. But it was of no significance, and I refrained from questioning him further.

"Well, many thanks for your company," I said, and gave him some money for a winter garment or two. And I said goodbye to him, and wanted him to turn back.

However, he was keen to go on with me a little farther. And to get me to agree to this, he suddenly said: Yes, the Captain *had* got hold of the engineer while he was here. This good, dim-witted soul had understood enough of the maids' gossip in the kitchen to have just about grasped the connection between the engineer and this cousin who came to stay; but that was as far as he got. However, it was he and no other who had guided the Captain up the river in search of the engineer.

"The Captain simply had to meet the engineer," he went on, "and I went with him up the river. 'What is there for the engineer to inspect on an ice-bound river?' the Captain asked me on the way. 'I can't make that out either,' I said. So we walked all day till about three o'clock. 'I wonder if he mightn't be in this cabin,' I said; 'I'm told his men stay here sometimes.' After that, the Captain didn't want me to come any farther—just told me to wait. Then he went up to the cabin and went inside. He'd hardly been gone more than a minute or two, then out he came from the cabin, and the engineer too. They spoke a few words together—I didn't hear what they said. Then all of a sudden the Captain threw up his arm in the air—like that—and fetched the engineer one, so he went flat on his back. Lord bless you, it must have been like an avalanche through his head. And not content with that, the Captain picked the engineer up again and fetched him another great crack. Then he came back to me and said, 'Let's go home now.' "

This set me thinking. I was amazed that the underporter, this man who had no enemies and bore malice to none, should have allowed the engineer to remain at the cabin without help. Nor had he shown a trace of disapproval in his account of the punishment. My guess was that the engineer had been miserly with him too, and had never paid for his services, but only acted the nabob and laughed at him and behaved like a whelp. Yes, that would be it. And perhaps this time it was no longer my jealousy leading me astray.

"But the Captain—he was the lad for giving tips!" concluded the underporter. "I paid off all my debts with what he gave me, I did and all."

When at last I had finally got rid of the underporter, I crossed the river; the ice was firm enough. Then I continued up the road, thinking about his story. That assault at the cabin— what purpose had it served? It settled nothing, beyond the fact that one of the parties was big and strong, while the other was a little runt of a sportsman with a big bottom. Still, the Captain was an officer, who had doubtless remembered vaguely that something of the kind was due. He ought, perhaps, to have remembered vaguely, while there was still time, that other things were due. Who can say? It was his wife who had gone in the river, and whatever the Captain might do now, she would never come back.

But even if she could have, what then? Assuredly, she had been born to her destiny. Both husband and wife had tried to patch up the damage and had failed. I remembered her as she had been six or seven years back: bored and already attracted, no doubt, to this man and that; but faithful and sensitive. Time continued to pass. She had no mission, only three maids in her home. She had no children, only a grand piano. She had no children.

And life can afford to be wasteful.

It was mother and child that went to the bottom.

Epilogue

A wanderer plays on muted strings when he reaches the age
of two score years and ten. That is when he plays on muted
strings.

Or I might put it like this:

If he comes too late in the autumn to the woods where the
berries grow, why then, he comes to them too late; and if one
fine day he no longer feels up to making merry and laughing
uproariously from *joie de vivre,* why then, it must be because he
is old; don't blame him for that! Besides, beyond question, it
takes a certain degree of brainlessness to remain permanently
contented with oneself and with everything. But favorable mo-
ments we all have. A condemned man sits in his tumbril on the
way to the scaffold; a nail in the seat irks him; he shifts position
and feels more comfortable.

It is wrong of a captain to ask God to forgive him—as he
forgives God. He is simply dramatizing. A wanderer who

doesn't each day find food and drink, clothes and shoes, house and home provided, according to his needs, feels just the right degree of privation when all these splendors are absent. If one thing doesn't work out, another will. And if that other fails to work out also, he does not go around forgiving God but takes the responsibility himself. He puts his shoulder to the wheel of fortune—that is to say, he bows his back before it. It's a trifle hard on flesh and blood, it grays the hair horribly; but a wanderer thanks God for life, it was fun to live!

I might put it like that.

Why, in short, all these exacting demands? What have we earned? As many boxes of candy as a sweet tooth could desire? Fair enough. But have we not looked on the world each day and heard the soughing of the forest? There is no splendor like the soughing of the forest.

There was a scent of jasmine in a grove, and a tremor of joy ran through one I know, not for the jasmine but for everything—a lit-up window, a memory, the whole of life. But when he was called away from the grove, he had already been paid in advance for this annoyance.

And there it is: the very favor of receiving life at all is handsome advance payment for all life's miseries, each single one.

No, a man should not believe in his right to more candy than he gets. A wanderer advises against all superstition. What is life's? Everything. And what is yours? Is fame? Pray tell us why! A man should not insist on what is "his"; to do so is ludicrous, and a wanderer laughs at anyone so ludicrous. I remember one such who never escaped that "his"; he laid his fire at high noon and finally got it to burn in the evening. Then he couldn't bring himself to leave its warmth for bed, but sat there making the most of it, till others got up again. He was a Norwegian dramatist.

I have wandered around a good deal in my time, and am now grown dull and withered. But I do not hold that perverse graybeard's belief that I am wiser than I was. And I hope, indeed, that I shall never grow wise; it's a sign of decrepitude. If I thank God for life, it is not on the strength of any increased maturity that has come with age but because I have always enjoyed being alive. Age confers no maturity; age confers nothing beyond old age.

I came too late this year to the woods where the berries grow, but I made the journey nonetheless. I have allowed myself this frivolity as a reward for being so capable in the summer. And I reached my goal on the twelfth of December.

It is true, no doubt, that I could have stayed down among the villages. Something would surely have turned up for me, as it has for all those others who have felt it was time for them to settle down. And Lars Falkenberg, my colleague and companion, has advised me to take a clearing, with a wife, two cows, and a pig. It was a counsel of friendship, the voice of the people. And consider—one of my cows could be a gelded ox for riding, and then I would have transport for the days of my toothless mumbling. But the scheme foundered, it foundered! My wisdom has not come with age; instead, I have come to Trovatn and the moors and forests, and am living in a logger's cabin.

What pleasure can there be in that? Ah, Lars Falkenberg, and ah, all the rest of you—never fear, I have a man who comes here every weekday with a loaf of bread.

So I saunter and saunter in circles around myself, enjoying myself, tasting solitude. I miss Bishop Pavels's seal, which I got from one of his descendants.* I had it in my waistcoat pocket this summer; but when I felt for it just now, I could not find it. Well, well. Still, I have received advance payment for this annoyance in once having owned the ring.

* Claus Pavels (1769–1822), Bishop of Bergen, wrote a famous autobiography and kept diaries of which five volumes were published by his grandson. The material published is rated very high, not least for its honesty; and possibly Hamsun's reference to Pavels's seal is a lament that he has become more personally reticent since the days of *Hunger*. In any case, there seems to be some connection between the honesty of the diaries and what Hamsun regarded as the dishonesty of much "literature."—Trans.

Literature, however, I do not miss.

Here am I remembering the twelfth of December and any and every date, while cheerfully forgetting more important things! In the first place, literature: the fact that Captain Falkenberg and his wife had many books in their home—novels and plays, a whole bookcase full. I saw it while painting windows and doors at Øvrebø. They had whole series of authors, and authors' whole series—thirty books. Why the whole series? I don't know. Books—one, two, three, ten, thirty. They had come one each Christmas, novels, thirty volumes—the same novel. Presumably the Captain and his wife read them, always knew what they would find in these Home Library authors—there were pages and pages about everything coming right in the end. Presumably they read them—how should I know? My God, how much literature there was—two men could not shift the bookcase when I needed to paint behind it, three men and a cook were needed to shift it. One of the men was Grindhusen; he turned red under the weight of Home Library authors and said, "I can't understand what people do with all these endless books."

As if Grindhusen understood anything about anything! Presumably the Captain and his wife had all these books so that none should be missing; there they stood, complete. It would make a gap if one of them was removed. They were all alike, all matching: homogenized poetry, the same novel.

There's been an elk hunter with me in the cabin. His visit was no great event; and his dog did nothing but snarl. I was glad when he left. He took down my copper pan from the wall, used it for cooking, and left it all sooted up.

Not that it is my copper pan; it was left in the cabin by someone who'd been here before. I merely took it and scoured it with ashes and hung it on the wall to serve me as a weather prophet. Now I sit polishing it up again, for it's a good thing to have: it goes dim without fail if there's rain or snow in the offing.

It occurs to me that if Ragnhild had been here now, she

would have stepped in and polished that copper pan. But on second thought, I would rather look after my weather prophet myself; Ragnhild could find something else to do. And if this place in the woods was our clearing, she would have the children, the cows, and the pig—but as for *my* copper pans, Ragnhild, I intend to take care of those myself!

I remember a married lady who took care of nothing, least of all herself. And ill she fared in the end. But six or seven years ago I could not have imagined anyone so sensitive and lovely toward another human being as she was. I was her coachman on a journey, and she was shy with me, although she was the mistress that I served; she blushed and looked down. And the strange thing is that she made me bashful too, although I was her servant. Just by looking at me with her two eyes when she gave me an order, she showed me beauties and values beyond those I knew already; I remember it still. Yes, I sit here remembering it still, and shaking my head and saying to myself, How strange it was—ah no, no, no! Then she died. What more? Nothing more. I remain. But her death should cause me no sorrow: had I not been paid in advance when she looked at me, undeserving as I was, with her two eyes? Surely that's how it is!

Woman—what do wise men know about woman?

I remember a wiseacre who wrote about woman. He wrote about woman in thirty volumes of homogenized dramatic poetry—I counted the volumes once in a big bookcase. Finally he wrote about the woman who left her own children in search of—the miracle of miracles! What, then, were the children? Oh, it was ludicrous, and a wanderer laughs at anything so ludicrous.*

What does the wise man know about woman?

---

* The willfully misleading reference is to Nora Helmer in *A Doll's House*— the *first* of the great series of prose dramas (of the major work only *Brand* and *Peer Gynt* are in verse) which Ibsen wrote in his fifties and sixties; this late flowering explains the slighting reference, on p. 274, to an unnamed "Norwegian dramatist." In 1890 Hamsun had attacked Ibsen to his face in a notorious public lecture.—Trans.

In the first place, he doesn't grow wise until he has grown old, and by then his knowledge of woman is confined to his memory. And, in the second place, he *has* no memory of her, because he has never known her. The man with a talent for wisdom busies himself, miser-fashion, with this talent and with nothing else, tending it and nursing it, displaying it and living for it. One doesn't go to woman for wisdom. The four wisest heads in the world, who have delivered their opinions on woman, simply sat and dreamed her up themselves; they were dotards, young or old, who rode their gelded oxen. They knew nothing of woman in her sanctity, woman in her sweetness, woman as a vital necessity; but they wrote and wrote about woman. Just think, without ever meeting her!

God preserve me from growing wise! Yes, I intend to mumble toothlessly to my deathbed bystanders: God preserve me from growing wise!

It's a pleasantly cool day for an excursion I've had in mind; the snow peaks are rosy in the sun and my copper pan points to fair. The hour is eight in the morning.

Knapsack, a good supply of food, some spare cord in my pocket, should anything break; money on the table, in case the man comes with a loaf for me while I'm away.

Oh yes, I've been giving myself great airs for my own benefit: I was going on a long journey, I must make meticulous preparations, I would need all my resourcefulness and powers of endurance. Yes, the man who is going on a long journey may give himself such airs; but they hardly match my case. I have no mission, no places I must visit; I am just a wanderer setting out from a logger's cabin and coming back to it again; it makes no difference where I am.

The woods are peaceful and deserted; everything stands there in the snow, holding its breath as I pass. At noon I see from a hilltop Trovatn far behind me; the lake lies there, white and flat, six miles of chalk in the snowy wilderness. After lunch I go

on again, I climb higher and higher, I approach the real mountains, but slowly and reflectively, with my hands in my pockets.
There is no hurry—I only need to find a spot where I can take
shelter for the night. Around three o'clock I sit down and eat a
bit more, as though I needed food and had earned it. But it is
only for something to do; my hands are idle, and my brain
inclined to fancies. It gets dark early; good, here is a snug cleft
in the mountainside, with plenty of wind-felled firs to make a
fire.

Such are the things I tell of now, playing on muted strings.

I am out early next morning, as soon as the sky lightens a
little. Snow begins to fall, soft and warm; there is a soughing in
the air. Bad weather brewing, it seems—who would have
guessed it? Neither I nor my weather prophet, twenty-four
hours ago. I leave my shelter and continue over moors and
marshes. Noon comes around again, and it is snowing. My
shelter last night was none too good: I had plenty of pine needles for my couch and I didn't get cold, but the smoke from my
fire blew all over me and interfered with my breathing.

But this afternoon I find a better place, an extensive, elegant
cave, with walls and a roof. There is room both for me and my
fire, and the smoke rises vertically. Here I nod and put down
my things, although it is early still and broad daylight. I can
distinctly make out hills and valleys and rocks leading up to a
bare mountain straight ahead, several hours' walk away. But I
nod as if I have arrived, and start laying in firewood and pine
needles for the night.

How completely I feel at home here! It was not for nothing
that I nodded and put down my things. "Was this your destina-
tion?" I ask myself as a joke. "Yes," I answer.

The soughing in the air has grown stronger; the snow has
turned to rain. It is strange: heavy, wet rain is running down
over the cave and soaking the trees outside; yet it is the cold
Christmas month, it is December. A heat wave has contrived to
visit us.

During the night it rains and rains, and the soughing continues in the forest outside, as if it were spring. Finally it fills my slumber with a pleasure so profound that I sleep a good sound sleep until far into the day.

It is ten o'clock.

The rain has ceased, but it is still warm. I sit looking out of my cave and listening to the forest as it bends and soughs. Then a stone in the mountainside opposite breaks loose and butts against a rock, which in turn breaks loose; thuds are heard in the distance. Then it turns to a roar, which echoes through me, and I see what is happening: the rock has loosened other rocks, it is an avalanche, stones and snow and earth go thundering down the mountainside, a swirl of smoke rises in the wake of the mighty train. The stream of granite boulders looks positively brutish—thrusting, slashing, teeming, streaming, streaming, filling up a chasm in the valley—and stopping. The last stones sink slowly to rest, and all is over; the thunder out there is silenced, and only my breathing resembles a slowly descending bass.

And now I sit once more and listen to the soughing of the forest. Is it the distant Aegean I can hear, or the ocean current Glimma? I grow weak from sitting and listening, memories well up within me from my life: a thousand joys, music and eyes and flowers. There is no splendor like the soughing of the forest, it is like rocking, it is like madness: Uganda, Antananarivo, Honolulu, Atacama, Venezuela . . .

But it must be my years that make me so weak, my nerves that join in the sounds I hear. I get up and stand by the fire to calm myself; for that matter, I could talk to the flame a little, make a speech while the fire dies. I am standing in a fireproof house, with good acoustics. Hm.

Then a shadow falls over the cave, and there is the elk hunter again, with his dog . . .

It is starting to freeze as I wander back home to my logger's cabin; soon the frost bites into moors and marshes, and makes the going easy. I saunter onward, slowly and indifferently, with my hands in my pockets. Why should I hurry? It makes no difference where I am.